THE GENESIS OF SEVEN

THE GENESIS OF SEVEN

SARA M SCHALLER

Sara M Schaller

DESIGNS BY SERAPHIM

The Genesis of Seven
Copyright © 2020 by Sara M Schaller

Published by Designs by Seraphim

This is a work of fiction. Names, characters, places, and incidents are either the product of the author's imagination or are used fictitiously. Any resemblance to actual persons living or dead, events, or locales is entirely coincidental.

ISBN 978-1-7325162-0-5 (hardcover)
ISBN 978-1-7325162-1-2 (paperback)
ISBN 978-1-7325162-2-9 (ebook)

Cover design by Sara M Schaller
Interior design by Sara M Schaller
Symbol Artwork by Adrianne Tamar Arachne
Edited by Bryony Leah

First Edition: July 2020

www.saramschaller.com

For the family unit—
Mom, Dad, & Anthony

I could never have done this without you.

In the Beginning he was one of us,

a brother amongst us in

our empyrean domain.

JORDAN

1

Abandon all hope, ye who enter here.

Those were the words Dante faced when he entered Hell. Perhaps if they were posted above the subway this afternoon, I would have proceeded with the same caution.

The New York subway system was a strange and peculiar place. An underground metropolis full of noise and activity, where anything and everything occurred. I liked to compare it to the Underworld as I imagined it worked in much the same way, with spirits being ferried across the River Styx like people being transported through the city. Yet the main difference between Hell and the subway was all those who entered typically resurfaced every day, sometimes multiple times a day, without being scathed.

Unlike me, whose life would be forever changed by the simple act of bumping shoulders.

It wasn't unusual to accidentally graze the arm of a stranger in the subway, but there was something different about this guy at the bottom of the station steps, almost like he was waiting for me to run into him.

"Sorry," I offered, pulling my MetroCard out of my pocket and looking up.

He was dressed in all-black, wearing a leather jacket with the hood pulled up so I could barely see his face. Instead of answering, he stared at me like I'd committed the worst crime known to man.

"I'm really sorry," I said once more. Clearly, this guy wasn't a local, or he'd be used to the bustle of Brooklyn Heights by now.

His response was to pull out a cigarette and lighter. He inserted the stick of tobacco between his lips and lit it. As he did, I noticed several rings on his fingers, but most memorable was the large skull tattooed across the back of his hand. It started at his wrist and ended near his knuckles.

Replacing the lighter and blowing smoke in my face, he stared hard at my necklace.

I coughed from the noxious fumes and grabbed at it, returning the pendant under my shirt. The impact of running into this guy must have made it fall out.

Still, he stared.

My necklace was a simple fleur-de-lis pendant on a silver chain. Sister Helen, the head nun at my orphanage, gave it to me as a birthday gift when I turned six. I was orphaned before I had the chance to know my parents, and I'd lived at the Holy Trinity Home for Disadvantaged Youth my entire life. The fleur-de-lis was the symbol of Holy Trinity. Sister Helen told me to wear the necklace always since it would bring me protection. At six years old, I didn't understand what she meant, but now, I realized its protection came from the devotion of the sisters themselves.

It was weird this guy was so fascinated by it. His sharp eyes held focus like he could see right through my shirt to the now hidden pendant. Maybe he simply liked it, but his expression did little to convey the feeling.

Deciding I'd apologized enough already, I turned away from him and approached the turnstiles. Swiping my pass in the scanner, I walked through when the light flashed green, then veered to the right and rounded a corner. When I glanced back over my shoulder, the man was not in sight.

There was already an A-line train pulling up as I neared the platform. Quickening my pace, I entered the car, claimed a seat, and made myself comfortable for the ride. But as I gazed to my left, through the glass window into the next car, I noticed the guy in black standing inside watching me.

Averting my gaze fast, I tried to settle my thoughts. Was he following me? Should I be afraid? Had I really run into him so bad he wanted revenge? One more glance into the next car. Though the guy was still there, he was no longer staring.

I really need to calm down.

It was just coincidence he was on the same train. This was one of the main lines. He was probably staring because he recognized me as the rude boy who ran into him. He meant me no harm. He apparently just wanted to intimidate me.

I tapped my foot up and down, anxious to get off the train. I didn't know why, but the guy gave me the creeps. When the car slowed, I jumped up, realizing this was my stop anyway, and exited the subway station as fast as I could.

On my walk to the movie theater, I couldn't help but look over my shoulder. It was a relief to see the guy wasn't following. Reassured, I bypassed the ticket booth and made my way inside.

Ethan was taking ticket stubs in the foyer. "Hey, Jordan." He stared disinterested at me for a few awkward seconds.

"Can you let me in?" I asked.

"I thought your final shift was last week."

"It was, but there was something wrong with my direct deposit. Marcus wanted me to come in and pick up my last paycheck in person."

"I see. Well, go on through then."

He motioned me forward, and I went in search of my ex-boss. I'd worked at the movie theater since I started high school, but now I was leaving for my mission trip, I had to quit. This place held a lot of memories because it was the movie theater Sophia and I always went to. The thought of her made me sad, but I couldn't dwell on it too long as I soon found Marcus sweeping up spilled popcorn. He led me into his office, handed me my check, and quickly went back to work.

I exited the theater and headed straight to the bank to deposit my check at the ATM. Typically, I would snap a picture of it on my phone, but I forgot my phone back at the orphanage. Once the slip of paper was out of my hands, I glanced at the time in the bank lobby and realized I couldn't be late for the farewell dinner the sisters were having for me. I set off immediately, reaching for my pass as I descended the steps to the subway.

"Sorry," I said as I bumped shoulders with another stranger. But a sense of déjà vu overcame me.

Looking up, I saw this man was also dressed in all-black with a hood covering his head, fingers decked with rings, and a similar skull tattooed across the back of his hand. Yet I had the distinct feeling this was not the same man. He stared at my chest like he was also trying to get a glimpse of my necklace. Creeped out and certainly not in the mood to seek this guy's forgiveness, I chose to ignore him and walked over to the turnstiles.

As I scanned my pass and entered the platform, however, I became vaguely aware that this guy *was* following me.

What had I done, infuriated some gang by running into one of their crew? I surely didn't have a hit out on me for running into him. It was the *subway*. People bumped into each other down here all the time! In fact, it seemed like a vital part of the public transport system.

My nerves led my thoughts on rambling tangents. Right now, what I needed was to think logically so I could arrive home safe. I sent up a silent prayer as I stepped into the subway car and remained standing in case I had to exit quickly. That seemed like a good, logical thought. Yet all I could think about was why this guy wanted to track down a kid who ran into his friend in the subway. I was an *orphan*. If they thought they could get money out of kidnapping me, they had another think coming.

The train stopped, and I exited the car. No guys in black followed, so I heaved a sigh of relief. I ascended the steps out of the station and headed down the street toward the orphanage.

When I entered through the main doors, I was met with darkness and silence—both odd attributes for an orphanage full of children. Passing through the hallway of offices, I walked through the second set of doors that led to the living quarters. Still, there was no one around.

I ran my hand along the wall in search of the light switch, but before I could flick it on, someone grabbed my arm.

I nearly jumped out of my skin and yelled out in terror before realizing it was Sister Helen. She had her finger to her lips as she pulled me down the hall to the back entrance. When we got to the door, she handed me a backpack, the duffel bag I'd packed earlier, and a slip of paper.

"I don't have much time to explain, but you need to go," she told me.

"Go? Go where?" I asked.

She pointed to the paper. "You must get to this address. Whoever is there will help you. They can protect you. It should be Michael, but I'm not sure."

I opened my mouth to protest, but she continued on.

"I know this all seems strange and confusing, but you need to trust me. The children and sisters have all been moved, so don't worry about us. You must only worry about yourself. You are our last hope."

Sister Helen looked at me with pleading eyes. I had so many questions, but I knew from her distressed tone I couldn't ask any of them. Following her order, I slipped the backpack onto my shoulders and gripped the duffel bag and paper in my hand. I placed my free hand on the doorknob ready to depart, but she wasn't finished yet.

"You never lived at this orphanage. Understand? For everyone's sake, it never existed. Jordan, I'm sorry our time together has ended like this, but you must get to that address," she stressed.

"I will," I promised.

"Good. Now, about your mission trip—"

Her words were interrupted by footsteps upstairs. Sister Helen's eyes grew wide, and she quickly opened the door.

"Go! Go!"

I stepped through it and froze in place in the back alley.

"Run!" Sister Helen shouted.

Somehow, my body obliged. My legs carried me down the alley-way, past dumpsters and trashcans. At the street, I stopped briefly to figure out where to go next. I glanced at the paper and realized I had a bit of distance to cover. The address was near Central Park, but the orphanage was in the opposite direction. In fact, the orphanage wasn't even in Manhattan. There wasn't time to figure out a route though. At the sound of running footsteps, I looked over my shoulder and saw two men dressed in black fast approaching.

Without a second thought, I broke into a sprint and headed right.

I'd never been chased in my life and soon realized I was the worst person for it. I kept running straight for blocks. Not once did I try to evade my chasers. I was merely in flight mode, running forward without a thought of where I had to go. The backpack hit my shoulders every time I moved my legs, creating a rhythm my heartbeat began to mimic. I was scared senseless, had no idea what to do, and was weighed down by the duffel bag, which gave me a weird, galloping stride.

As I raced on, some unknown part of my brain took over and told my legs to veer left into an alleyway. My chasers passed by, unsuspect-ing, though they soon backtracked and followed. At that point, my run became a series of quick turns and dashes through side streets and alleys in an attempt to evade them.

Breathing hard, heaving the cursed bag, and almost tripping over my own feet, I came to a standstill in front of a chain-link fence. Did this *seriously* have to turn into some iconic movie chase? I groaned as I sized up my new enemy, wondering why I never took gym class seriously. Surely, completing the rope climb—something I'd never successfully achieved—would come in handy right about now.

At the last second I decided to backtrack, but the two chasers blocked my path. One was a big, burly man, and the other was the second guy from the subway, who was much taller and leaner than his accomplice.

Frustrated, I ran up to the fence and swung my duffel bag through the air. It landed surprisingly safe on the other side of the chain-link barrier. Without a moment's hesitation, I ran and jumped at the tall gate, latching onto it with my hands. Flashbacks of the rope climb came to mind, and I knew this wasn't going to be easy. In a struggle, I scrambled up as my chasers approached.

By some miracle, I made it to the top, and I was preparing to swing my leg over and ring that fictitious bell when a hand gripped my ankle. When I looked down, a menacing skull tattoo met my gaze.

Nearly falling backward, as the burly man yanked and pulled, I gripped the fence harder and kicked out at my attacker. "Let go of me, you creep!"

I thought I was doomed when he grabbed at the backpack with his other hand. But the strangest thing happened. As soon as he touched it, he yelled in pain and ripped his hand back. Quickly, I pulled myself up and over the other side of the fence, scrambling down a reasonable distance before jumping to the ground. Dismounting always was easier than climbing. Catching my breath, I picked up my duffel and took off once more, ignoring the men on the other side of the fence who were yelling and arguing with each other now.

I spotted a subway station at the end of the alley. The only way I was going to get to this address was with some transport. This time, I paid attention to every step I took, making sure I ran into no one who might come after me later. When I slid through the turnstile, I walked over to the map. I could take either the A-line or the C-line into Manhattan, but I didn't know which stop to get off at. Glancing at the clock, I noticed the C-line would be here any second. I took off running through the underground tunnels and made my way to the platform, not stopping once since the train was already there.

I'd just made it inside the car when the doors closed, barely missing my duffel bag.

I collapsed into one of the few remaining seats and closed my eyes, trying to reestablish a normal breathing pattern. After a few minutes, I rummaged through my duffel bag for a hoodie, realizing I couldn't trapeze around town without any sort of disguise. I put it on, zipped it up, and pulled the hood over my head. Hopefully, this would be enough to throw those guys off.

With the backpack on my lap and the duffel at my feet, I settled into the ride. Every stop was a nightmare as people disembarked and new passengers arrived. I didn't know who was following me, but I kept my eyes peeled for any hooded guys dressed in all-black with skull tattoos.

Of course, trouble arrived at the stop before mine.

When the doors opened, almost everyone left, like a message had been sent out to evacuate the cars. A glance to my left and right revealed four guys dressed in black had entered the cars next to mine. I hopped up with my belongings and ran for the door, which chastised me to, "Please stand clear," as I fled.

I raced through the tunnels and spotted the sign for the street entrance, quickly mounting the steps to the sidewalk. As we were uptown, there was more activity here. I pushed my way through the crowds, trying to get as far from the subway station as possible.

Then, I saw them. Two more guys dressed in black, right in front of me. I was about to spin around and head in the other direction when the other four appeared from the subway.

I was done. I was tired.

Illogically, I ran straight ahead, right at the two guys. I figured two was better than four, and these men in particular had never seen me before. But I stuck out like a sore thumb—hooded, running, and carrying more baggage than any normal person. The second I passed by, they caught on and turned to follow.

At least I'm getting close.

At least I'm headed in the right direction.

At least let me make it there alive.

This mantra helped more than I knew. As I ran, I looked up at the street signs and saw I was crossing onto Central Park West, the exact street I needed. There was no time to search for building numbers, so I kept on running and tried to scan the entrances as I passed.

Footsteps behind me grew louder as six pairs of feet pounded the pavement. The thump of my Converse hitting the sidewalk mixed into the fray, adding an irregular beat since I was still galloping awkwardly with the weight of the bag.

At the sight of a huge fancy apartment complex up ahead, I knew the building number would be clearly displayed on the entrance. As I approached, I looked up and read the metal letters spelling out the number thirty-four. Glancing down at the paper clutched in my sweaty hand, I realized this huge fancy apartment complex was where I had to be. I sent up a prayer for my miraculous salvation and raced up the steps, making straight for the elevator. With a barrage of people chasing after me—now the footmen and front desk security guards since the hooded subway chasers were nowhere in sight—I squeezed in between high-class residents just as the elevator doors closed.

They all stared and tried to step away like I was a hoodlum or a thief. I glanced down at my appearance and figured their assumptions were valid thanks to the rip in my jeans, my sneakers covered in dirt, and my hoodie drenched with sweat. Ignoring them, I opened my fist and looked closer at Sister Helen's crumpled piece of paper. There was only the building address, no apartment number.

Great. I'd come this far, and now I had no clue which door to knock on. I ripped the piece of paper in half and shoved it in my pocket, cursing myself and the situation. An elderly couple backed into the corner at my outburst, and when the door opened, everyone exited quickly.

If I didn't do something soon, these doors would close, and I'd be arriving back downstairs to a mob of people who wanted my head. I searched the floor numbers, hoping for some sign that might tell me which one to press, but there was nothing.

I was about to lose all hope when the "P" button consumed my gaze. Sheer gut instinct moved me to press it, and I prayed it would work out.

When I arrived, the elevator chimed, and the doors opened. "Penthouse," the mechanized voice announced as I stepped off into the hall.

A door in front of me was the only thing in sight other than some decorative plants. Swallowing hard, I walked up to it and knocked. I stood there wishing someone would answer.

After a pause, a unique-looking man opened the door. He was tall, with medium-length black hair styled away from his face. He wore a suit without the jacket but complete with tie and vest. His eyes captured mine, and I noticed their unusual amber color.

"Can I help you?" he asked.

"Are you Michael?" I answered, remembering the name Sister Helen had given.

"No." The hint of a smile graced his face. "I'm Gabriel."

JORDAN

NEW YORK CITY, PRESENT DAY

"Who are you?" Gabriel asked.

"My name is Jordan Conway. May I come in?"

He looked at my large duffel bag, backpack, and generally disastrous state and said, "Sure," as he opened the door wide.

I brushed past him and walked into the apartment, grateful for the sanctuary. He closed the door and locked it, then turned to face me where I stood in the middle of his living room, still clutching my bag.

Unsure of what to say, I blurted out the first thing that came to mind. "Do you play?" I pointed to the violin sitting in the corner.

"Yes, it's my profession."

"Oh, so you're in an orchestra?"

"Not exactly. I started out that way, but I'm a soloist now."

"You must be good then."

He ignored the comment. "Why don't you make yourself comfortable? Can I get you something to eat? You look like you could use some food," he offered, noticing my raggedness.

I placed my duffel on the carpet. I knew I couldn't just come out with the reason I was there, so I said, "I guess I could eat."

"Great. Follow me." Gabriel headed into the kitchen.

The place didn't feel like a penthouse. Its living room, kitchen, and dining room where all visible as part of the open floor plan. In the kitchen, I noticed there were two hallways—one to the right, one to left—branching off from the main living space. The extra square footage possibly made it a penthouse, but the awesome view through the kitchen window and the oversized balcony definitely contributed to the title.

While Gabriel explored the contents of his cabinets, I removed the backpack and set it down on one of the stools lined up along the island.

"Do you have anything to make?" I asked as he scrambled around.

"Not much. I could make you some eggs?" he offered, peering into the fridge.

"That works."

"Would you like some toast with that too?" He held up a loaf of bread from the pantry.

"Sure."

Gabriel went about preparing the food, taking a frying pan out from the cabinet and cracking the eggs into it. He put two slices of bread in the toaster and returned to the eggs.

"How did you get up here?" he asked.

"I jumped in an elevator at the last second," I explained. "The other residents' swipe access must have still registered when they left because I had no problem coming up."

"I see." He concentrated on the cooking, and a beat of silence ensued.

I couldn't wait any longer. "So…Gabriel, was it?" I asked.

"Yes," he replied, turning to look at me.

"What exactly is going on here?"

"I don't know. You tell me."

"Sister Helen sent me. She gave me a piece of paper with your address on it and said I would be safe here…that I was their last hope. These guys chased me the whole time. I thought it was because I bumped into them on the subway earlier, but now I get the feeling that's not the reason."

Gabriel didn't seem to understand. Then, the toast popped up, and his attention was back on the food as he slid the pieces of bread onto a plate alongside the eggs. He placed the food in front of me, offering a fork and knife.

"Thanks," I said.

He started to clean up so I could eat, but I was nervous, and when I got nervous, I tended to blurt out whatever came to mind.

Jokingly, I asked, "Are you, like…a vampire or something?"

Amused, he glanced up at me from the sink. "No."

"That's good." I fumbled with the fork in my hand.

"Is the food all right?" he asked since it remained untouched.

"Yeah," I replied. "Aren't you hungry?"

"No. I already ate."

"That's something a vampire would say."

Gabriel chuckled. "If you're so concerned about me being a vampire, I could give you some garlic to put around your room before you go to sleep tonight."

"Are you saying I can stay here?" I searched his face to see if his words rang true. I'd only just met this guy, and I wasn't sure if I could trust him. But I also had nowhere else to go.

"Yes," he said, placing a spatula in the dishwasher. "Now, these men who were chasing you—what did they look like?"

"Couldn't say. They were dressed in all-black and wore hoods that covered their faces," I explained. "The only things that stood out were the skull tattoos on their hands."

He stopped scrubbing the pan and turned to me. "Did you say, skull tattoos?"

"Yeah," I replied in distraction, wiping up egg yolk with the toast since we were comfortably talking now.

"How many men were there?"

"Six."

He stared at me. "You said Sister Helen sent you. Who is she?"

"She's the head nun at the Holy Trinity Home for Disadvantaged Youth. It's an orphanage," I explained. "I've lived there my entire life. My father died before I was born, and my mother died shortly after giving birth. Sister Helen said you would know what to do. She gave me that backpack."

"Do you mind if I take a look?" he asked, drying his hands on a dish towel.

"No, feel free." I rose to put my plate and utensils in the dishwasher.

Gabriel walked over to the backpack and examined it.

"It was the strangest thing," I continued, coming to his side. "One of the guys in black grabbed onto it. I thought I was doomed, but it was like it burned him or something because he let me go."

"That makes sense. It's been doused in holy water," Gabriel replied.

"Excuse me?"

"Do you know what's inside?" he asked.

"No. Sister Helen gave me the bag. I didn't have time to look."

"Did she give you a key?"

"No...why?"

"Because there's a lock around the zipper. There's no way to open it without a key." Gabriel's brow creased in thought.

"Wait a second... Can we go back to the holy water?"

My question brought his attention back to me. I could tell he was sizing me up, trying to figure out if he could trust me, much like I had moments before. Abruptly, Gabriel walked back to the living room and indicated for me to take a seat on the couch. He stood before me and began to speak.

"How well do you know your Bible?" he asked.

"Well enough," I responded hesitantly. My knowledge of the Bible was slightly better than the average person because of the sisters, but it was nothing compared to the knowledge they had.

"What do you know about angels?"

"Not much other than the four archangels. Michael, Raphael, Uriel, Gabri—" I stopped and stared at him, sensing the direction this conversation was going. "You're not saying..."

He nodded.

"You expect me to believe you're an angel? And not just any angel, but Archangel Gabriel?"

"Yes."

His one-word answer bewildered me, and suddenly, I wasn't so sure if I could trust him. This guy was a complete stranger, I was in his house, and no one else knew where I was. More intimidating was the knowledge that if I couldn't stay here, there was nowhere else for me to go. Perhaps I could track down Sophia, but I'd left my phone at the orphanage, and she was staying at her roommate's house anyway. I had no idea who the girl was or where she even lived. The only option left would be to stay on the streets, which I didn't want to do because those guys were still out there, and I wasn't so sure I could defend myself against them.

I figured playing along with Gabriel was my best option for now, so I exuded a sense of calm in the hope of hiding my panic. "Where are your wings? If you're an angel, shouldn't you have wings?" I leaned my head to glance at his back.

"Yes, I do have them. No one can see them though, not until I reveal them."

"Interesting…" It was a cop-out reply.

"I can tell you don't believe me," he said.

I chuckled. "How do you expect me to?"

Gabriel shook his head and smiled. "I don't know. I thought your open-mindedness about vampires was a good indicator you have a mind for the extraordinary."

I could tell he was trying to joke around, possibly even get on my good side, but this was too unbelievable. "How exactly are you here?" I asked. "I mean…if you want me to trust you, maybe you could explain how this is all possible?"

"It's difficult," he said with downcast eyes.

My voice shook. "Well, could you try? Because I feel like my life's been turned upside-down."

Gabriel took a moment to compose himself before he spoke. "Many centuries ago, seven of us archangels were sent down to Earth to guard humanity in the ages to come. We were scattered across the world, on every continent, and were told to wait and watch for a sign that would indicate it was time for us to act. We spent many years waiting and watching. We witnessed many atrocities. Yet no sign came.

"During our time on Earth, we knew we were not to interfere with the problems of humanity. We had been sent to guard, but we could not involve ourselves in any atrocities or acts of evil. As time went on, we assimilated into society because we were never called back, and our role here became obsolete. With no obvious sign and no means of participating in the struggles of humankind, we began to lose hope and faith…until now."

His explanation didn't convince me, but his last words piqued my curiosity. "What do you mean?"

"You. You must be the sign we were told to wait and watch for. Clearly, whatever is in that bag is important to the fallen forces, and if it's important to them, it's important to us. Sister Helen entrusted you with it for a reason. It's now time for us to finally act."

"Hold on, hold on," I said, getting up from the couch. Nothing was making sense, but his mention of Sister Helen reminded me of her words: *"Whoever is there will help you…they can protect you. You need to trust me."* My trust in Sister Helen was a million times greater than my trust in Gabriel, so I knew I had to stay here, to follow this through and figure everything out. "Before we go any further, I have some questions I want to ask."

"Ask me whatever you like," Gabriel said.

"All right." I paused a moment to think. "When you say evil, you mean what, exactly?"

He swallowed hard, clearly uncomfortable. "I had a brother once, a fellow archangel who fell from Heaven—"

"Wait. You're not about to say what I think you are, right?"

"If you mean, am I insinuating the evil I'm fighting is Satan, then yes."

I rubbed my hands over my face and sat back down. *Sister Helen*, I reminded myself. *Do this for her.*

"So, the devil was the one chasing me?"

"No. Those men who were chasing you are fallen angels. More specifically, they are the top-ranking fallen angels who directly interact with and execute Satan's bidding. The skull tattoo is their identifier. In addition to Satan, only the six of them have it because it marks their rank."

I took a deep breath. "How was I able to escape them?"

Gabriel sensed that was a rhetorical question and remained silent. After a few long seconds, I found the courage to speak again.

"Where do I fit into all this? You said I was the sign you've been waiting for, but why did Sister Helen give me the backpack?"

He nodded. "A very good question. However, that's where things get more speculative."

"How so?"

"Judging by the symbols on that lock," Gabriel said, pointing to the backpack, "it would seem Sister Helen was part of the Sacrarium." At my blank look, he elaborated. "The Sacrarium is an order of people who have been entrusted to protect the holy bloodline and anything relating to it. They believe there is one remaining descendant alive today."

I gazed at him, mouth slightly agape, as I processed his words. "The holy bloodline? Of Jesus and Mary Magdalene? Isn't that a myth or something?"

He smiled. "Now you see why I called it speculative. To some, the idea is blasphemy. To others, it does not concern them. To a select few, it is every part real. I do not know if the bloodline exists or not. To the Sacrarium, it does. History has called them many names and attached certain agendas to their order, but I've heard the Sacrarium that is active today is nothing like those of ancient times. They are merely here to protect the bloodline since it has been persecuted for centuries. Because of their involvement, the members of the order are persecuted as well, to the point of near extinction—which is why you might be their last hope."

"Me?" I asked. "But I know nothing about them."

"I understand that. As I said, it would seem Sister Helen was part of this order, and it seems she wanted you to be as well. Why else would she have given you the backpack? She must have thought you would know what to do."

"But I don't. I have absolutely no idea what I'm supposed to do with that thing! All I know is, it nearly got me killed."

"I believe you," Gabriel reassured me. "For whatever reason, Sister Helen ran out of time to train you. She was obviously threatened by the fallen forces if she had to flee and sent you here."

"You said you weren't part of the Sacrarium. Why would she send me here? How would she even know about this place?"

"Those are difficult questions I have no answer to. However, some people, such as dedicated religious ministry, can sense my celestial energy. I've never met Sister Helen, but the Sacrarium has ways of knowing things that even escape me. Somehow, they must have discovered me and my brothers' presence on Earth. When you arrived, you asked if I was Michael."

I nodded.

"They obviously thought he would be here, which means they know about more than one of us."

"Okay, so they have ways to find out about you all… But why would she send me here and not to another member of the Sacrarium?"

"There are two possible answers. One, there are no members of the Sacrarium left. Two, no else but us can combat an evil such as Satan and his numbers. We've done it before, and we will do it again. I surmise Sister Helen thought you would be most safe with those who could not only defeat Satan, but also protect you."

"Well, that would make the most sense. Fighting the devil and his demons is what you're supposed to do, right?" I smiled, finding some humor in the situation, but Gabriel was unfazed and obviously didn't agree.

"Yes, but it's slightly more complicated than that."

His seriousness erased the smile from my face. "I'm sure it is."

Quiet filled the room. Gabriel glanced at the clock on the mantel and said, "It isn't quite late yet, but you must be tired after everything that transpired tonight."

I followed his gaze. He was right, it wasn't late, yet I suddenly felt like all the energy in my body had been drained, probably because I was coming off an adrenaline high from the chase. Tiredness crept in. I knew I wouldn't be able to survive a night on the streets. I had to make a decision: *Do I stay, or do I leave?*

I went with gut instinct. "I wouldn't mind some sleep."

Gabriel led me down one of the hallways to the spare room, where I placed both of my bags on the floor and turned to look at the man who claimed he was an angel.

"If you need anything, let me know."

After he left, I stood staring at the empty doorway. I still wasn't sure if I trusted him. He seemed like a decent guy, but that was the problem. He *wasn't* a guy. Well, he had the physical form of a man, but why would anyone go around calling themselves an angel?

Sighing in frustration, I rubbed my hands over my head. My brain was not in the mood to figure all this out. Nothing made sense. How could Sister Helen be a part of some secret society? She was the cheery nun who had always been the mother I never had, the one who chased away my nightmares and made everything right again. That's what was frustrating. She had sent me into the unknown, thrown me right into evil's path, without so much as a backward glance. It was unlike her, and because of this, I knew she was in over her head. Sister Helen would never put me in harm's way.

My emotions battled against each other. I knew I had to do this for her—whatever *this* was, or wherever it would take me.

I dropped my arms to my sides, closed the bedroom door, and took a shower. When I finished, I crawled into the guest bed and shut off the light on the nightstand. I should have fallen asleep right away, but I couldn't quiet my mind.

JORDAN

3

New York City, Twelve Hours Ago

I couldn't believe summer was already over. It felt like I graduated just yesterday from Sacred Heart High School, yet here I was, two months later, preparing to leave for my mission trip to Africa. My plan surprised most people when they asked what I would be doing after high school. Typically, they wanted to hear which college I would be attending, but college didn't seem like the right step for me yet.

I turned away from my empty closet and looked at the packed bag on my bed. Almost everything I owned fit in that single duffel. As an orphan living at Holy Trinity, it wasn't like I had many belongings.

A knock on the half-open door drew my attention away from the bag. It was Sophia. Her long, wavy blonde hair swayed as she entered the room. She wore sandals with white shorts and a blue blouse that accentuated her equally blue eyes.

"Sorry to intrude," she said in her singsong voice, "but the car's here to take me to the train station."

"You're leaving already?"

"Yes. It's about a three-hour train ride, and I want to get there before tonight."

"But orientation isn't until tomorrow morning," I protested.

"I know. I just want to be early."

"A whole day early?" I questioned with a smirk.

"Of course." She stepped into my open arms for a hug. "I'm going to miss you," she confessed.

"Me too," I replied, releasing her. "But this is your time to start fulfilling your dreams, so don't worry about me. Harvard is lucky to have you, and you deserve to be there."

"Thanks. I'm still going to miss you," she said, tears in her eyes.

I grabbed her for one more hug. "I know what you're thinking," I murmured in her ear. "This isn't goodbye."

She stepped back and looked at me. "Promise?"

"Promise." I meant it. "Now, if you don't move into your dorm until tomorrow, where are you staying tonight?"

"I'm staying with my roommate, Dafne. I met her in July. Remember I told you, we got along really well? Her parents don't live far from campus, and they suggested I come early since I have no one else to help me move in."

With all this talk of parents and no help, I knew Sophia was upset. "Don't let it get to you, and definitely don't think about it."

"Easy for you to say. At least you had parents who wanted you."

I looked at her skeptically. "That's not fair, Sophia. They wanted me, but they're dead."

Shaking her head, she realized the fault in her words. "I know, I'm sorry. I shouldn't have said that. I just hate that my mom abandoned me."

Before I could respond, Dane, the boy I'd shared this room with for my entire life, kicked the door open, much like he did every time he entered our room, and proceeded to insert himself into our conversation.

"Dead parents or no dead parents, I don't see how anyone could want you."

"Dane!" Sophia exclaimed, coming to my defense.

"What?"

"Apologize."

"What for?"

"For being impolite."

He shrugged off her remark.

"Don't worry about it, Sophia. Whatever he says doesn't bother me," I told her. And it was true. I didn't let Dane's snide comments get to me. Though he and I never got along, I was still civil to him, even if he never returned the sentiment. As kids, I knew we were never going to be close friends, so I gave him the space he needed and would go play downstairs. That was how I met Sophia.

We were both five years old when I found her in the games room one day, playing cards by herself. She had only just arrived at Holy Trinity and hadn't made any friends yet. I asked her if she wanted to play UNO instead. At first, she hesitated, but soon, she agreed, and our friendship was solidified.

As for Dane, I knew he was a lost cause. I couldn't force him to return my respect, so I tolerated his antics. It wasn't like I could switch rooms or ask for a new roommate. Holy Trinity was at its capacity, and I simply had to deal with the situation I was given.

"Every time I find the two of you together, you're always discussing your sob stories," Dane scoffed. "It's pathetic you're both so hung up on people you've never even met."

"That's not true!" Sophia exclaimed. Instinctively, she grabbed at her necklace and rubbed the pendant. It was a St. Michael medallion and was related to her mom, but I wasn't entirely sure how since Sophia hated talking about her. In fact, Sophia hated talking about any memories from her childhood. "I was five years old when I came here, so trust me, I remember my mom," she told Dane. "Thinking about her isn't pathetic. What's pathetic is you. At least I express my emotions and try to deal with them. Instead, you lash out at everyone around you and ignore the fact you hate it just as much as I do, that you have no idea why your parents didn't want you either."

"Maybe they didn't want me. I'll never know because I was barely a few months old when I was left here. But who cares? They had no part in my life, just like your mom, so why should I spend my time fantasizing about them?"

"Sophia?" Sister Helen called from downstairs. "The car's waiting."

Dropping the chain around her neck, she called back, "Coming!" Sophia turned to me once more and gave me a quick hug. "Keep me updated about your mission and write me whenever you can. I want to know everything, and when you get back, we need to meet up no matter what."

"Absolutely," I agreed.

With that, she exited the room without so much as a glance in Dane's direction.

I walked over to the window to watch the driver load in Sophia's luggage. My friend waited on the sidewalk with Sister Helen, the two exchanging a heartfelt goodbye.

"Are you ever going to tell her you like her?"

"Dane, would you stop with that already? I don't have feelings for Sophia."

"Sure, you don't."

I ignored his comment and remained fixed to the window until the sound of a drawer slamming pulled my attention away. I looked over at him. Dane was grabbing his things and stuffing them in a bag. Apparently, he was leaving now too.

I observed his tall figure bent over to reach for shoes in the closet. He had always been taller than me until two years ago, when I finally caught up to his height. He was more muscular though, and I didn't think I would ever match him in strength. His black hair fell into his eyes—an odd look, since he always kept his hair so well-groomed. He wore black jeans with a gray t-shirt and combat boots. The beginnings of a tattoo peeked out from under his left sleeve.

He looked up, and his black eyes registered annoyance when he caught me staring.

"Would you leave me alone?" he demanded.

"I didn't do anything."

"Well, stop staring at me," he complained. He rubbed his angular jaw, a usual gesture whenever he tried to think something through. I imagined he was trying to decide if he should bring his posters with him, the ones plastered over every inch of wall space on his side of the room.

"I guess you're leaving now too?"

"Yeah. The sooner I get out of here, the better. I cannot wait to leave this place."

"You came of legal age in July. Why did you wait another month to leave?"

"The apartment complex I wanted to move into was full. It's close to where I work, so I waited until they had an opening." Abruptly, he stopped and shook his head. "Why am I telling you this?"

"Because you want to be my friend after all?" I teased, smiling.

He flipped me his middle finger and continued to pack.

Shaking my head in disbelief at his rude gesture, I figured I would just leave him alone, but my curiosity overcame me fast. "Do you have any roommates?"

He ignored me and stood on his bed to take down the posters.

"Okay... Probably not then. I mean, who could possibly want to live with you?" I blurted out the words before I knew what I was saying.

He gave me a mean glare. "Who says I'm living with anyone?" he replied, jumping down from the bed. "Although, I do have friends, unlike you."

"You mean those guys you hang out with who look like junkies?"

He stopped his packing to give me another mean glare. "You know nothing about me, so stop judging me with all your assumptions. They might be junkies, but that doesn't mean I am." He paused. "I've got my shit together more than you think. I've saved enough money to afford an apartment on my own, busting my ass like I did working all those jobs. It might be a studio, but it's better than this place. I already have a job set up for myself too, working at a tattoo shop. What do you have to show for yourself other than some asinine idea you want to help people? It's time to grow up, Jordan."

He zipped up his duffel and swung it over his shoulder, ready to leave. Before he could though, I offered my hand. Dane stared at it.

"Although what you just said was hurtful, I'm going to look past it. I egged you on in the first place. I also want to wish you the best of luck."

Dane was hesitant to shake my hand, seeking deception in my words. But there was none. I truly meant what I said.

He quickly grasped my hand and shook it. Of course, he had to get in one last dig. That was who Dane was, and no one would ever change him.

"You too, when you figure out what you want to do with your life." Then, he let go and left the room.

I heard Sister Helen giving him a brief goodbye on the way out and walked back over to the window to see Sophia's car door closing. I lifted my hand to wave, not sure if she could see me, and watched as the car disappeared down the street. Seconds later, Dane exited the building and started off along the sidewalk. He rounded the corner and was gone.

Dane was right. It was time to grow up. He wasn't so confused by the transition like I was. He actually knew what he wanted from life. He'd been a skilled artist ever since we were children, able to draw anything and everything. In high school, he was fascinated with tattooing and got some even before he legally could. They were always in places where the sisters couldn't see since they would be furious if they found out. But he had discovered something he was passionate about, to the point he'd learned how to tattoo and now had a job doing the very thing he loved.

I left the window and sat on the edge of my bed. Seeing the room empty made me realize my childhood was truly over. It was officially time to move on, but I had no idea what I wanted to do with my life.

Out of all the people I knew, I thought Sophia would be the least surprised to learn I wanted to embark on this adventure rather than go to college. Helping people had always been something I was drawn to—so much so, I frequently gave money to the homeless and volunteered at soup kitchens and for charities. The kids at school thought I was insane for doing these things so willingly. They assumed it was because I'd lived in a religious orphanage my entire life and the sisters forced me to be charitable. I had to explain that being a good citizen and a decent person was not a requirement of the residents at Holy Trinity.

Sophia had always understood I enjoyed helping people, which was why her surprise perplexed me. She'd persisted in trying to convince me to apply for college. At one point, I even gave in and let her help me pick out schools. I settled on Cornell, NYU, Fordham, and Columbia. She forced me to put Harvard on the list because that was where she wanted to go, although Cornell was my top choice. I really liked the location, and it had such a great selection of programs I knew I would find something to interest me.

I wasn't sure I would get accepted though. I had good grades and test scores, but most of these schools were elite. Sophia believed I was smart enough to get in. I had to remind her several times, she was the smarter one, the valedictorian. It didn't seem to stop her from pushing me to apply.

Although I didn't get in to Columbia or Harvard, I was offered admission to Cornell, NYU, and Fordham. It was a tough choice because I didn't want to throw away an amazing opportunity, but after doing some research and thinking it over, I deferred my acceptance to Cornell for two years. They let students do this if they had a good reason to take a gap year, and a mission trip was definitely a good reason. This meant I could have the best of both worlds.

Sister Helen agreed it was the best solution. Sophia wanted me to just go to school, but I knew I was meant for a different path, one less traditional. I needed these two years off to answer my mysterious call to help others first. Apparently, Dane didn't think it was the right thing to do either, but who cared about what he thought?

Glancing at the clock on my bedside table, I realized I'd better leave now to pick up my paycheck so I would be back in time for dinner. I made my way downstairs, past two rowdy eight-year-olds who knocked me against the railing. After righting myself, I continued through the wide double doors into the front part of the building, which housed the offices.

Sister Helen looked up from her desk when I knocked on her door. "Can I help you, Jordan?"

I gazed upon her face. Her blue eyes, strong cheekbones, and silver mane of wild curls. She had this way of smiling that wasn't a full smile but a mere perk of the lips expressing her most genuine emotions. Her bold, spunky personality was unlike any of the other sisters. While most of them wore full habits, Sister Helen preferred a long skirt with a white button-up shirt and a solid black vest. Nothing ever covered her hair. Never.

"I just wanted to let you know, I'm going out to run an errand. I'll be back in time for dinner," I assured her.

"Excellent. The other sisters and I are really looking forward to it, though farewell dinners are such a bittersweet occasion. We've prepared all your favorite food."

"That sounds great, Sister Helen. I'm really looking forward to it too."

"See you later, Jordan. Be safe."

With a grateful smile, I pulled her office door closed.

GABRIEL

4

After the shower turned off and the light in the guest room flickered out, I sat in the living room composing music until the nighttime news came on. Then, making sure the volume was low, I watched the breaking headline announce a fire was burning at an abandoned orphanage in Brooklyn. Understanding inherently that it was Holy Trinity, I turned off the television. Jordan didn't need to know until morning.

I waited a little longer to be sure he was asleep before rising from the couch and walking to my office on the opposite side of the apartment. My storage chest sat below the window and responded to my celestial energy when I rested my hand on it, softly clicking open. I reached inside and grasped a long gold horn. After opening the window, I pressed the horn to my lips and blew. Notes flowed through the city and out into the sky, the sound capturing only the attention of those the call was meant for, drifting past humans and finding the ears of archangels.

I hoped they would answer, because it was finally time...

Time to deal with everything that happened in Heaven.

GABRIEL

5

"Gabriel! You must come quick!" Raphael exclaimed.

"What is wrong?"

"We have all been sent a message to gather in council."

My brow creased. "In council? What for? I received no message."

"Your message was brought to the Watch Tower. The Cherubim thought you were on duty. I flew down quickly to find you. The message was brief. All it said was, we are to gather in council," Raphael explained, concern on his face.

"What do you think it means?"

"I am not sure. But it must be serious."

"Right." I carefully placed my violin in its case and stowed it away in my designated cabinet. "We must go."

Raphael and I strode out of the Sanctuary of Music, passing by the other six sanctuaries containing each circle of vocation. All angels in the Third Choir were gifted certain skills that determined which circle they would be placed into. The circles were grouped into seven categories: healing, home, teaching, nature, art, power, and music.

I was placed as an angel of music, but this was unusual for an archangel as many of our rank were placed into the other circles.

The sanctuaries were spread out next to each other in a half-arc shape along the valley. Above the entrance of each sanctuary was a symbol representative of the vocation housed in each. There was a caduceus, a flame, a scroll, a tree, an artist's palette, a helmet, and a music note.

In the distance, the sanctuaries were overlooked by two cathedrals on the hills and by three towers on the edge of Low Heaven. The cathedrals housed the Council of Principalities and the Council of Angels, but Raphael and I were headed for the three towers—the middle of which held the Council of Archangels. It was flanked on either side by the Watch Towers, where two archangels stood on duty throughout day and night, watching over the world.

We flew immediately to the middle tower. These structures, unlike the sanctuaries and cathedrals, looked more like circular observatories, with wide-open entranceways permitting us to fly directly into them. Once we landed, Raphael rushed forward to a large wooden door that held thirteen different keyholes. All of them but two were lit, indicating the owners of the keys were already inside. Raphael and I were the last two remaining.

We inserted our keys in the proper places, and the door creaked open.

Sitting around a large circular table, upon which the sky and all of its stars were reflected, were the eleven other archangels who had been appointed by Father to sit on the council. We did not know why He had chosen the thirteen of us in particular, but we all suspected He saw favorable qualities in each of us. Father had based our appointments on the astrological constellations He founded when creating the sky and all of its stars.

Raphael and I walked into the room, headed to our respective seats, as the door slammed behind us. Everyone heard the locks click, shutting us in and preventing anyone on the outside from disturbing us. I sat down in my chair with my wings comfortably situated. The backs of all the seats were tall and slender, allowing them to run up the middle of our backs so our wings were not affected or confined. Each seat had a symbol inscribed on the slim back relating to the astrological constellation we represented. To my right sat Chamuel, and to my left was Tzaphkiel.

Immediately, Metatron began to speak. "Thank you all for answering the summons and arriving so quickly. I appreciate your swiftness and welcome your presence to this council meeting."

"And we welcome yours, Metatron. I do not wish to speak for everyone, but I think our swiftness was due to the summons coming from the Cherubim. Usually, most messages are carried to us from the Second Choir, not the First," Raziel replied.

"You are right, Raziel, and because of this, I am sure you all suspect the summons involves something serious."

I glanced at Raphael. He had warned me about the same.

"Unfortunately, your suspicions are correct," Metatron continued. "I received notice that another object has gone missing."

A hum of voices filled the room as my comrades began to speak all at once, concern furrowing their brows.

Uriel could be heard above the noise as he asked, "What was taken this time?"

We turned to Metatron, all of us on the edge of our seats awaiting his answer.

"The Castle Key."

"What would anyone want with that?" Tzaphkiel said.

"To unlock the castle tower," Ariel offered.

"Yes, but why?" I asked, glancing back at Metatron.

He returned my gaze. "Unfortunately, the Cherubim have divulged no more detail than that. What they have asked is for us to be vigilant and increase our watches in order to possibly discover who..."—he hesitated—"or what is stealing these items."

At the mention of thievery, concern deepened on my comrades' faces. Some even let out gasps of disbelief. Samael was the only one who remained resolute. He neither contributed to the conversation nor expressed his emotions. When he caught me looking, I averted my eyes.

Raziel demanded, "How can this be? First, a book was taken from the Sanctuary of Teaching, and now, the Castle Key has been stolen, presumably from the Hall of Law. There is obviously a pattern occurring here, and I am afraid High Heaven is the next target, especially with the Seventh Day Gathering coming up."

"Raziel, please calm down," Metatron cautioned.

"No, I will not calm down. Thievery goes against everything Heaven was created for. It goes against everything *we* were created for, and I am afraid to admit it, but one of us angels must be the perpetrator."

A hush fell over the room. Samael looked at all of us with a bemused expression, letting out a little chuckle.

"Is our distress amusing to you, Samael?" Raphael said.

"No, I just cannot believe Raziel is repulsed by the idea of thievery when he himself is a liar."

"What?" Raziel shouted.

"All right, everyone, we need to relax," Chamuel offered, eyeing Raziel, who stood from his chair in defense.

Samael ignored him. "You are going to act innocent, as if you do not know what these objects mean? What they signify?" Samael asked Raziel.

"What are you talking about?"

"You know what I am talking about!" he yelled, rising from his seat.

"Samael…" Michael warned.

"No! I will not relent. He knows."

"I do not understand what he is accusing me of," Raziel pleaded to no one in particular.

Samael shook his head in frustration.

"If you think you know something, Samael, would you please care to enlighten us?" Jophiel interjected.

At first, Samael hesitated. When he finally spoke, he chose his words carefully. "There is a great power in our world that Father has created…a great potential for someone to possess that power if they know how to discover it. The only way to do so is to read the book that was taken. I have heard it contains information about things beyond our knowing…that it divulges all the necessary components to wield this immense power."

"Enough!" Metatron bellowed, his voice reverberating through the room. I flinched in my chair, not expecting such a passionate outburst. "I suggest you sit down and no longer discuss this foolishness."

"Why?" Samael asked.

"Because you do not fully understand what you are talking about."

"So, it is true? The book? Have you been lying to us?"

"Stop this nonsense! I have not been lying to you." Metatron was frustrated, his jaw clenched.

"Why are you so upset with me mentioning it?"

"Because you are causing dissention!"

"They have a right to know. Unless you do not want them to…"

"That is not the reason," Metatron was quick to answer. "The book that was stolen is off-limits to everyone except angels of teaching, and even at that, we are not supposed to access it. The fact you know so much about what it holds raises my suspicions that *you* took it."

Samael glared at him, opening his mouth to retaliate, but Ariel spoke before he could.

"Why can we not know about it?" Ariel asked.

"Please tell us," Tzaphkiel coaxed.

Metatron took a moment to compose himself. "The reason you are not supposed to know about it is because Father forbids it."

"Why?" I asked.

"Because the book contains principles beyond our knowing, and for that reason, Father wishes for it to be kept secret. There are things mentioned in this book no angel understands—myself included. As an angel of teaching, I might have the ability to devise their meaning, but Father will not sanction it. I suspect the only one who truly knows what is in that book is Father, but He is not likely to reveal that to anyone. Not even to me. While what Samael was saying is true, there is a side to this power that leans toward darkness. In the wrong hands, this book could be disastrous to many."

"Like who?" Ariel asked.

"To us, to Father, to humanity. The possibilities of danger are endless. As an angel of teaching, it is my job to *protect* this knowledge, not *use* it. I am sorry I was not straightforward from the beginning, but the promise of power can pollute the mind of any being, which is why Father does not make it known. If I were you, I would never speak of this again." He resumed his seat.

"Zadkiel and Raziel are angels of teaching too," I pointed out. "Do either of you know about this book?"

"I know where it resides within the sanctuary, and I have seen the pages of it once, along with Metatron and Raziel. But beyond that, I have little awareness of its meaning," Zadkiel explained.

"I knew it existed, but I never paid attention to it either. I knew it was there, but I also understood that it needed to be ignored," Raziel said.

Fanatical, Samael spoke up. "None of you care that they withheld this information from us? That they lied?"

"Why would we? You heard what Metatron said," I replied.

"I know. He warned us it is dangerous. But the power…"

"Please, let this rest," Metatron pleaded.

"Why? Would you not want that power?"

"Stop! Why are you so obsessed with this?" I asked Samael.

"Because we have an immense potential for power, yet we never use it. All our energy goes into serving Father rather than ourselves. We were given the ability of free will but no one expresses it. Order and stability are so ingrained in us that none of us can decide for ourselves or create our own destiny. We have the capacity to choose for ourselves, to act for ourselves, yet our choice is always second to Father's agenda."

"Samael, tread lightly on the accusations you are raising," Sandal-phon warned.

Everyone seemed to take notice. Sandalphon was usually the quiet one. For him to speak out meant Samael's words were a concern.

"Why? I am merely stating, we are creatures with free will and we should not be subjugated to Father. Just because He made us and the divine order of things does not mean we have to follow His every command. I do not understand why He would not want us to possess the power in that book when He already has the same. Unless He prefers to make us feel like inferior servants who should consistently do His bidding."

"End it!" Michael roared, rising from his chair.

Samael was surprised by his emotion. "Why?"

"Because what you are saying is treasonous."

"You mean true," Samael contested.

Chamuel interjected before Michael could react, standing up from his seat and raising his arms out in a manner to resolve the tension. "We must all remain calm."

"How can you dismiss this? Do you agree with him?" I asked.

Samael looked toward the angel expectantly.

"No, of course not. I merely think we all need to settle down. Fighting or arguing, or whatever you call this disagreement, will not help us. We must maintain a united front. Because of this, Samael, I suggest you eradicate these thoughts from your mind."

Samael curled his hands into fists and clenched his jaw. "None of you understand. He would not have made us this way if He did not want us to express our thoughts."

"Samael, please," Jophiel tried. "Father allows us to voice our opinions, our thoughts as you say, but to a certain extent. The ideas you are speaking of are too rebellious and, quite frankly, should not be declared so liberally."

"That is exactly my point! We can only do things to a certain extent. There are always limitations put on us. Meanwhile, Father can just *summon* us and *command* us to do anything. None of you see the error in this rationale."

There was complete stillness in the room. The majority of us stood out of our chairs in defense against Samael. The few who remained seated stared in bewilderment.

"Father is not here, the First and Second Choirs are not here. We can communicate freely and truthfully without being judged. This is the time to speak if you feel subservient," Samael persuaded.

"If you are trying to insinuate we are thinking the same but are simply too fearful to say anything, then you are wrong," Zadkiel replied. "However, I cannot speak for everyone."

"No, you cannot. But you are absolutely right, Zadkiel. None of us are having these seditious thoughts," I interjected.

"Gabriel, your words are making it impossible for me to see how everyone else feels. By attempting to control the conversation, you are preventing others from voicing their true opinions," Samael admonished.

"Fine. But judging by the tension, the unease, and the worry you are inflicting upon every one of us in this room, you clearly cannot see we are all frightened by your words, not inspired," I said.

Samael gazed around the room. "None of you agree with me? None of you feel the same?"

"No, we do not. Now, if you would *please* give this up, we may all be able to salvage ourselves from the treachery we have been exposed to," Metatron concluded. He stood and exited the room with the rest of us close on his heels.

GABRIEL

Heaven, In the Beginning

6

After leaving the council room, I flew to the Watch Tower, where I took my place upon the parapet and marveled at the world below. Although time passed in mornings and evenings down there, no such measure of time was relevant in Heaven. The home of Father's celestial beings was always full of light, and night and darkness never penetrated here. The view was remarkable, just as Father had created this new world to be, but the moment was tarnished by Samael's outlandish ideas. I did not agree with him in the slightest, and I knew somehow, deep down, he was planning on doing something foolish. Something that would change the very nature of our world.

Because of my concerns, I decided to write Father a note about what had occurred. Once Chamuel released me from watch duty, I flew to my room, which was located in one of the other towers. When I landed in the circular entranceway, I descended several flights of stairs until I was on the correct floor. Inside, Zadkiel sat at his desk, rubbing his forehead as he analyzed some scrolls. He looked up when I entered.

"Do you need the room?"

"No. Just need some parchment," I told him. We shared the room, and we were always mindful to give each other peace when needed. Right now, it seemed Zadkiel needed some, so I collected parchment, ink, and a quill, and then left.

I flew outside and landed in the valley. Taking a seat on the ground, out of the way of passersby, I began composing my message, telling Father of the events and accusations that occurred at the meeting. When the task was complete, I looked up. Sending this note was a betrayal and a necessary loyalty all at once. I did not want to make Samael feel like he could not confide in me, but these inner instincts were raising warning bells I had to address.

Putting my lips together, I whistled. A small brown sparrow came flying through the air and landed upon my outstretched finger. I admired its beauty, then transferred the bird to my shoulder and rolled the small bit of parchment into a scroll. The bird flew to my bent knee, anticipating I was going to attach something to its leg. I fastened the note securely, and it flew off, already knowing the intended recipient.

For a long while afterward, I sat thinking about what I had done and all its implications. My thoughts led me to ponder Samael's words. *Is Father really controlling our ability to choose for ourselves? Do I feel subservient? Is the book as dangerous as Metatron warned?* I shook my head, trying to expel the thoughts. Samael's ideas were like a plague spreading through my mind. I would not succumb to his false assertions.

I touched the band of letters that wrapped around my upper arm and was reassured by its presence. Father had marked all of us with emblems. By touching mine, I knew who I was and what purpose I served. This emblem was my name spelled out in angelic script. All angels had one scrolled around their left arm. I mused at the other symbol imprinted on my body, the astrological sign of Gemini. It graced my left wrist. Only the archangels on the council had these marks.

I was so absorbed in my thoughts I did not register Samael in the trees to my right. Standing, because I did not wish for him to see me, I saw Michael approaching and sat down again fast to ensure neither comrade detected me. I tried to occupy myself by admiring my surroundings, but this did not keep my attention for long.

Michael walked up to Samael, holding a piece of parchment in his hands and looking upset.

"Ah, Michael," Samael said upon seeing him. "I am glad you got my letter. Well, what do you think?"

"I do not know what to think, Samael. I thought I expressed my dissent during council. All I can say is, these principles you have written down go strongly against what we have been taught. We were made to be good." Michael gestured to the letter.

"What do you mean? You think I am something else...something bad?"

"I do not mean that. As your brother, I am only trying to advise you to stop this nonsense."

"You do not agree with me then?" Samael's stance changed. "Michael, I trust you more than any of the others. I wrote to you thinking it would be a better form of communication because I thought you did not want to voice your opinions in front of the council."

"I am sorry if I gave you the wrong impression, Samael, but no, I do not agree with you. Now, listen. I need you to come with—"

"Here." Samael plucked a fig from the tree they were under and handed it to him.

"No." Michael pushed his hand away. "This is not a moment for fun. This situation you now have involved me in is very serious. You have not acted right since you returned from Eden, and I think you need to go to Father immediately."

"Judging by your lack of enthusiasm, I take it you do not want to be involved in my…fun. Is that what you call it?"

"No, I do not want to be involved, but I *am* worried about you and think you should seek help. I can come with you. You do not have to go alone. You have done nothing wrong yet, and I am sure He will forgive you."

"Why would I go to Him? He cannot help me. No one can. Besides, I will never be forgiven."

"What do you mean?" Michael asked.

"Apparently, you are like the rest of them who abhor my company and spurn my ideas," Samael said, admiring the fruit in his hand.

"You are misunderstanding me. I am trying to *help*," Michael countered.

I watched Michael and Samael secretly, knowing I should not be there. I repositioned myself on the ground to make my departure as stealthily as possible. However, a fallen branch snapped beneath my foot, alerting them both to my presence.

Samael stopped the conversation. He turned to look at me and stared directly into my eyes. I saw so much anger and hatred in them, two emotions I never thought would enter into this Paradise. He quickly reached out and snatched the letter from Michael's hand. The violent action pulled Michael's attention back.

"Samael!" Michael called to his retreating figure.

He did not stop.

GABRIEL

7

HEAVEN, IN THE BEGINNING

From that moment on, the trust between Samael and Michael was broken.

Samael knew many of us suspected him of stealing the missing objects and sought allegiance elsewhere. I saw the anger and hatred lurking inside, and I knew he was waiting for the precise moment to show his true colors.

After receiving no response from my first message to Father, I wrote Him twice more with updates. I emphasized more than anything that I thought the extreme change in Samael's behavior was most worrisome. On my third attempt, I finally received a response. The brown sparrow I sent my first message with found me sitting on one of the two hills in Low Heaven that had a wonderful view of the world below. He landed on my shoulder, and I lifted my finger to him so he could jump on. Then, I carefully detached the small piece of parchment from his leg with my other hand.

The moment it was untied, he set off again. I unrolled the message and read its contents.

I will take care of it.

The words spelled out before me in angelic script offered no sense of calm. While I was content He had finally taken my warnings, there was still unease rising in me that His response did not reduce.

When I looked up, Michael was walking toward me. He sat down beside me on the ground, and I knew I had to reveal my apprehension.

"I know you are worried," Michael began. "I am too. That anger and hatred you see in him, I see it also."

"It was never there before."

"I know. I know it better than anyone. I just do not understand what changed."

"Samael did not reveal anything to you? In the letter, perhaps?"

"No. That letter only contained more ranting and raving, much like the council meeting. I took it seriously then, and I am taking it seriously now. You heard our conversation. I tried to appeal to him. I tried to let him know I was still there, but he pulled away."

"He pulled away from all of us, Michael. There is nothing you can do if he does not want your help."

"I know. I just feel like I failed him as a brother."

"You did nothing wrong. You offered your help. I know it must be hard for you since the two of you were so close," I reasoned. Not only were Michael and Samael on the council, they were both in the same vocation as angels of power, meaning they were skilled fighters ready for combat.

"You speak the truth, Gabriel, but I just feel betrayed. He was like a brother to me. Not in the sense we are all brothers and sisters in Father's realm, but like a *real* brother. I know that sounds trivial."

"No, it does not. I understand. You two were similar in many ways.

You formed a bond, but now, he has forged his own path—one you cannot tread because you do not feel the same. This has revealed a difference between the two of you. You take your position as an angel of power seriously, devoting yourself to Father and obeying His will. Samael has the same position but has turned his attention to himself, lusting for his own power and control rather than using his abilities to protect others."

Michael nodded in agreement but did not speak.

"I just try to look back and wonder where this new behavior started. What triggered this defiance, this change of heart?"

"I wonder the same sometimes. Did you notice, he has not been acting right since he returned from Eden?" Michael said.

"No, I did not, but now you mention it, he has been different. Did he tell you about anything that happened there?

"No. When he returned, he told me everything was fine. But he has not been right since."

"Well, I composed several messages and sent them to Father in order to warn Him about Samael's behavior."

"And?"

I handed him the small piece of parchment.

"Ah," Michael replied.

I nodded. "I want to help Him, but I have no idea how to do that. Between Samael and these missing objects, my warnings seem very insubstantial."

Michael became silent. I knew he wanted to say something but was holding back.

"What is it?" I asked.

"With everything going on with Samael, I forgot about the missing objects. Raziel is probably right. Whoever the culprit is, they are most likely targeting High Heaven next, which means the Seventh Day Gathering serves as a perfect distraction."

"That is logical…and I suspect you are right," I said, thinking the matter over carefully. "I cannot believe how unwise I have been." I stood up and paced. "If only I paid more attention to this before. I forgot about Raziel's words, but if I had remembered, I could have warned Him more precisely."

"Gabriel, you tried. You did all you could. I imagine if you included more details, the answer would have been the same," Michael said, rising from the ground. "I will see you soon. I realize I have to release Ariel from watch duty. I briefly forgot we are all taking extra shifts because of the missing objects."

I watched him leave, paralyzed by the idea the inevitable was coming, and there was no way to stop it. It seemed like time—something I never took note of—was suddenly moving so fast, because I soon found myself standing in the valley outside of the sanctuaries, where a group of archangels had formed to fly to High Heaven together.

Raphael was making sure all the angels of healing were present, while Chamuel and Tzaphkiel guided the angels of the home. Jophiel was trying to coax the angels of art out of their sanctuary, many protesting about leaving masterpieces and inventions unfinished. Zadkiel stood aimlessly among the angels of teaching, while Metatron and Raziel took lead of the group. Uriel and Sandalphon already had the angels of nature ready to proceed. Michael and Ariel were standing in front of the Sanctuary of Power, conversing with one another with troubled looks on their faces. I was alone, as there were no other archangels who were angels of music, so I made my way over to them.

"What is wrong?" I asked.

"Samael is not here," Ariel explained.

"Have you looked for him?"

"Yes, we sent out a search party and even looked ourselves. There is no sign of him," Michael said.

"Where could he be? Do you think he left already?"

"Of course he did. It is exactly the type of stunt he would pull after that council meeting."

At Ariel's words, I looked at Michael.

"We must go. There is no one else to wait for," he replied, walking away to inform everyone we were ready to depart.

Metatron was displeased by Samael's absence. Michael silenced him with a stern look.

With that, we all spread our wings and took off into the air. It was exhilarating, flying through the realms of Heaven, especially with so many of us. All the eye could see was a sea of white wings, and the mass of angels only grew in size as we passed the two cathedrals and the Principalities and Angels joined us. All of us made up the Third Choir of the Celestial Hierarchy, known as Heaven's messengers.

Once we mounted the tallest hill, we quickly arrived in Middle Heaven, where our ranks grew ever more as the Dominions, Virtues, and Powers merged with our flock. These angels comprised the Second Choir, known as Heaven's governors. In their realm, the terrain changed into mountains and cliffs. Unlike Low Heaven, this domain had barely any ground or clouds to stand or walk upon, forcing all the angels who resided here to fly in order to get around. As we flew over the region, the beauty of three tall cliffs that held the councils for the Dominions, the Virtues, and the Powers struck my sight. These buildings were known as halls, and they had pillared entranceways and long steps leading up to them. The architecture of the halls matched the formal nature of the angels who inhabited Middle Heaven.

Our flock began to break left, gaining momentum and speed to make the elevated ascent into High Heaven. It was refreshing to have such a journey and to be able to spread my wings for a longer period of time. The wind blew through them, ruffling my feathers and reviving the life in them. We burst through a span of clouds, and the sight before us was breathtaking. A radiant light glowed throughout this realm and encased every inch of High Heaven in almighty awe. It was a kingdom of clouds, which centered on a large castle in the middle of the sky. This fortress rested on an enormous cloud. The spires and turrets gleamed, and the white marble façade dazzled the eye as it sparkled against the light.

Everyone flew past the castle and continued to the right, toward a cloud that was the designated gathering place. All of us began to pull up. I stretched my wings down to either side and gracefully landed, slightly disappointed our meeting would not take place in the castle. Instead, we were out in the open air.

The highest rank of angels, the Seraphim, Cherubim, and Thrones, were already gathered. These angels formed the First Choir, known as Heaven's counselors.

Once we were all together, the festivities ensued.

Every so often, Father arranged the Seventh Day Gathering for all His divine beings to attend. He had created a similar day for human-kind simply known as Sunday, meant for worship, rest, and spending time together. In Heaven, our gatherings did not occur every seven days. Instead, the timing of them was more random, and usually, there was a large gap before we had one again. This gathering in particular was taking place much sooner than any of us expected, and I surmised Father had made the decision because of the missing objects. Not only would a gathering keep up morale among the angels, it would alert us to anyone who was suspicious or who might be missing.

There was always music, singing, laughter, and camaraderie, and this time, it was a welcome distraction from all the worry about Samael. However, even as I played my violin in the symphony, those anxious feelings returned. I tried to calm myself by getting lost in the music, but to no avail. Instead, I focused on what the others were doing.

Metatron was having a debate with angels from the Second Choir.

Tzaphkiel was dancing to the music along with other angels of the home.

Chamuel and Jophiel were having a conversation with some Cherubim.

Zadkiel sat alone, reading a scroll.

Ariel was introducing Uriel and Raphael to other angels of power.

Grace, Hope, and Peace, three Virtues, were serenading Raziel and Sandalphon.

Michael was brooding by himself, alert and on watch. *At least I am not the only one worrying about a potential threat.*

I brought my attention back to the task in hand and filtered out the activity around me. A sour note from a flute had us stop in the middle of a ballad, as angels of music never made such a mistake. The other angels at the gathering carried on as if they had not heard it, but the angels of music assembled around me were upset.

"Who misplayed?" Griel demanded.

"Sorry," Araziel confessed.

I gazed into the face of my comrade, recognizing the signs of nervous distraction. "Araziel, it is nothing to be ashamed of. All angels of music make mistakes sometimes."

Griel huffed, knowing "mistakes" and "angels of music" were two concepts that did not belong in the same sentence.

Araziel ignored her. "Thanks, Gabriel. These missing objects have me on edge."

We all raised our instruments again and started the song over. Halfway through, a thought struck my mind. *How does Araziel know about the missing objects? That information was not revealed to everyone…* I glanced at my comrade. He played his flute but seemed anxious, like he was expecting something to happen. I knew he did not enjoy playing in front of large groups, but his earlier comment lingered in my mind. *Perhaps he overheard one of us talking.*

Of course, that had to be it. There was no other logical explanation.

GABRIEL

8

HEAVEN, IN THE BEGINNING

Once the celebration ended, Michael and I stayed behind in the hopes of talking to Father. We wanted clarity and reassurance, but instead, we had to settle for talking to the Head Seraphim, Seraphiel, who promised to relay our worries to Him, telling us repeatedly He had everything taken care of.

We left shortly after that, realizing we simply could not do any more except call a council meeting and let the others know our concerns. On our arrival in Low Heaven, Michael went to check on Cassiel and Haniel, who were on watch during the gathering and might have seen Samael. I headed to the council room and sent out the message we needed to meet.

In a short amount of time, all our comrades filled the council room. All except Samael.

"As Head of Council," Metatron began, "I call this meeting to attention. Since Michael and Gabriel called upon us, we shall now give them the floor."

"Thank you," I responded. "As you can all see, Samael is not among us. He was not at the gathering either. We fear he is missing. Michael and I are concerned because the last time we all saw him, he was expressing unfavorable ideas, and his disposition had obviously changed. We believe him to be dangerous."

"Dangerous? How so?" Ariel asked.

"Well, considering his anger and rebellious language, he might try to do something to seek Father's attention," I explained.

"But the Seventh Day Gathering is over," Ariel said.

"Yes, but that should not matter. We need to take action. We need to prepare."

"I am sorry, but I thought we all thought the thief would strike during the gathering. That did not happen, so why are we preparing now?" Tzaphkiel asked.

"Because Samael is missing," I replied.

"Isn't he the thief?"

"There is no evidence to prove that," I pointed out.

"Correct, but why else would Samael feel the need to leave unexpectedly, unless he thought we were onto him?"

Seeing the conversation was veering far off course, I tried to reign it in. "Everyone, I understand you are all under the assumption Samael is the thief. I cannot give you an answer regarding that situation. We are here because he is missing, and judging by his recent change in temperament, we believe him to be dangerous. For these reasons, we need to prepare ourselves. Now, I have written several messages to Father to warn Him about Samael. Regardless, I still think we need to put together a plan to ensure our safety."

"What was Father's response?" Metatron asked.

I looked at Michael, knowing this answer would be our undoing.

"He told us He would take care of it."

"Then He will take care of it, and we should not worry. I am concerned about Samael too, but Father might have already located him, and He could be dealing with the situation as we speak," Metatron reasoned.

"Right," I suggested. "But—"

"Look, I understand you all think you know Samael," Michael interrupted. "You can believe in the comforting possibility Father is resolving this situation, but no one knows Samael like I do, and my instincts tell me we need to prepare for an attack. As the leader of our army, I am asking the council's approval to put some procedures in place. You do not have to agree. You do not have to participate. I simply need your verbal support. I know we must take Father's words into consideration, and I am not trying to disobey Him, I just believe we should be ready. I want to protect us, and I want to make sure we are safe."

"Then we shall put it to a show of hands," Raziel said. "All in favor of Michael and his wish to act?"

Hands went in the air, seven in total, including Michael's and mine.

"All opposed?"

The five remaining hands rose.

I was pleased the odds were in our favor. My happiness did not last long.

"As Head of Council," Metatron began, "I reject this tally."

"What? Why?" I blurted.

"Gabriel, I simply cannot let you and Michael do this. There is no reason to act other than your belief Samael has become dangerous, which we cannot prove. Yes, we all witnessed a very worrisome outburst, and I will be the first to admit I was concerned about his interest in the stolen objects. However, you have consulted with Father, and He said He would take care of it. We cannot disregard that just because Michael has suspicions. I feel horrible about this, but we cannot do anything." Metatron's words, his body language, even his facial expression revealed he did not want to let us down. He had a duty to fulfill though. As Head of Council, it was his job to determine how we would act, so he had to reject the tally because it went against his responsibility, our orders, and the structure that made up our world.

"Fine." Michael sighed.

"I am sorry," Metatron apologized, looking directly at Michael.

He nodded his head.

"Our meeting is adjourned," Metatron concluded.

Everyone began to leave. I stood up, ready to exit, when Michael met my eyes and shook his head. It was a sign to stay. The others who had shown their support saw it too and came to stand by my side. Raphael, Uriel, Jophiel, Chamuel, Zadkiel, and I knew no action meant ignorance, and ignorance led to vulnerability. None of us were about to let either of those happen.

The seven of us acted together, without council consent, by making arrangements in the event of Samael's return. We discussed strategy, and later, gathered supplies and weapons in the Sanctuary of Power.

Then, we began to warn other angels about the potential threat.

GABRIEL

9

Heaven, in the Beginning

In a brief moment of solitude, I realized I never returned my violin to the Sanctuary of Music after the celebration. Retrieving the instrument from the council room, I landed in front of the sanctuary and walked through the portico into the main hall. I headed for my cabinet and had just secured my violin in its proper place when I overheard two voices having a tense argument.

"You idiot! I told you to steal the scepter during the celebration. Why did you not listen to me?"

"Because that seemed like the worst possible time to do it! Everyone was in High Heaven, where the scepter is kept."

"Yes, but they were not anywhere near the castle. You could have taken it without being detected."

"Easy for you to say. You are not the one doing all this sneaking around."

I moved closer to see who the culprits were, and as I was about to turn the corner on the last row of instrument cabinets, one of the voices said, "Did you hear that? Someone is here."

With my presence now detected, I hesitated no longer and rounded the corner without a second thought. To my surprise, Araziel stood before me, but with no companion.

"What are you doing here?" he demanded.

"Putting away my violin," I said. "The better question is, what are *you* doing? I heard you! If you planned to take some scepter, did you steal the book and the Castle Key too? Why? And who were you talking to?"

My barrage of questions was left unanswered as a deafening roar came from outside. Naturally, I turned toward the sound. I knew I had to investigate but not unless Araziel came with me to explain himself.

When I brought my attention back, however, he was gone.

I stood there in confusion until another deafening roar sounded out. Running for the exit, what I saw upon leaving the Sanctuary of Music was pandemonium. Angels of all kinds were running and flying in every direction, terrified and confused. No one knew who the attacker was because the threat was from within our ranks. Defenseless and with nowhere to take cover, everyone was overwhelmed as the traitorous forces invaded. Hundreds had already been injured as the rebels set fire to the sanctuaries.

Through the blaze, I saw Metatron, Raziel, and Zadkiel desperately trying to extinguish the flames that threatened the Sanctuary of Teaching, home to all of Heaven's divine wisdoms. Most of the other angels were abandoning their sanctuaries to seek safety.

All I could see was chaos. Familiar comrades had turned into enemies, their wicked, malicious expressions revealing a hidden nature. All that was good and light had been erased, leaving corruption and darkness in its place. I had never seen this before, but I knew evil had been introduced into our Paradise.

The anarchy continued. Explosions could be heard above us in the other two realms as rogue angels annihilated all that symbolized our heavenly Father's will.

Samael's plan was becoming clear. He had separated his forces between the three realms in order to cause more chaos and destruction, but he had taken most of his rebels with him to High Heaven. Apparently, he thought to secure mass quantities of anointing oil as well because there was no other way to account for the raging fires and loud explosions. Michael and I had not discussed procuring oil because it would do more harm than good. The oil was located in every edifice throughout Heaven. However, larger amounts were stored in the Forge in High Heaven. Samael must have stolen some, along with flints, to produce the flames destroying our world.

I was pushed to the ground by a stampede of angels trying to escape the rampage of insurgents. As I tried to get up, a helpful hand appeared through the chaos. I was not surprised to see Michael standing before me, resolute and unwavering in all the madness. He was prepared for battle, with his longsword attached to his hip.

We shared a look, knowing we were the ones who had to stop this rebellion.

Quickly, Michael took command. He dispatched soldiers to collect the resources we had gathered in the Sanctuary of Power—shields, helmets, swords, spears, axes, bows and arrows. There were even unique weapons, such as a scythe and a club, since he had collected whatever he could get his hands on.

Our preparations proved useful; it did not take long for our army to assemble and strike back. Since there were not as many rebels down here as there were in the other two realms, the angels of power rallied behind Michael and began to dispatch the rebel forces. While they were engaged in combat, I rallied some of the remaining angels to put out the fires.

By the time we had accomplished all this, a semblance of peace had returned to Low Heaven. Even though the pure and marvelous beauty of the region had been tarnished, flames no longer consumed it, and the dissidents had been struck down or had fled.

There was no time to think about the condition of our realm though, as the injured lay in agony on the ground. Raphael and the angels of healing were already attending to the wounded. One of the cathedrals had been secured and was now acting as an infirmary. While everyone helped to regain some control, Michael gathered willing, able-bodied troops. He was preparing to embark to the other realms.

Suddenly, something changed in me.

I had to fight back.

No, I *needed* to fight back.

Michael turned to look at me as I approached.

"I am going with you," I told him.

"So are we," Uriel said, closing in behind with Raphael, Jophiel, Chamuel, and Zadkiel.

With no time to argue, Michael did not object. The six of us grabbed weapons and joined the ranks of angels. Having assembled his army of thousands, Michael signaled us into formation for take-off. I gripped the scythe, somehow the only weapon remaining, and waited for his command.

"Wings up!" he shouted, and within seconds we were in the air.

It did not take long to arrive in Middle Heaven. The sight was devastating. The Second Choir seemed to be the only ones who remained steadfast in their loyalty, and because of this, many of them had been struck down by Samael's horde of angels. The rebels were no longer present—they had enacted their damage and had moved on to High Heaven, where the real battle was taking place. Nevertheless, fires raged, and the wounded lay helpless on the ground.

At our arrival, one of the Virtues, Justice, made his way toward us. "How is Low Heaven? Is it secure?" he asked.

"Yes. There is some damage, but we regained control and are tending to the injured," Michael explained.

"Good. As much as we need help here, you must continue on. Most members of the First Choir turned to Samael's side. Those who remain are dwindling fast, and now, they are severely outnumbered. I am not sure what end he seeks, but Samael must not get into the castle or beyond the gate. You must go. *Now*," Justice pleaded.

"We will, but not before we get you some help," Michael insisted.

Hastily, we sent a message for aid down to Low Heaven, then all took flight again.

The closer we got to High Heaven, the more impossible it became to see. Smoke blackened the sky, an unusual sight for a place typically filled with serene light. Before our surroundings came into view, a whizzing noise filled the air.

"Arrows!" Michael shouted.

All at once, our army broke off into groups that veered away from the oncoming assault. I stayed with Michael and my fellow council members, dodging the arrows and trying to locate a place to land.

We rapidly dropped altitude, diving into the black smoke, as our surroundings came into sight.

Justice was right. The First Choir had been divided as the rebellious Cherubim tried to obliterate the brave throng of remaining angels. I surmised they had turned on us because they were second in the Celestial Hierarchy, only one rank standing between them and all the power Father granted the Seraphim. Some of the Thrones aided the Cherubim, although most of them were rallying with the Seraphim to fight against the defectors. As for the other rebels, they continued to wreak havoc by burning anything in sight, their purpose merely to cause ruin.

Despite the madness, we knew we had to find Samael. The castle had already been overtaken by the rebels, and with a deafening shock of sound, it seemed they were trying to smash their way through the Heavenly Gates. None of that mattered. When the loyal forces saw our numbers, their resolve was strengthened.

Our army landed as one, and on impact, we were thrown into the throng of battle. We clashed, struck, stabbed, and pierced our way through enemy forces that did not stand a chance against us in size or determination as we fought to avenge and recapture our home.

When we had gained the upper hand, Michael sent the loyalists among the First Choir with half of his army to attend to the rebels at the Heavenly Gates. The other half of the army, plus me and my comrades from the council, were to follow Michael and recover the castle.

We neared the structure that once looked so beautiful and marvelous. Now, it was tainted and tarnished where smoke had blackened the white marble, and the glorious turrets had begun to crumble from destruction. At the sight of it and the leering insurgents who stood on the steps, an uncontrollable power overcame me. These traitors had to be vanquished. They had to be *punished* for what they had done.

As the rebels surged forward to engage us in combat, an untapped force unleashed.

I barreled into their ranks, swinging the scythe with uncanny speed and accuracy, landing my blows to wound, not kill. Although I was frustrated, although I wanted them punished and eradicated from our heavenly Paradise, my hand could not slay the rebels. I was not the one to determine their judgment, but I would be the one to stop them.

Soon, we were up the steps and gaining ground into the entranceway. At some point, I found myself fighting next to Michael, his longsword and my scythe scattering the rebels. Both of us knew Samael was somewhere inside this castle, and we had to find him quickly, otherwise the war would continue. But the castle was enormous, and it would take too long to locate him unless we knew where we were going.

Zadkiel and the others managed to fight their way to us, and before either Michael or I could speak, Zadkiel shouted, "The tower!"

"What?" Michael questioned.

"The tower! Samael must be in the tower! If he is going after the last object, that is where it resides. Metatron told me before we left," he explained.

We all knew flying up there would be nearly impossible with the constant deluge of arrows and the sheer number of enemies we would have to get through. We had to keep fighting our way up.

"The grand stairs," I said, taking in our surroundings. It seemed the staircase was the best choice, a path to the tower with fewer rebels defending it.

The seven of us braced ourselves and entered the throng once more in order to get through. We swiftly made progress and were nearing the last group of opponents when Ariel dived in front of us to engage them first.

"Go!" she shouted, indicating the stairs.

We all ran, and once we were on the second floor, the din of battle faded and was replaced with an eerie quiet. We made our way down the hall, trying to reach the southern end in order to mount the spiraling steps to the tower. We crept along the passageway in silence, expecting to encounter enemy forces. When we reached the bottom of the stairway without any interference, we knew something was wrong.

"This must be a trap," Raphael whispered.

"No, not a trap," Michael responded quietly, "just an impossible siege. Samael most likely has the best of his troops residing on the upper landing of these stairs. The moment we set foot there, we will be outnumbered."

"How do you know for sure?" Chamuel wondered.

"Trust me, I know."

"Then, what is the plan? Someone needs to get to the top of the tower," Jophiel said.

"We go up together, but while all of you are dealing with the rebels on the landing, I'll find a way around you and go up further to confront Samael," Michael said.

Without any more discussion, we began our ascent, stopping briefly before the landing to prepare ourselves for the onslaught. Within moments, we reached the last step and barged into the room, wanting to be on the offense rather than defense. Sure enough, there were more rebels here, and as we commenced battle, I saw Michael slip by and continue up the stairs.

We were clearly outnumbered, but that did not stop us. The six of us had made it to the center of the room and formed a circle with our backs to each other. Each of us relied on the other. If one went down, the circle would be broken, and the rebels could easily surmount the rest. None of us were skilled fighters, but we all somehow turned into soldiers in that moment, each pulling energy from the others, able to find the courage and strength to carry on.

We fought for what felt like an eternity. All of us were growing exhausted, and the fact Michael had not returned yet was a worry. Our outcome looked bleak, especially as we all began to take on minor injuries.

Then, a miracle happened.

The ground began to shake at our feet. Light returned outside, and an almighty presence could be felt in the air.

Father had arrived.

As His wrath and power permeated around us, the rebels abruptly stopped fighting and fled. Only two remained in the room, turning the odds in our favor. Three against one, we managed to easily seize their weapons. I ran up the remaining steps in search of Michael while the others bound the rebels.

A loud noise reverberated along the stairwell, the clinking of swords and an intense battle. I did not want to distract Michael, but I also knew he might need the help. Moving through the unlocked door, I saw him falter in a moment of fatigue and weakness. Samael struck the hilt of his sword to Michael's chest, and he fell to the floor.

I was about to rush forward when Michael yelled, "What are you going to do, kill me?"

Samael froze in mid-swing with his sword over his head and looked down at Michael.

They stared at each other for quite some time until Michael calmly said, "There is no way out of this. You realize that, right?"

Samael lowered his sword and, consumed by an outburst of rage, spun toward a small empty pedestal at the far side of the room. "It was supposed to be *here!*" he growled. "It was supposed to be easy! I was supposed to take it!"

"Well, you failed," Michael said. "Did you really think Father would leave it here—whatever *it* was—after the other two objects went missing? He is no fool. He probably moved it in an attempt to avoid something like this."

"That is impossible! I was not the one who took the other objects. There is no way He could have suspected me," Samael barked, turning back to face Michael.

"That is not true," Michael said, regaining his footing. "Gabriel and I made sure of that."

A look of realization crossed Samael's face. His anger resurfaced as he lifted his sword and aggressively resumed battle. Michael was ready. With a ferocity I had never seen before, he executed blow after blow, and within two sword strikes and a swift wing sweep, he had Samael on the ground, disarmed.

Michael kicked Samael's sword away from his outstretched hand

and placed his blade on his opponent's throat. Samael looked up at him. I could not say what passed between them. However, their eyes were thick with betrayal as Michael returned Samael's glare.

It was the look of enemies, not brothers.

"You are coming with me," Michael said. "It is time you pay for what you have done."

Sensing the battle was over, I eased my way over to the defeated angel and picked up Samael's sword. Michael took his right arm and pulled him up, then bound Samael's wings and hands behind his back, pushing him toward the stairs. I followed behind as they descended.

When we approached the landing, the others were beginning to descend as well, their bound rebels in tow. Once we finally made it back to the entrance, all that remained was the wreckage. We walked out onto the front steps and headed over to the amassing group of angels.

It seemed many of the rebels stopped fighting when Father Arrived. The loyal forces had easily defeated those who had not. With order somewhat restored, the Seraphim rounded up the insurgents and brought them to the edge of High Heaven. As we walked with the instigator in our possession, rows of angels stopped to stare.

Somehow, the Seraphim had managed to corral all the rebels together by making a barrier to keep them from fleeing. As we approached, I noticed the barrier was made of divine light, meaning Father had something to do with it.

Seraphiel stepped forward and took the two rebels Uriel and Raphael were holding. She escorted them to the barrier and urged them inside. Then, she turned back to us and looked pointedly at Samael.

"Well, it seems your attempts at supremacy have failed. Now, if you would please tell us where you placed the missing objects, we can get on with your punishment."

Samael glanced at her disdainfully. "I did not take them."

"Lies will not be tolerated."

I interrupted before she did anything too serious. "He is telling the truth."

All the angels present set their eyes on me.

"And how, Gabriel, do you know?" she asked.

I told her about my encounter in the Sanctuary of Music, how I presumed Araziel was the one who stole the book and the Castle Key since he was talking to someone about stealing the scepter. At the mention of his name, the angel tried to hide among the masses of insurgents, but not before Seraphiel spotted him. She signaled one of the loyal Seraphim to retrieve him. Tired of fighting, the insurgents gave up Araziel in the hopes of sparing themselves.

"Gabriel says you stole the objects. Where are they?" Seraphiel asked.

"The book is in the Sanctuary of Music, in my instrument cabinet. As for the Castle Key, I used it to open the tower door," Araziel confessed.

"And where is it now?" she demanded.

He fidgeted as his nerves got the best of him. I noticed he was gripping something in his hand.

"Araziel, give it to her," I said.

Seraphiel saw my gaze rooted to his hand, so she grabbed at it and forcibly pried the Castle Key out. She handed it over to one of her comrades.

"Take this to the Forge. It must be destroyed immediately."

The other angel took the key and retreated to the castle, where the Forge was located.

Thinking the interrogation was over, Araziel relaxed considerably—until Seraphiel set her sights on him once more.

"Gabriel said you were speaking to someone about the objects. Who was it?"

"Why...Samael, of course," he said.

Samael opened his mouth to protest, but I spoke before he could. "That is not true. I am positive the voice was distinctly feminine."

Seraphiel looked at me. "Are you sure?"

"Yes, without a doubt."

She glared at Araziel. "Who was with you?"

He squirmed and hesitated, but his fear got the best of him. "Gabriel is right. It was a female. Her name is L—" He did not have a chance to finish as an arrow struck him in the chest. His body convulsed, and he struggled to breathe.

There was only one explanation for such a reaction. The arrowhead was poisoned.

Before any angels of healing could react, a burst of light flashed, and Araziel disappeared. This was what happened when an angel perished. Our energy receded into the universe in either a sudden flash or a gradual fade depending on the injury.

Alarmed by the attack and the tragic conclusion, everyone went on high alert again, eyes peering over the battlefield in search of the assassin.

"Find whoever did that," Seraphiel ordered.

Members of her rank took to the air and chased after the mysterious assailant. With tensions rising, Seraphiel turned to Samael. She analyzed his figure.

"Where is it?"

Confused, Samael said, "What?"

"*Your* key. The one for the council room."

He remained silent.

"Do not make this worse than it already is. Tell me!"

He simply looked at her with a defiant air.

Before she could say or do anything, Michael released Samael and grabbed at his neck, latching onto a chain Samael wore and giving the necklace a rough yank. It broke away. Michael held the chain up, showing the key hanging on it.

Seraphiel took the necklace out of Michael's hand and led Samael to the barrier, but not before Samael glanced one last time at Michael. The look went beyond betrayal. Now, it was full of a violent hunger for revenge, as Michael's act put Samael in a vulnerable, inferior position.

We all knew that Samael hated to be powerless.

Before Samael was secured inside the barrier, Seraphiel cut his bindings. Then, she forced him inside, and the apprehension finally began to dissipate. The two angels who chased after the assailant came back with a female rebel who had fled the battle. None of us recognized her, but she was hastily escorted to the barrier, the distaste toward her palpable. The Seraphim angels rejoined the First Choir, and we all stood there waiting for something to happen.

None of us expected the loud crack that pierced the air. Nor did we expect the thunderous shaking that ensued. With a blast, a large void opened up directly beneath the barrier and consumed the rebel forces.

In the blink of an eye, our rogue brothers and sisters were gone.

SATAN

10

We fell for nine days in a constant state of agony. When we finally struck the end of our fall, the moans of the fallen sliced through the cold air.

Confusion and discomfort marred my comrades' faces as they absorbed their unfamiliar surroundings. They did not stir or move because none of them knew what to do. They were frightened and sore from the violent landing.

But their anguish was nothing compared to mine.

My screams tore through the dark, causing the others to cower in fear at my palpable fury. I shrieked in unbearable pain on the stone floor, a slick sweat covering my body and chilling me to the bone. My once beautiful wings were burnt, immobile, and lay useless at my sides. The acrid smell of burnt flesh and the gritty taste of putrid smoke overcame me.

This dismal place was my new kingdom.

This dismal place was Hell.

I attempted to move, and at the slightest motion, my entire body erupted in pain. I cried out and twisted my head. Lying face-up, I tried to assess my condition.

My torso was bare, and so too were my feet and both legs. My body was damp with sweat and blackened by soot. There was a constant pain rooted in the center of my back where my wings sprouted out from my body. They must have taken most of the damage. It was impossible to control our fall, and there was no way to protect them from the raging fire and snapping wind.

We had dropped from Heaven in a fiery blaze that landed us here. The fire still burned around me even though it was freezing. I was breathing in ragged gasps and saw my breath in front of my face.

Squeezing my eyes shut, I wished this was some temporary nightmare, not my permanent reality. These feelings of self-pity were soon replaced with anger, and I pounded my fist upon the floor. Once more, I screamed, but this time with rage. I *hated* that I could not move. I *hated* the pain that seared through my entire body. I *hated* how weak I felt.

I refused to yield to the rage.

Instead, I sought control.

I opened my eyes to view my surroundings. It seemed I was alone. I could hear the moans of my fallen forces, yet they seemed distant and far off. The fact I was in a cave-like space made me doubt my perception of sound. Everything echoed around me, especially my screams.

I knew I had to get up, to take charge, but it was difficult to muster the nerve and to overcome the pain. My last moments in Heaven had happened so quickly they had left me with an unsettling realization.

I could never return.

The thought struck me with great fear. Heaven was my home, and it had been stripped away from me in an instant. My comrades had turned against me. My closest brothers had turned against me. *Michael* had turned against me.

I slammed my hands upon the ground again as I thought about his betrayal. Pain erupted from the action, radiating up my arms and infusing my entire body with its ache. I screamed. Not only from the pain of my predicament, but from the duplicity in Heaven and the magnitude of everything I had lost.

With my hands still curled into fists, I rolled my head back and forth on the cold ground, numbing myself to the ache, and considered what to do next. This place could never become Heaven, but perhaps it could resemble it in certain ways. I had to make it my new home. But what could it become? How would I transform a world so atrocious into something meaningful?

First, I needed to overcome my punishment. If I ignored it and acted like the pain did not exist, I could get up.

With this mindset, I abruptly tried to stand.

In seconds, the agony was insurmountable, and I soon found myself on the stone floor again, this time on my side and crawling into a fetal position. I gave myself a few moments to let the pain settle. Clearly, I was too ambitious.

If—*when*—I regained control, a new order would need to be implemented…a hierarchy of sorts, one I had command over. This would give me everything I wanted: power, control, and a kingdom that resembled what had been stolen from me.

A stabbing pain erupted throughout my body, interrupting my thoughts of the future. I succumbed to it and lay upon the ground, immobile. All I could do was close my eyes and yield to my punishment, find solace in the emptiness within.

It felt like days passed as I lay there. I knew this had to end.

Placing my hands flat on the ground, I braced myself and slowly raised my torso, biting back the ache. I moved one knee, then the next, and became lost in cries of anguish.

I remained in that position, on all fours, for quite some time. Stealing a glance over my shoulder at my wings, I just as quickly looked away. The sight of them repulsed me, made me sick, because I was not certain I would ever be able to use them again.

Forcing those thoughts from my mind, I concentrated on the task at hand and placed one foot flat on the ground. My back spasmed at the pain, and my roars of anguish filled the air again. Breathing heavily, I braced for the next foot when I heard laughter.

Anger flared inside me like a red blaze.

"My, my, what a sight this is…" a female voice said.

"Leave me alone," I growled, clearly in a position that did not command the bravado I desired.

When no response came, I resumed my attempt, thinking the unknown female had left.

A hard kick to my back alerted me she had not. Her action sent me collapsing to the ground once more in paralyzing pain. I was again incapacitated, screaming pathetically.

"You are not what I thought you were," she continued, drawing near to my limp body.

I rolled onto my back to face her, but she stayed in the shadows. I could not find the words to speak, so she persisted with her demoralizing words, letting them drip over me.

"So pitiful, incapable, and *weak*." She lingered on the last word, knowing it would terrorize me.

"I am not weak," I groaned.

Then, her figure appeared before me as she knelt beside my face. She forcibly grabbed my chin with her gloved hand and said, "You most certainly are."

I jerked my face away, ignoring the twinge of discomfort, and demanded, "Who are you?"

"You don't remember me?"

I squinted through the dark. As my eyes adjusted, I was able to see she had long black hair. It was hard to recognize her because she was dressed in an entirely black dress, scorched in places from the fire during our fall. The high neckline remained intact. However, the hem of her dress had been burned, exposing her bare feet and ankles. It was long-sleeved, though the right sleeve was torn, and the left had completely disappeared.

A glint of metal drew my attention to her left hand. It seemed she wore some type of jewelry, perhaps a ring, but it was impossible to see exactly what since she had on black gloves that camouflaged her fingers. A battered pouch hung from the belt around her waist, the leather gleaming in the shadows.

Her face was the only thing I could distinguish. Her skin was pale and it shone through the dark. She had an angular jawline and hollow cheekbones, but most remarkable were her eyes, an unnatural mix of brown, green, and a hint of blue.

Those eyes seemed familiar.

At my blank expression, she smiled. Grasping my hand, she raised it to her mouth and playfully bit one of my fingers. All at once, I knew why those eyes were so familiar.

Dismayed, I pulled my hand from her grasp, ignoring the dull pain.

"You," I said.

She laughed at my outrage and shock.

"How is this possible? You were a snake."

"Oh, honey," she teased, rising from the ground. "I'm always a snake."

"You know what I mean!" I snapped, confused and angry.

"Oh, please, you are unbearable. Yes, I was a snake physically when you stumbled upon me in Eden. I was doomed to that form forever... until you came along. When you cut me with your blade, you freed me from bondage." She indicated a scar down the side of her left arm. It was long and jagged, the fleshy tissue raised and deformed.

Her story irritated me. It had not happened so romantically.

"You bit me, and it changed everything," I retorted.

"I bit you, and it showed you everything," she corrected. "All the knowledge you needed to gain insurmountable power, yet you failed." She looked down at me. "You must be in a lot of pain. I can't imagine what that Hellfire is putting you through."

"Hellfire?"

At my question, she began to retreat.

"Where are you going?" I shouted.

"To find some other angel with the strength to run this place."

I gritted my teeth and, in one movement, rose to a standing position. I roared through it all as a way of releasing the pain instead of letting it consume me.

With my feet planted firmly on the cold ground, I turned stiffly to face her. "Why? Am I not good enough?"

She seemed surprised at my audacity but then smirked, her skeptical expression shifting. She was impressed.

"Maybe I underestimated you," she said, drawing near to my side.

The closeness worked to my advantage. I grabbed her by the arm and slammed her against the wall of the cave, gripping her neck firm in my hand.

"First of all, do not ever underestimate me. Do you hear? I will show you how capable I am of ruling this place."

She sneered, but something akin to fascination flashed through her eyes.

"Second, do not ever touch me like I am your pet again, because I will remind you how that feels. And finally, none of this will ever replace what I had. *You* will never replace them. No one will ever replace them. I thank you, since I now have my own domain to rule." I stole a look around. "Though, I must say, it's an awful comparison to everything I lost." Releasing her, I stepped back.

She automatically leaned over and grabbed at her throat. I realized my touch had burned her skin, which was now starting to heal before my eyes. After a few seconds, she regained her composure and set her sights on me.

"You will never frighten me, so stop trying." She stood resolute, like I had never laid hands on her.

"Fine. But I can obviously hurt you."

She chuckled. "Perhaps. You can hurt anyone with that Hellfire running through your veins, especially if you don't control it. Knowing you, I'm sure you'll let your anger take charge instead of your mind."

She started to leave, but I grabbed her arm once again and turned her to face me. As my touch burned her a second time, she shrugged out of my grasp.

"Explain," I demanded.

"Why should I? There's nothing in it for me."

I contemplated her words. "What do you want in exchange?"

She smirked. "Oh, now you're bargaining? Well, let me think…" She posed with one finger on her mouth in mock deliberation.

"You find this amusing, do you? Either tell me what you want, or leave." I knew that giving her this ultimatum would speed her decision.

"Fine. You really do take the fun out of everything." At my stern glare, she relented. "All right, all right. I want your blood."

"Excuse me?"

"Your blood. I want some of your blood."

"What for?"

"Divulging information to you is not part of the deal."

Once again, I contemplated her. I knew I could not trust her. She *was* a snake after all, in every way but form. Besides, how much did I really need to know about this Hellfire anyway?

My curiosity got the better of me. "Fine. You can have some of my blood in exchange for information. Now, speak."

Reluctantly, she began to explain. "When you fell, He sent you down in a blaze. If you haven't noticed, it's absolutely freezing down here even though the fire continues to burn. That's because it's Hellfire, a unique type of fire created by Him. It now runs inside of you, literally. That is why it was so hard for you to stand. It's your punishment, to be wracked with pain that will never go away because it resides inside. And since you are immortal, it is a punishment that will last forever."

"No one is truly immortal. Not even you or me," I said.

"That may be true, but I intend to live for quite some time. Now, it's my turn," she said, eagerly reaching for my hand.

"Wait." I pulled back. "I have a question."

She looked annoyed.

"When I burned you before, that was Hellfire?"

"Yes. At any skin-to-skin contact, Hellfire latches onto whoever you're touching. Based on your sudden ability to stand, you're learning to control it."

I did feel better. I was still stiff and slow to move, but at least the agonizing pain had subsided. I guessed He had not expected that outcome. The thought pleased me.

Suddenly, I felt a pinch of pain and realized she had taken my hand and pricked it with a sharp claw she wore on her finger like a ring. Gazing down, I saw she wore a claw on every finger of her left hand, which must have been the glint of metal I saw earlier. Her gloves seemed to act as a barrier to the Hellfire since my touch was not burning her.

Blood oozed out of the small wound and, ever resourceful, she produced a small vial from the battered pouch at her hip. She uncorked the bottle, placed my finger to it, and squeezed so more blood would come out. When she had her desired amount, she released my hand and sealed the vial, then turned to leave.

"That is it? That is all you wanted?"

She looked at me over her shoulder. "You have no idea what you just gave to me."

My anger flared. "What do you mean?"

She smiled. "It's amazing how powerful the blood of an archangel is."

I did not understand what she was insinuating, but I could not let it get to me. Instead, I asked her one more question.

"What is your name?"

"Lilith. And yours?"

"You know my name."

"But that's not your name anymore, is it?" she challenged.

I stared at her. Once again, she smiled. That smile was becoming quite irritating.

To prove her wrong, I tried to say my name aloud, but the words would not form on my lips. I looked at the band of letters gracing my left arm, which spelled out my name in angelic script. All that remained was an impressive scar where the letters had been burnt off. The other emblem I had been marked with, the astrological sign of Ophiuchus, was in a similar state on my left wrist.

"Your name is Satan now," she said, pulling my attention away from my hand. "There are more items I need than just the three I sought in Heaven."

"What do you mean? You told me all that was left was the scepter."

"I know. I did that intentionally. I couldn't have you knowing everything."

"Why not?"

"Because I needed to see if I could trust you."

"And can you?"

She pondered for a moment. "Possibly."

I rolled my eyes. "So, what else do you need?"

"Thirteen stone spheres. Each archangel on the council was assigned one."

I stared at her. "You are lying. I would know about this."

"Really? After everything that happened, you think you can believe Him? You know He withheld things from you."

"You do not have to remind me. Why should it be my concern?"

"Because the spheres are needed to obtain immense power, and the only way you will have leverage over the blessed is if you recover yours."

"How? Where is it?"

She grew silent.

"Lilith! Tell me what to do," I demanded.

"You will have to figure that out for yourself." She moved to walk away.

Reaching out, I grabbed her right hand, my fingers latching onto the glove. Effortlessly, Lilith eased her arm back, pulling free from the garment and evading my grasp. Then, she was gone.

Perhaps I should have put up more of a fight. She seemed to know more than I did about my current situation. In fact, she seemed to know more than I did about everything. My anger boiled at the thought. When had I ever been this needy and dependent? It was time to change.

Since I had learned to deal with the Hellfire, I decided to explore my surroundings and find my fallen comrades, but at the cave's entrance, I ran into an invisible barrier. Obviously, this was one of His attempts to imprison me. Lilith had passed through without a problem.

The thought of Lilith spurred me to think about my ability to burn her. Holding her glove in my hand, I channeled the Hellfire from within, directing my anger at the barrier as I placed my free hand on it. It glowed as the fire began to combat with the invisible wall. But it would not budge.

I dropped my hand to my side, giving myself a moment to summon more strength from within. The red blaze rose inside me again, and I knew this time, I would succeed.

Once more, I placed my free hand on the barrier, adding more force as the barricade fought my advances. Yet it could not resist the Hellfire. I was more powerful.

When the barrier dropped, I was not prepared for the sight. Sprawled out in front of me was an entire wasteland of rock and fire. The temperature remained freezing, and the fallen lay everywhere. Their moans, screams, and shouts of torment were a cacophony of pain and terror.

I stood there looking on at them and could not find an ounce of sympathy. They were not consumed by the Hellfire like I was, they were just disoriented and scared. I walked out into the wasteland among them, and the noise gradually ceased. When I stopped in the middle of their vast multitude, I raised my arms wide.

"This is our new kingdom." I paused to let that sink in. "Believe me when I say, I am just as appalled by it as you are, yet we must accept the consequences of our actions and make them work to our advantage. You may see this new domain as a shortcoming, but I see it as a new beginning with endless possibilities. However, I will never be able to lead without capable and faithful comrades at my side. What I see before me does not bode well in this regard. Mere moments ago, you were all fierce warriors fighting for something you believed in. Now, you all lie helpless at my feet. What kingdom will I be able to turn this Hell into if you all do not try to stand? My courage and strength sustained me as I tolerated unimaginable pain to emerge as your resolute leader. Will you now rise for me, so we can rally and fight back against these obstacles the blessed have doled upon us?"

Initially, my encouragements produced no action. One figure, however, slowly rose among the rest. He had been a faithful companion in Heaven and remained behind to fight even after everyone else fled. His name would not form on my lips as none of our given names could be spoken aloud anymore. That did not matter because I had been renamed, and so too would my fallen angels.

Lucifer, I thought. His name would be Lucifer. A bearer of light in all this darkness as his courage to stand proved his loyalty to me.

I stared at my lone companion, nodding my head in approval.

Apparently, my earlier words slowly sunk in. Others began to rise. I raised my arms wide once more, turning in a circle as they chanted and cheered in exhilaration. These were the fallen heroes I remembered well.

In all the excitement, a small black figure appeared above us, drawing my attention as it gracefully descended through the air to land upon my left arm. I was surprised by the raven's presence since He had created all these creatures. To have one navigate its way into our domain was a sign.

The raven looked into my eyes. We had work to do, but this meant freedom.

SATAN

11

HELL, In the Beginning, Centuries Later

It took time. Several long years passed, but I finally managed to turn this place into something. Throughout the ages, people called it many names. Pandemonium. Inferno. The Underworld. To me, it was always Hell.

My first course of action after that fateful day was to appoint additional leaders so I would not have the burden of dealing with the insignificant woes of every inhabitant in Hell. The leaders I selected were my allies in Heaven and some of the fiercest warriors. They were cunning, devious, and brave. They became known as The Six, my closest companions who executed my bidding. I marked them and myself with a skull tattoo, wanting a visual symbol to convey our rank but also instill fear. I had skull rings forged to authorize the distinction of leadership, since bestowing rings to signify roles was common practice in Heaven.

Once The Six were appointed, I split Hell into nine sections. The architecture of our realm made the execution of this easy. There were nine enormous caverns, each with its own maze of connecting caves that could be transformed into living quarters. I assigned a cavern to each of The Six, with mine at the top. Cavern two became Pride, led by Lucifer. Cavern three was Envy, led by Leviathan. Cavern four, Gluttony, belonged to Beelzebub. Mammon led cavern five, Greed. Asmodeus took charge of Lust in cavern six. Laze became Belphegor's domain in cavern seven.

I named our cities after the deadly sins since the blessed in Heaven could not fathom the evil down here, and I wanted to celebrate what made us different from them. Although I accepted the anger that lived inside of me, I was by no means going to let it define who I was. Rather than name my own cavern after it, I instead called it Elysium, home to me and my brethren of fallen angels. This title spurned its divine connotations, which pleased me immensely.

The five rivers of Hell resided in cavern eight. This place was uninhabitable due to the rivers' potency tempting unsuspecting creatures into their watery depths. Belphegor discovered this the hard way. Unable to resist the allure, he waded into the River of Lamentation and was immediately consumed by shrieking wails that pierced the cavern and echoed off the stone walls. With some difficulty, the others managed to fish him out. The only lingering effects the river had on him appeared to be his diminished senses and gullibility.

At first, I had no idea what to do with the ninth cavern, but as spirits spontaneously began to arrive, I had no choice but to use it for them. There, at least, they were as far from me as possible. I named the cavern Misery because it was a cave of condemnation, where they lived out their sentences of torment.

Naturally, spirits wanted to escape Misery because not only was their existence defined by torture, but what existed beyond caverns eight and nine was far more appealing. The Six and I had transformed our caverns into a metropolis. Many fallen angels would visit Misery to tease spirits about what lay beyond their doom, some of them brazen enough to attempt an escape. But anyone who tried had to traverse the Rivers of Hell, which never ended in success.

Spirits who fulfilled their sentences were somewhat liberated, able to move up to one of our cities. They were not permitted to choose which, but instead had their destinations assigned by Murmur, a fallen angel I had appointed because of his clear talent at asking the right questions and making spirits confess to the sins they had committed. Any spirits whose sin was anger remained in Misery for eternity. There was no place for them in Elysium. Besides, I highly doubted any of them had an anger lurking inside like mine.

As soon as Murmur decided where to send a spirit, Mulciber would escort that spirit to the appropriate city to ensure they did not wander or fall prey to the treacherous rivers. Mulciber possessed an enormous strength unlike any other fallen angel, which allowed him to deal with spirits, especially riotous ones. However, he was not immune to the rivers and required the help of Abbadona, another fallen angel. She was particularly special because she used to be a Seraphim. I was unsure what had turned her to my side during the war, but I knew she now regretted her insurrection. Since she had embraced evil, even for a short time, she could never return to Heaven, yet her change of heart gave her the ability to face the rivers. They had no effect on her, and because of this, she lived permanently in cavern eight, keeping watch for any spirits who tried to escape.

In addition to these three fallen angels, there were a handful of others I had appointed in numerous jobs throughout Hell, or who I called upon for favors because it was impossible for me and The Six to do everything.

Once spirits were relocated, they were expected to work and contribute to their city. They were no longer tormented, but if they went against the order of things, punishment or even a return to Misery was sanctioned.

We soon discovered the caverns were not separate from each other. Caves to the right connected them together. On the left, more caves led to a vast expanse of nothingness I termed The Pit.

The Pit opened at the top to my throne room in Elysium, which was connected to my private quarters. These access points between cities were beneficial to The Six and me, for they allowed us to traverse regions. They posed a problem, however, for the liberated spirits. I did not want them to freely travel between cities, so I needed security at each access point. I appointed feral creatures known as hellhounds to stand guard. These hounds lurked in the depths of Hell and fed on spirits' pain and discomfort. They were the perfect deterrent.

With order established, The Six came to love the names I had given their cities and as such, claimed their specific sins with dignity. They each fashioned jewelry and marked themselves with tattoos to portray their distinctions. I did the same. What we were really trying to do was reclaim parts of our past to bring stability and sanity to our new lives. The Six had never received any type of honor in Heaven, so they were thrilled about their leadership in Hell. They created our so-called "deadly sin rings" as a way to commemorate their distinction. The rings celebrated the sins with animals, each in the shape of a certain creature.

Lucifer chose the black jaguar. He believed this animal represented strength, stealth, and valor—the perfect choice to symbolize pride.

Leviathan decided upon the dog. More specifically, a three-headed dog, since he had found such a creature lurking down here in Hell and adopted it as his pet. Little did he know the beast was envious of itself, each head jealous of the others.

Beelzebub chose the boar. He said this animal represented gluttony best.

Mammon picked the frog, and quite frankly, I had no idea why. He was a peculiar creature though, so I rarely questioned him. I supposed frogs were a good symbol for greed, as the animals could be covetous.

Asmodeus selected the bull, feeling these passionate creatures represented his sin of lust.

Belphegor went with the goat, saying simply these animals were lazy. There was no further explanation. It was not in his nature to enlighten others. I suspected goats matched his stubbornness more than anything else.

I did not know which animal to pick to symbolize my deadly sin. The Six suggested a bear since it seemed fitting for anger. I agreed, and they had a ring fashioned for me.

I continued to wear the ring that was given to me in Heaven too, which designated I was a member of the council. It was silver with filigree embossing, and a black onyx stone was placed on top where the band of metal joined together. My cross necklace had crumbled into metallic dust when I fell, branding my skin just below my collarbones. The other objects that belonged to me, such as my sword and chest, remained in Heaven, and I imagined those were destroyed as well.

I did not care. None of those things were any use to me now. Just like His markings.

To hide the scar from the astrological symbol on my left wrist, tattooed flames covered both of my arms. These flames signified the Hellfire that was my curse and greatest superpower. To cover the scar from the band of letters spelling my name in angelic script, I had tattooed my upper left arm with a series of skulls to indicate my rule over The Six and Hell in general. As a reminder of my fall and what my wings used to be, I had tattooed a series of feathers on each of my shoulders. Once all of these were done, I filled the gap on my upper right arm with a bear to stay in keeping with my deadly sin.

All of these markings and material objects did not only capture our personalities but helped to provide a sense of structure and reaffirm who was in charge—something even The Six needed to be reminded of every so often. Yet I never wanted to be like Him, ruling oppressively without allowing anyone to express their freewill. There was a fine line I had to ride to maintain a balanced chaos.

I was proud of myself, for I had done what I had set out to do: create a kingdom of my own that the blessed would fear.

With the foundation laid, it was time to frolic in our freedom. We had endured a lot. Pain, punishment, and hardship. But now, from here until eternity, we would raise Hell and show those blessed bastards just how evil we could be.

JORDAN

12

Rolling over in bed, I peeked at the clock on the bedside table. *Wow, ten a.m. already? The sisters never let me sleep this late.*

My eyes closed once more, and I snuggled closer to the blanket. I was just drifting back to sleep when I remembered the events of last night and sprang up in an instant.

The unfamiliar room filled my vision. I blinked a few times until my eyes adjusted to the morning light, then sat in bed pondering my situation. I felt lost and utterly alone. Nothing was as it should be, and I still didn't know if I believed Gabriel.

The rational part of my mind knew there was no way he could be an angel, yet a tiny voice inside my head told me to believe him. He certainly seemed like someone I could trust. The fact I hadn't been killed in my sleep was a good indication. His story still remained unreal though.

Then again, who else would have been chasing me?

Shaking my head, I expelled all these thoughts. There would be no way to find out if any of this was true unless I actively sought the information. So, I got out of bed, though my hunger was driving me too, and headed for the door.

I left the guest room and walked down the hall. The apartment was silent, and Gabriel was nowhere to be seen. I came to a stop in the living room and sighed. So much for my grand idea to seek out more information.

I was approaching the kitchen, ready to locate some food, when Gabriel appeared.

"Good morning."

I flinched at his surprise entrance and turned away from the fridge to face him.

"Sorry to startle you. I was in my office," he said, pointing down a hallway to his right. "You must be hungry. I sent for some food since I have nothing of interest. Unless you want eggs again?" He approached the kitchen table, where a plate sat covered with a metal lid alongside a glass of orange juice and fancy silverware.

"Whatever works. I'm not picky."

"Great," he responded, removing the metal top.

Underneath was a stack of pancakes with butter, maple syrup, and bacon. At Gabriel's eager expression, I sat down at the table, placing the formal cloth napkin on my lap and eyeing the delicious breakfast.

"Gabriel, I appreciate you doing this, but where did this come from?"

"Tony brought it up about ten minutes ago. I figured you'd be hungry when you woke up."

"Who's Tony?"

He paused. "He's my friend. We help each other out sometimes. His daughter is a caterer, and he asked her to set aside one of her breakfast dishes for you."

"I see."

I couldn't resist the pancakes, so I stopped asking questions and dug in. Gabriel was a strange guy, and no amount of explanation was going to change that. In fact, his explanations just made him more mysterious. As I devoured the food in front of me, I could sense he wanted to tell me something.

Swallowing my last mouthful, I washed it down with some juice before asking, "What is it?"

He remained standing in front of me with his hands behind his back. "I'm not sure how to break the news to you, but there is something you need to see." He stepped forward and placed a newspaper on the table, motioned for me to read it.

I saw it was today's paper, and the main headline was, "ABANDONED ORPHANAGE BURNT DOWN: ACCIDENT OR ARSON?" My heart sank. I read through the article, the front-page picture revealing that it was Holy Trinity. The thought of Sister Helen in peril because of me made me sick to my stomach. When I was done reading, I sat there numb.

"It said there were no causalities. I'm sure she made it out okay," Gabriel reassured me.

I shook my head. "This is all wrong. Nothing makes sense. They said in the article the building was abandoned for years. How is that possible when I've been living there for the past six?"

"It's obviously a cover-up."

I turned to him. "Sister Helen told me before I left that none of this ever existed. I didn't understand what she meant at the time, but now…"

"As I told you last night, if she is a member of the Sacrarium, they have the means to make things go away."

I sighed. More and more events kept happening with no real explanation.

My thoughts were interrupted when a noise from outside directed my attention. It caught Gabriel's too.

"Stay here," he warned, approaching the sliding glass door that led to the balcony. He unlatched the lock and stepped out, closing the door behind him.

A loud ruckus ensued.

I cautiously advanced toward the sliding door, uncertain whom or what was creating the clamor. Peering through the glass, to my surprise, I found Gabriel surrounded by a flock of birds.

"What are you doing?" I asked, sliding open the door.

I caught him off-guard. He jumped and quickly turned to face me.

"Nothing. Go back inside," he replied, composing himself.

"Why?"

"Because I said so."

"I've only known you for a short time, but now you decide to become secretive?"

Obviously guilty, he relented. "They have come with messages," he said.

I wanted to laugh since "they" were several birds of prey perched along the railing. How could they possibly know to deliver a message? Gabriel turned to face them as I stepped onto the balcony. The eagle raised a warning cry.

"Don't come any farther," Gabriel warned. "Your presence will make them temperamental."

"All right." I planted my feet firmly in place and leaned against the door. "Would you care to explain what's going on?"

He sighed. "I sent out a call last night, to my brothers. They were supposed to answer in person. Instead, they have sent these messengers." He moved toward the bird closest to him, which happened to be a falcon, and untied the rolled-up paper from its leg. The bird immediately flew off.

Gabriel continued his progress down the line of birds, untying the pieces of paper as he went along. There was a hawk, an osprey, an owl, a crane, and the eagle. When each scroll of paper was freed, the bird took flight and departed.

As the last bird took to the sky, I released a deep breath I hadn't realized I was holding. Gabriel's frown conveyed these messages did not contain good sentiments.

"What do they say?"

He raised his head and looked at me. "They're not coming."

"But isn't it their duty?"

"Yes," he said through clenched teeth, barging past me into the apartment, where he paced the length of the kitchen.

I followed him inside and sat down on a stool at the counter, peering at the discarded notes from his brothers. None of them were in English. Instead, the messages were written in some kind of odd-looking language.

Gabriel stopped pacing and rested his hands on either side of the sink.

"What now?" I asked.

"I'm not sure."

I wanted to let him think, but I had far too many questions. "Why did those specific birds come and not some everyday pigeons?"

"Because each archangel on the council has an affinity to a certain bird."

"Council?"

He looked at me. "In Heaven, there are nine types of angels. Each rank has a council whose members are chosen by Father. There are twelve archangels on the council—thirteen until Satan fell. I am one of these members, and since we are messenger angels, we have an affinity to a specific bird. For instance, mine is the sparrow. The birds that arrived this morning are connected to each of my brothers. There are other things we have an affinity to also, such as stones or places."

I nodded my head, trying to keep track of all the information.

"Listen, Jordan, I know the things I'm telling you are difficult to fathom, and I apologize if I'm not telling you everything at once. But I don't want to make things more complicated than they already are. Forgive me if I don't explain everything right away."

"All right."

"You still don't believe me, do you?"

I looked away. "I don't know what to believe anymore. Some of the stuff that's happening validates what you're saying, but I don't one hundred percent believe you yet."

"I understand."

"You do?"

Right there in his kitchen, I received all the validation I needed. As I turned my head back to look at him, I was affronted by the sight of Gabriel with wings fully outstretched. I blinked in utter disbelief, and just as quick, the wings were gone.

"Did you just…?"

"What?" he asked with a sly expression.

"Your wings. Did you just…?"

He waited.

"Never mind."

"You're sure?" He grinned like a fox.

"Positive. Anyway, I know I keep asking this question, but really, what now?"

"Well, if my brothers refuse to come to me then I suppose we'll just have to go to them."

"You mean, we're going to get them? I thought you didn't know where they are."

"I don't."

"Then how are we going to them?"

"I'm not entirely sure, but I might have an idea." He departed the kitchen and strode down the hallway to his office, returning with a large map, which he began to unfold.

I helped him, and once I took over the unfolding, he went back to his office for some tape. Gabriel grabbed one side of the map while I held the other and applied tape in order to stick it to the wall. Then, he merely gazed at it. Figuring I was the one who needed to take action, I went down the hallway he had just come from and walked into his office in search of a marker. I found one sitting on his desk in a decorative pencil holder.

Returning to Gabriel, who was still staring at the map, I located New York and made a big X mark. This got the angel's attention.

"What are you doing?"

"Marking your location. You told me there was one of you on each continent, right?"

"Correct."

"So, if you're in North America, the remaining six should be elsewhere." I glanced at him. "There are six others we're trying to find, right?"

He nodded his head.

"Okay." I stepped back and examined the map. My eyes roamed over countries and oceans until they landed on Antarctica.

"Gabriel, if the seven of you were placed on every continent, does that mean someone is in Antarctica?"

He laughed. "I certainly hope not, but I'm not entirely sure. I would guess no, since there is only a small population of people there, lessening the forces of evil." He strode closer. "I predict there might be two stationed in Europe."

"Why do you think that?"

"Because Europe is an old continent and throughout history has endured a number of malevolent attacks, thus increasing the need for protection."

"That would make sense. Although the same could be said for Asia."

We both fell into silence as we realized the daunting task of locating Gabriel's brothers.

"Wasn't there some precaution put in place so you could find each other?"

"Yes, it was to send the call. I did that, and they refused to come."

"What call exactly did you send?"

He left my question unacknowledged as he once again departed to his office. Several seconds later, he returned with a long gold horn.

"I sounded the Horn of Assembly," he explained.

I grasped it and almost immediately dropped it due to its weight. Gabriel lifted the object from my hands with ease.

"Okay. Well, did you play the right song?" I asked, grappling for words. At Gabriel's skeptical look, I knew I had failed. "I don't know the proper word, but did you sound the correct call?"

"Yes," he said seriously.

"I'm not doubting you, I'm just trying to cover all of our bases. So, is there some kind of secondary precaution?"

"No," he responded just as seriously.

I let out a heavy sigh and turned back to the map. Suddenly, an idea struck my mind.

"Gabriel, you told me before that you each have an affinity for things, like places or..." I tried to remember his words.

"Stones."

"Right!" I exclaimed, but when I turned to him, he was nowhere in sight. I headed to his office, and when I entered, he was rummaging through some chest below the window. "What are you trying to do now?"

"Find my rosary beads."

Puzzled, I asked, "Why?"

"Because we need to seek guidance." With that, he left me once more. Attempting to keep up was becoming quite the frustrating task.

I went back into the living area, where Gabriel cleared the kitchen table and took the map down from the wall. He spread it out over the surface, then sat diligently with his rosary beads wrapped several times around his right hand. I realized a mysterious ring had been placed on the map.

"Can you just hold on one moment and explain to me what you're doing?"

"I'm sorry, I'm getting ahead of myself."

It was about time he finally acknowledged that.

"This ring"—he pointed to the object on the map—"will guide us to my brothers. Each of us was given one. Although the stones and metal vary, the bands were forged from the same fire. None of us ever take them off. I thought if I placed my ring on the map and prayed, it might reveal to me where the rest of them are located."

In that moment, my resolve waned. The person sitting before me was clearly an insane man. Or maybe I had gone insane, since everything in my reality no longer made sense.

What Gabriel said was completely illogical. But of course, he had to prove me wrong.

The ring started to move independently, in slow circles around New York City. Gabriel sat before the map with eyes closed and both hands grasped together tight. His mouth was moving, but his voice was barely a whisper as he spoke in some foreign language, which I presumed was Latin. Mesmerized, I paid no attention to the map. He must have sensed this, as he reached for the marker and handed it to me without opening his eyes or fumbling his words.

I brought my attention back to focus on the task at hand, however bizarre it seemed. The ring was still circling over New York, but it was moving faster now. Its pulsating movement and the sound of Gabriel's chanting whisper lulled me into a hypnotic daze that was broken only by a sudden jolt from the ring. It jerked to the right, across the Atlantic Ocean, and commenced circling once more around England.

I hastily moved some chairs out of the way so I could lean over the table and get a better look at the map. Upon closer inspection, the ring appeared to be revolving around Oxford. I grasped the marker, prepared to note the location. The ring moved, continuing its journey across Europe.

I quickly marked Oxford with an *X* and a *#1*.

The ring neared Australia and rotated over a remote area in the middle of the continent. I moved around the table, trying to procure a better angle. It was above the Gibson Desert. Ready to mark the site, I waited for it to move. Sensing my preparedness, the ring slid out of sight, heading west.

I marked the Gibson Desert with an *X* and a *#2*.

Scanning the map, I found the ring hovering over Africa next. Practically climbing on top of the table, I scrutinized the exact location. It was Botswana.

As the ring zoomed off again, I marked Botswana as *#3*, but it worried me the location was not a specific city or town.

Looking to my right, I saw the ring circling over a new site, so I climbed off the table and moved in that direction. It had centered on Tokyo, Japan.

When the ring moved, I labeled Tokyo as *#4*.

I returned my gaze to the map and searched for the ring. Gabriel was right. It was back over Europe. In my excitement, I strode to the center of the table, nearly running into him in his chair. I saw the ring come to a stop above Rome, Italy. Before I could even approach the spot, it was on the move again.

I labeled Rome with a *#5*.

Sensing the ring's urgency, I scanned the map for its last site. It was circling so fast that it was almost impossible to decipher where it centered. Finally, the ring stopped and lay immobile on the map.

São Paulo, Brazil. I marked it with an *X* and labeled it *#6*.

Exhausted, I sat down in the nearest chair. Gabriel had finished his foreign whispering and had just now opened his eyes. He unclasped his hands and turned to me.

"Did it work?"

"See for yourself."

He stood and gazed at the map, eyes growing wide as he took in each location.

I picked up his ring and handed it to him, ready to ask my famous question. "What now?"

He glanced up. "We go to Oxford. I hope you have a passport."

JORDAN

13

NEW YORK CITY, PRESENT DAY

Considering I hadn't unpacked, preparing for our global adventure should have been easy. However, I couldn't find my passport. I knew I'd placed it securely inside my duffel when I was preparing for the mission trip, but now, it was no longer there.

I was panicking. There would be no world adventure if I didn't find it, and it wasn't like I could just go to the post office and get a new one today.

I stomped around the guest room in search of the tiny blue booklet. It looked like a bomb had gone off as I'd thrown practically everything out of my duffel in the process.

Gabriel knocked and entered. "Still no luck?"

I looked up from the near-empty bag in front of me with a manic gleam in my eye. "No."

"Well, that poses a problem."

"I know." I shoved my arm into the duffel bag to retrieve its last contents from the bottom, and I was about to give up all hope when my fingers brushed against thick paper. I frowned.

"What?" Gabriel asked.

"I don't know, I think I found something," I told him, pulling out whatever I had touched.

Buried underneath a pile of clothes at the bottom of the duffel was a large manila envelope with my name on it.

"I take it you didn't put that in there?"

I shook my head, unable to speak.

Sensing something was wrong, Gabriel asked, "What is it?"

"It's Sister Helen's handwriting. I would recognize it anywhere. She had to sign all my permission slips when I was little."

Gabriel came closer to my side, inspecting the envelope. "You should open it."

I hesitated. "What do you think is inside? It's an awfully big envelope for just a passport."

"You'll have to open it to find out. Who knows, maybe the key for the backpack is in there?"

At that, my hesitation vanished. I gripped the envelope and dashed from the room toward the kitchen counter, needing a large surface to spread out the envelope's contents. Gabriel followed on my heels and stood by my side while I took a seat on a stool. I raised the tiny metal brackets and lifted the flap, gently shaking it until everything came sliding out across the counter. On top was my passport.

I turned to Gabriel, realizing Sister Helen must have moved my passport on purpose so I would find the envelope. He motioned for me to continue.

Moving my passport aside, the next thing that caught my gaze was another envelope addressed to me, this one much smaller in size. I tore open the seal and pulled out a two-page letter.

Dear Jordan,

I am sorry for leaving you as I did, without proper explanation of the events presently occurring. My deepest regret is never instructing you properly and leaving you to face the unknown. By now, I am sure you have made it to one of the archangels. Please trust and have faith in him. Hopefully, he, or all of them together, will teach you what you need to know in order to discover the truth. I haven't much time to write this since the fallen are closing in, but I assure you not to worry about me. I will be just fine.

However, I must address two things. First, you are not going to Africa. At least, not yet. Every few years, the Sacrarium relocates to evade Satan and the fallen. We possess something he dearly wants. I have an inkling of what the object is, but I have never seen it. I only know that it was placed inside the backpack and entrusted to me for protection. Satan has been tracking us because of it, so the need to stay on the move is vital to our survival. You might remember how we changed locations twice in your childhood. This year, we were supposed to do the same. But you had just graduated high school and were researching mission trips, and I knew I needed to keep you safe. I made up the opportunity in Africa. Really, all I was trying to do was to get you to one of the archangels. I figured he could train you and explain all this. I'm sorry for misleading you, Jordan. I know how excited you were for the trip.

When you left to run your errand, I was alerted our

location is compromised and the fallen are near. I have to ensure the safety of the other children, so the sisters and I have begun our move prematurely. It's going to be far too late to explain anything when you arrive, but I imagine the fallen have already connected you to us because of your fleur-de-lis necklace. It is a symbol linked to both Holy Trinity and the Sacrarium. You are in danger without this knowledge, Jordan, so I've found an archangel who lives closer. I hope you made it to him safely. As for Holy Trinity, it still exists, but not as you know it, so please do not go searching. Instead, listen to the archangels. They will guide you in the right direction.

Now, most importantly, your parents... I knew them. In fact, they were dear friends of mine. On the night you were born, I assisted your mother to the hospital. She needed help in such a vulnerable state, and your father had already passed. Her demise that night was unforeseen and heartbreaking. However, your mother was always prepared. She must have sensed something was wrong because she came to the hospital with a portable safety box full of documents and possessions that she wanted you to have, which she gave to me along with a letter when we arrived on the ward. She told me to read it if something happened to her, and this gesture seemed strange at the time, but with hindsight, I understand her intentions.

Those items are what I have included in this envelope. She did not want you to have them until you were eighteen, but she stipulated you were to have a monthly allowance in order to care for your needs. That is why you were always slightly more spoiled than the other children in the orphanage.

Jordan, I must go, but I cannot express how sorry I am for not telling you any of this sooner. I was respecting your mother's wishes and trying to keep your well-being in mind. I hope you can forgive me. Always know, I will be praying for you. And always remember, the truth resides inside.

Sister Helen

I remained frozen in place. Not only did this letter validate everything Gabriel had said, it also held knowledge about my parents.

Gabriel sensed my shock. "May I?" he asked, indicating the letter. I passed it to him.

He read through it while I sat there in silent distress, unsure of what this all meant. Eventually, Gabriel set the paper on the counter, with a glance at me to determine my emotions.

"I'm not sure I can proceed," I confessed, staring into space rather than at the items strewn in front of me.

"I can't imagine how difficult this is for you."

I nodded.

"Yet," he continued, "I think Sister Helen and, most importantly, your parents would want you to continue on."

Once more, I nodded. Swallowing the lump in my throat, with a heavy sigh, I reached for the pile of papers. A debit card slid out from the stack. I grasped it and saw my name engraved across the plastic. Sister Helen must have set the account up for me. As I shuffled through the rest of the documents, I soon realized they were bank statements. It became apparent my parents had left me quite a fortune.

I sat numb, sifting through the documents in disbelief. A statement for a college trust fund my parents had set up. A deed to a house they must have lived in, which I now owned. My social security card and birth certificate. My parents' death certificates.

The more I went through the pile, the more overwhelming it became. I stood up and walked away from the counter, running my hands through my hair. I felt on the verge of a panic attack as the shock finally set in.

Gabriel came to my side and led me to the couch, where, obligingly, I sat down. He disappeared briefly and returned with a glass of water.

"Drink," he insisted, trying to calm me.

I grabbed the glass and swallowed some water. "I haven't even finished looking through all of it and I'm already a mess."

"Your reaction is to be expected, especially after discovering everything your parents left behind."

We sat in silence and let the minutes tick by until I eventually found the courage to return to the counter. I realized I had gone through most of the pile and all that was left were two clear plastic bags. One was filled entirely with photos. Sighing, I set it aside. The last thing I needed right now was to see my family and what my life could have been. The other bag held only two items: a man's ring, and a necklace. I pulled the ring out first, admired its simplicity. It was a black band with green jasper in the middle and gold interspersed throughout the stone. I placed it on my right ring finger, and, surprisingly, it fit. Feeling a sense of comfort, I left it on and went back to the necklace, lifting the chain to eye-level to examine the plain silver cross.

"You should always wear that." Gabriel broke my reverie. "It will bring you protection."

I realized he was leaning against the counter. "Really?"

"Yes. The fallen cannot touch anything holy or sanctified."

"Hence the holy water."

"Correct. Some angels wear a cross or another religious symbol, depending on their faith, for the same reason. It's a way to arm ourselves against the fallen."

I noticed the glint of gold shining around his neck. Presumably, the cross he mentioned. But my attention was drawn to Gabriel's wrist, where he absentmindedly rubbed his fingers over a mark that peeked out from his shirtsleeve.

"You have tattoos?" I asked.

He quickly moved his hand away. "Some. Not many. Not tattoos in the traditional sense. These are more like divine markings."

I smiled. No matter what he wished to call them, they were still tattoos. I slipped the silver necklace over my head since the chain was large enough, and the movement revealed my other necklace.

"The fleur-de-lis," Gabriel remarked.

I grabbed at the chain and unclasped it resentfully, setting the jewelry on the counter. "That's what caused this mess."

Gabriel looked skeptical. "Jordan, you cannot blame yourself. Sister Helen said in the letter that she knew their location was compromised."

"Yes, but I led the fallen right to her."

"You didn't know. How could you if Sister Helen never told you anything? Besides, it seems everyone made it out safe."

"I know. I just feel guilty... There's so much running through my mind."

"Like what? Perhaps it will be better if you vocalize your concerns."

"Like the fact Sister Helen knew my parents. Does that mean they were members of the Sacrarium?"

Gabriel shrugged. "I don't know. It's possible."

"Do you have to be born into the Sacrarium?"

"I don't believe it's a requirement, but I'm sure it helps."

"I see. Well, I'm not entirely sure I want to go around flaunting this anymore, so I'll just put it in the bag," I said, taking the necklace from the counter and placing it in the now-empty plastic bag.

"What else are you concerned about?"

I fixed my gaze on Gabriel. "It's not concern exactly, but she was sending me to Africa, to one of your brothers. We just discovered one of them is there, and to think they're expecting me is hard to wrap my mind around."

Gabriel nodded. "You're right. Which means we don't know what each of them is involved in."

"What do you mean?"

"Whoever is in Africa was obviously in contact with the Sacrarium, but why? Who's to say none of the others know things we do not?"

"I guess I see your point, but we shouldn't dwell on that too much. We'll be finding them soon enough, and I'm sure once you're all face-to-face, everything will be revealed."

Gabriel sighed. "You're right, I'm getting ahead of myself. Anyway, you shouldn't worry about it either. When we get to Africa, I'm sure we'll have more answers."

I nodded and started gathering everything together, returning all the items back to the manila envelope.

"What about the pictures?" Gabriel asked.

"I'm not ready for them."

"It's your choice. One day, you will know when you need them."

I nodded in agreement. "You know, there was no key."

Gabriel looked confused.

"For the backpack," I explained.

Recognition graced his face. "I had completely forgotten about that in all this."

"Me too. I wonder what object Sister Helen was referring to in the letter. Whatever it is, Satan seems to want it badly."

"Indeed. There are many objects Satan wants, so I'm unsure what it could be. What's more peculiar is why the Sacrarium would have it unless someone gave it to them. Sister Helen did say the backpack was entrusted to her...but that just leads to more questions. As for the key, it will reveal itself in time."

I nodded in distraction.

"What did Sister Helen mean by, 'the truth resides inside?'"

Smiling at the memory, I explained, "She always had this saying that she would repeat to all the kids at Holy Trinity whenever we had doubts about ourselves or were upset about being orphans. We were teased and bullied sometimes because of it, so Sister Helen would remind us the truth resides inside, deceit lies without, and the journey to both is obscure."

Gabriel pondered the words. "That doesn't make much sense."

"Exactly. That was her point. It always made us think about the saying rather than dwell on our doubts or insecurities."

"I see," Gabriel said, though I suspected he didn't truly understand.

JORDAN

The wheels of the plane hit the tarmac as we descended from the air. I grinned at the sight of Heathrow airport, excited to finally see more of the world. Add my angelic situation into the mix, and what more could an ordinary teen want?

Gabriel insisted on flying first class and took the aisle seat. By all accounts, he was the ideal travel companion, but he hadn't slept a wink in the entire seven-hour flight.

He noticed me scrutinizing him and turned his head. "Yes?"

"Nothing. I was just wondering why you didn't sleep."

"How do you know I didn't sleep? I could've been sleeping when you were."

The thought hadn't occurred to me. "True, but I just get the feeling you didn't."

"You're right, I didn't," he said nonchalantly. "I don't need to sleep… or eat, for that matter."

"What? Why haven't you told me this before?"

"Because it never came up. Though you must have been suspicious to accuse me of being a vampire."

I laughed at the memory, then realized it only happened two days ago. Time sure went fast when you were in the company of an archangel.

Everyone around us stood up to retrieve their carry-on bags, and I realized we'd made it to the terminal gate. Gabriel stepped into the aisle and opened the compartment above his head, retrieving the backpack, his garment bag, and both of our raincoats. I stepped into the aisle too and took the backpack and my jacket.

"Thanks."

We departed the plane and began our trek through the terminal, following the signs for Customs and Baggage Claim. Making it through the first without a hitch, we stood in front of the baggage carousel eagerly awaiting our luggage.

"Did you bring a camera with you?" Gabriel asked randomly.

I glanced at him to determine what had spurred that question and realized he was plain curious. "No. I figured pictures would be forbidden, given you're some celestial super entity no one should know about."

He laughed. "You have a wild imagination. You know that, right?"

"Yeah. A lot of people tell me that."

A moment of quiet passed between us.

"You know, I was really nervous going through security in New York," I blurted out.

"Why's that?"

I pointed to the backpack on my shoulders. "Because of this. We don't know what's inside. For all we know, it could be a weapon."

Gabriel smirked. "I highly doubt Sister Helen gave you a weapon to protect."

Nodding, I said, "You have a point there, but you know what I mean. I was afraid it would set some alarm off and raise suspicions."

"That's highly unlikely. Whatever is inside is a holy, sanctified object, and such things do not show up on human radar."

"Really? So, an X-ray wouldn't show anything?"

"No."

The bell of the carousel interrupted our conversation, announcing the arrival of our bags. We watched as bag after bag passed before us.

"Gabriel, I know we're going to Oxford, but where exactly are we going, and who are we intending to meet? The ring gave us locations, not specific addresses or the names of who would be there."

"I wondered when you were going to ask that," Gabriel replied, briefly leaving my side to retrieve his bag. When he returned, I waited expectantly for an answer. "We'll talk about it in the car," was all I got.

With a sigh of frustration, I walked away to pull my duffel from the pile of bags it was stuck underneath.

"Where to now?" I asked when I returned to his side.

Gabriel remained standing. "We need to wait for the chest."

"Oh, right." I'd forgotten about the enormous chest Gabriel insisted we bring, the same chest he'd pulled the golden horn from. I could only imagine what other paraphernalia lived inside.

As suitcases streamed out of the carousel, I could tell Gabriel was growing impatient. Scanning the baggage area, it dawned on me that his chest might not come out with the other bags. Several peculiar-looking items awaited collection in a small office across from us.

"Gabriel, I think your chest might be over there."

He picked up his things and strode over. I followed close at his heels.

"Wait here," he said, leaving me outside with the luggage.

He spoke to the woman at the counter and after showing her his identification, Gabriel pointed to his chest, which could be seen from the counter with piles of luggage around it. A stressful conversation ensued. It seemed like Gabriel wanted to retrieve the item himself, but the woman refused to let him. Instead, she approached the chest and tried to move it, but it wouldn't budge. Gabriel rolled his eyes. She asked her male coworker for assistance, who tried to help her to no avail. Really losing his patience, Gabriel stepped behind the counter, grasped the chest with both hands, and left the office.

The man and woman stared after him, stunned.

Chuckling to myself, I asked, "Should we get a cart?"

"No," Gabriel replied. "If you don't mind pulling my hand luggage, I can take the garment bag and chest."

"Sure."

With our luggage situated, I followed Gabriel through the airport and out into the parking garage, where I stopped suddenly.

"You have a car here?"

"Yes," he replied, not breaking step. "I have a car in New York too. I don't drive much there though." He finally stopped in front of a silver Lexus RX. Unlocking the car, he began to load his chest and bag into the trunk.

I stared in disbelief. "You can drive?"

He looked at me in curiosity. "Yes."

"A stick shift?"

"Yes," he said, exasperated. Striding over, he took his other bag and my duffel and loaded them into the trunk as well.

He continued to amaze me, and it was in moments such as this I didn't attempt to ask for an explanation.

"Are you getting in?" he asked from the driver's seat.

I nodded, unable to decide what to say. I made myself comfortable in the passenger seat, located on the left side of the vehicle, and placed the backpack on the back seat behind Gabriel. He went about inputting our destination into the GPS.

"Do you have a phone too?" I wondered.

He raised an eyebrow. "No. I hate technology. But I'm not foolish. I realize I must adapt to changing times, so I know how to operate such things even if I don't possess them."

"I see. Well, I had a phone, but I left it behind in my room at the orphanage. I guess either Sister Helen took it with her, or it burnt to a crisp in the fire."

The GPS beeped, and a robotic female voice with a British accent said, "Proceed to the route."

Putting the car in reverse, Gabriel eased out of the parking spot and exited the garage. Once we were on the highway—he told me they were called "motorways" in England—I couldn't wait any longer for him to answer my question.

"So, where exactly are we going? And who will be there?"

"When you think of Oxford, what comes to mind?"

I sat and thought for a moment. "The university, I guess."

"Exactly. And what happens at a university?"

I looked at him strangely. "Learning?"

"Precisely. Which means we're searching for an angel of teaching."

"An angel of teaching? What does that mean?"

"Every angel in the Third Choir is gifted with a certain talent and categorized into circles of vocation. I am an angel of music."

"That explains the violin."

"Right. Out of all of us who were sent here, Zadkiel is the only angel of teaching."

"Zadkiel? That's a unique name. Now, go back a minute. What do you mean by the Third Choir?"

"There are three choirs of angels in Heaven that are made up of three groups of angels. In a sense, it's a hierarchical designation."

"Hierarchical?"

"Yes, a hierarchy. Think of each group as being on a separate tier, with the most important angels on the top tier, and each lower tier being slightly less important."

"Okay, but the Third Choir is the lowest?"

"Yes."

"Then why are you here and not the angels who are higher up?"

"Because we are messengers. Most importantly, because our ranking does not convey the seriousness of our duty."

"Interesting… So, essentially, you do the dirty work?"

His head teetered back and forth. "In a way."

Settling deeper into my seat, I tried to keep myself busy by taking in the scenery. The next thing I knew, I was opening my eyes as we drove through a quaint town, which I guessed was Oxford. The cobblestone sidewalks and old buildings certainly seemed like the right fit.

I rubbed my eyes. "Are we here?"

"Yes, just trying to find some decent parking."

When he found a spot, Gabriel parked the car and pressed the ignition button to cut the engine. I got out and shut the door.

"Bring the backpack with you," he instructed.

"Why?"

"I don't want to leave it unaccompanied in the car."

I grabbed the bag from the back seat and slipped on my jacket since it had started to drizzle.

"Ready?" Gabriel asked.

"Sure." Though, I was unsure of how his brother would react to us showing up unannounced.

We set off down the street, passing teashops and bookstores. The university was ahead of us and grew larger in size as we walked. Students all around us sped by on their way to class.

"Where do we go?"

"I'm not entirely sure." Gabriel eyed his surroundings. "We need to find a directory of faculty."

"The library might have that on their computers."

Gabriel stopped a student passing by. "Excuse me?"

"Yeah?" the guy answered.

"Where is your nearest library?"

"Over there." The guy pointed. "Follow this path a little way. It should be on the right."

We thanked the guy and set off in the general direction. When we found the library, I took the lead.

Walking up to the circulation desk, I asked, "Excuse me, is there a computer I can use? I'm a prospective student and I'm trying to locate a certain professor."

"Of course." The librarian came around from behind the desk and escorted us to a computer station. She logged on for me and pulled up the university's directory.

"Thank you."

"Absolutely." She smiled. "Let me know if I can assist you with anything else."

Gabriel stepped to my side when she left. "That was smart. Good thinking."

"Thanks. Now, you said his name is Zadkiel. I highly doubt he goes by that, but let's go to the *Z* page."

There were several *Zachary* and *Zacharia* entries. None of them seemed right.

"Wait," Gabriel said.

I stopped scrolling.

"There." He pointed to a name onscreen.

It read Zak Leid. I chuckled at the anagram, then covered my mouth to quiet myself since we were in a library. Gabriel shot me a look.

"What?" I whispered. "I thought your last name was bad enough."

I remembered the moment I first saw Gabriel's passport. I found it funny he went by Gabriel Maestro, given his musical talent.

Entertained by my amusement, Gabriel picked up a tiny wooden pencil and a small piece of paper. He wrote down the office number associated with Zak Leid.

"Okay, are we done here?"

"Yes," I said, logging off the computer.

We left the library and headed to the Humanities building. The vast lawns were deserted since everyone was taking shelter from the persistent rain. I pulled my hood closer to my face and followed Gabriel, nearly running into him when he stopped just shy of the building's steps.

"Zadkiel!" he called out to the back of a solitary figure hurrying up the steps.

At the mention of his name, the figure halted.

Turning slowly to face us, Zadkiel stared at Gabriel. The two of them remained in that position for quite some time, sizing each other up while the rain drenched each of them. I noticed Zadkiel was of average height, with dark brown hair covered by a flat cap. He wore dress pants and a sweater with a sports coat over it, and his equally dark brown eyes registered both shock and annoyance at the sight of Gabriel. He turned his back to us and continued his trip inside— though, this time, at a slower pace.

"What are you doing here?" he asked in a British accent when Gabriel caught up and began to walk in step with him.

I trailed behind them, close enough to hear everything they said.

"You know why I'm here. You didn't answer the call. None of you did."

Zadkiel stopped. "No one answered?"

"No, which is why I had to come find you."

They resumed their stride, navigating the halls to Zadkiel's office.

"Gabriel, I'm sorry to disappoint, but I'm not going with you. I don't want to be a part of whatever is happening. I have a life now."

"A life! None of that should matter. We have a duty to fulfill."

We arrived at Zadkiel's office door, and the angel pulled keys out of his leather shoulder bag to unlock it. "I understand that, but—"

"Professor Leid!" a girl called, walking quickly down the hall toward him.

Sighing, Zadkiel turned to her. "Hello, Margaret. How are you?"

"I'm good. I was wondering if you had time to discuss some questions I have about today's lecture?"

Looking at Gabriel, he said, "Unfortunately, I'm unavailable. A family emergency has come up."

"Oh, I'm so sorry to hear that. Well, I'm sure we can meet another time…" The girl glanced at me and Gabriel, clearly wondering how we were related to the professor. The sour look on her face as she waved goodbye showed her annoyance at us for interfering with her time.

Zadkiel stepped into his office, gesturing Gabriel inside. I followed suit, closing the door behind me.

The office was spacious and cozy, its walls lined with floor-to-ceiling bookcases, with two armchairs for guests and a reading nook in the corner. There was a large window speckled with raindrops that illuminated the space in a blue-gray tone. On top of the neatly organized desk was a reading lamp, and when the angel switched it on, it bathed the mahogany desktop in a warm orange glow.

Zadkiel turned to face us after placing his bag, hat, and jacket on a coat rack. "Gabriel, nothing you say will change my mind." Then, he noticed me. With a frown, he asked, "Who's the boy?"

We spoke at once.

"I'm not a boy—"

"His name is Jordan—"

Silence ensued. Zadkiel's eyes landed on the backpack.

"What's inside the bag?" he asked, looking to Gabriel.

"We're not sure. It was sealed shut."

He adamantly shook his head. "No. I will not be a part of this."

"Zadkiel, you don't understand. Jordan is the sign we were told to wait and watch for."

"I do understand, Gabriel!" he exclaimed. "Truly, I do, but the energy of whatever is inside that bag makes me nervous."

"Why?" Gabriel stepped forward. "I detect it too, but that only means it's powerful."

"No," Zadkiel whispered. "It's different for me. As an angel of teaching, I have encountered such an item before. You have too, Gabriel, although indirectly."

I could tell Gabriel didn't know what Zadkiel meant, which reassured me, because I had no idea what they were talking about either.

"What are you saying?" he asked. "What do you think is inside?"

"The Book of Prophecies. The last time it surfaced, you know what a disaster it caused for us. It started a war and brought destruction to Heaven."

"But...that can't be. How could it have gotten here?"

Zadkiel scoffed. "Gabriel, don't be so foolish. You know as well as I do, Father has many means to make things happen. Sending the book to Earth is not beyond Him."

Clearly understanding, Gabriel nodded. "Well, Satan's after it again."

"Of course he is. It's become his obsession, especially now he's locked in Hell."

"When did that happen?"

"I'm not sure. It's been several years. He has Lucifer doing his bidding, which is why most humans confuse the two. Lucifer is the one who has been on Earth lately, not Satan. And they are most certainly not one and the same, as you and I well know."

"How do you know about this?"

Zadkiel chuckled. "Because I'm an angel of teaching. We are constantly aware of the knowledge that pertains to our world even if we no longer dwell there." He looked at me. "Where does the boy fit in?"

They might have been talking in English, but everything they were saying was utterly foreign to me. I looked to Gabriel for an answer.

"A member of the Sacrarium gave him the backpack. He was then chased by The Six."

Zadkiel sized me up. "And he made it out alive?"

I shrugged. "I think I was just lucky."

"I'm sorry, I don't mean to offend. It's just…although you're quite tall, you seem a little scrawny to fight the fallen."

Great. Now I was being judged by angels. I knew I wasn't particularly muscular or athletic, but I had time to grow yet. Still, both Gabriel and Zadkiel seemed strong and capable of vanquishing fallen angels, unlike me.

Gabriel continued to explain my situation, telling Zadkiel all about Sister Helen, the orphanage, and the situation with my parents. "I was hoping you could teach him," he finished.

"*Me?*"

"He needs to be trained. I only know so much, and when I do tell him things, my explanations are quite horrible."

"They're not horrible," I said to make Gabriel feel better. "This whole situation is just confusing. Like now, for instance. I have no idea what you're talking about."

Gabriel could see the frustration in my eyes. "Jordan, I'm sorry. It's—"

"Not time for you to know," Zadkiel interjected.

I opened my mouth to protest.

"We are not trying to keep secrets from you," he continued, holding up his hand to stop my rebuttal. "We are merely trying to protect you until you're ready to know the truth. Now is not the time."

"Why not?"

"Because neither Gabriel nor I have the tools to teach you at the moment. And without the proper tools, your learning will suffer. I can tell, you are very bright and perceptive, Jordan, but your mind is not in the right place yet. We will know when you are ready to be taught because you will come to us with the right questions. For now, you must take this journey and give yourself time to perceive and analyze the situation. Take in what we are saying and try to be open-minded. Do not let anger or frustration rule you because that leads to dark paths. When the questions arrive, I will be there to teach you the answers."

"Does that mean you're coming with us?" I tried to process his words.

"Yes. From the moment I saw Gabriel, I knew I would be leaving with him. He never takes no for an answer."

Gabriel shrugged, a tiny smile showing on his face.

"So," Zadkiel asked, "who else have you found?"

"Just you so far," I supplied.

He sighed.

"We know where the others are," Gabriel said.

"Not specifically," I corrected.

Gabriel rolled his eyes.

"Sorry, I just feel he should know the magnitude of the situation."

"Why me first?" Zadkiel asked.

"Your location was revealed to us first," Gabriel explained.

"Who was second? Or, *where* was second?"

"Australia," I said. "The Gibson Desert, to be more precise."

Once again, Zadkiel laughed. "Only one of us would be caught dead in the middle of a desert."

"I was thinking the same," Gabriel replied.

"Who?"

"Uriel," they answered in unison.

"Does he like the heat or something?"

They both laughed.

"No," Gabriel said. "He likes nature."

"Let me guess, he's an angel of nature."

"Correct." Zadkiel smiled.

"I suppose we have to go to Australia then?"

"Yes, we will, but you need rest first," Gabriel warned.

"You can stay at my place," Zadkiel offered. "I just need to gather a few things first."

He went about his office collecting books and tidying things up. Half an hour later, he finally announced, "All right, everything seems to be in order." There was a considerable number of books stacked up on his desk and even more in his arms.

"Do you need help?" I asked.

"Yes, please. Here are some tote bags to put all the books in." He opened a drawer in his desk and pulled out the bags, which he handed to me. "While you do that, I'll put these books in my shoulder bag." He gestured to the ones in his arms.

As soon as all the bags were full, the three of us left his office, Zadkiel closing the door and locking it on the way out. We headed out of the Humanities building and down to the parking lot, where Zadkiel scribbled his address on the slip of paper he handed to Gabriel. He then readjusted his load and took the books from me.

"I'll see you there. And I'll make sure to have something for you to eat."

I smiled gratefully.

Zadkiel loaded his belongings into a black Mini Cooper and zoomed off, soon out of sight. The thought of angels driving still perplexed me. Then again, I was in Oxford, England with two arch-angels, in possession of a mysterious backpack I'd been trusted to keep safe from Satan, and everything I'd known about my life so far was turning out to be one big lie.

Maybe angels behind the wheel wasn't such a big deal after all.

SATAN

Freedom was a fickle thing. It was the answer to everything yet left a gaping ache in your soul when taken away. I had been free for centuries, able to roam from this forsaken realm into the human world without restriction, but now, that ability had been taken from me.

I wanted to know why, so I requested the services of an ancient seer and sorcerer, but neither spirit was delivered to me by Leviathan. Now, I had to traverse to the nether regions of Hell and find them myself.

Exiting my private quarters, I strode through the cavernous hall and entered the throne room. When two demonic servants came scrambling over to me, I instantly realized my mistake.

"Master, master," they screeched, hobbling in my direction.

"What?" I demanded without slowing down.

"You have an audience, sir."

I stopped abruptly, and the two idiotic demons almost careened into me. I glanced over my shoulder at the neatly lined-up spirits eagerly awaiting my presence. Standing nearby was Balberith, a fallen angel I'd appointed to tend to the spirits in the throne room. His job was to watch them, record their requests, and then escort them back to where they belonged. The demons often assisted him.

"Tell them I'm busy," I barked, continuing on my way.

"As you wish, master." They retreated back to the waiting spirits who, at my lack of interest, were growing restless.

"Wait, please!" one of the damned shouted.

I ignored him and kept walking.

He broke away from the crowd, evading Balberith as he tried to pacify the unsettled spirits, and approached me.

"I've been working my sentence for five hundred years," the spirit said. "I was supposed to be freed centuries ago. Please, listen to me," he implored, reaching out for my arm.

That was a big mistake.

As his fingers encircled my wrist, the Hellfire began to burn him. He cried out in agony but was unable to let go. Whenever someone involuntarily touched me, it was always an interesting sight to see. The Hellfire latched onto them like a magnet, refusing to release its prey until some force pulled them apart. Usually, that force was me, but this time I didn't intervene.

While he screamed and writhed in pain, I waited for his plea.

"Please," he gasped finally.

I glanced at the number branded on his wrist. The mark was a nine, which infuriated me even more.

"You think I should have sympathy for you when you've escaped from Misery and entered Elysium?"

His stare bore into mine, and there was a gleam of fear in his eyes.

My anger flared. The Hellfire increased. In a matter of seconds, the spirit disintegrated before my eyes into a pile of dust.

I brushed my hands together to get the residue off. "Clean this up," I demanded.

"Yes, master." The two demons rushed to the pile of dust and began to sweep it into The Pit with their hands.

"Does that always happen when someone touches you?" a brave spirit asked.

"Do not speak unless spoken to," Balberith demanded.

I raised my hand to silence him and stared at the female spirit who had spoken, admiring her tenacity. "Yes, at any skin-to-skin contact."

"Then I'll make sure to never touch you," she responded, turning her back and exiting the throne room. The other gathered spirits followed her lead, understanding I was in no mood to be benevolent.

Balberith quickly rushed after them.

With the spirits gone, I could get back to the task at hand. Yet I remained frozen in place. That woman had reminded me of someone. Lilith, with her flashy eyes and sleek hair, her stubbornness and determination, her curiosity and insight. I hadn't seen her since my fall centuries ago, but her memory was always at the forefront of my mind. She was like a poisonous drug, infecting my soul and causing addiction. The only cure or fix was Lilith herself. She was unforgettable.

Shaking the image of her from my mind, I crossed the stone floor and made my way to The Pit, the bottomless hole that spanned the levels of Hell, which I often used as punishment for anyone who defied me in the throne room. The spirit who had touched me deserved the Hellfire because his presence up here was a clear act of resistance to the order of things. A trip through The Pit would have been insufficient for an offense so severe.

SATAN

Stepping up to the hole, I placed my feet along the ledge.

When I fell from Heaven, my wings were so badly damaged I thought I might never be able to fly again. However, in the years since, they had fully healed. They had changed in color, from white to black, but that didn't bother me. I was just satisfied I could still use them.

I closed my eyes and breathed in and out deeply, then dove head-first into the void.

My body descended through the air like a bullet, fast and precise. When I came near to my destination, I spread my wings and eased up, slowing my freefall. The cold air ruffled my black feathers, a sensation I reveled in. Landing on a jutted cliff edge, I tucked my wings safely behind my back and strode forward, through the cave that acted as an entryway into Envy.

As I journeyed through the dark cavern, I sensed someone watching me. Stopping in my tracks, I listened for any noise.

A guttural growl echoed through the large cave as three snarling mouths came snapping at me from the dark. I evaded their attack and shouted, "You damn dog!"

Recognizing my voice, Cerberus instantly stopped his advance and lay before me.

"Good boy." I patted each head, otherwise the beast was likely to get jealous.

At my caress, Cerberus closed all six of his eyes in a sign of affection. Though I usually scorched anyone I touched, the Hellfire did not affect Cerberus. I wasn't entirely sure why, but perhaps it had to do with his thick hide and bristly fur.

Skirting around the large three-headed dog, I exited the cave and was thrown into the throngs of the city. Spirits of all types passed me by, frolicking in their partial freedom. My arrival in the metropolis was recognized, however, as some residents stopped their activities and others bowed low to the ground.

"As you were," I said, though most continued to stare in awe.

Ignoring them, I traversed the city until I came upon the area known for magic and divination. It was surprising how many witches, wizards, and the like fell prey to jealousy. A large number landed in this city compared to others, but not all magical beings were condemned to Hell. Plenty of good ones were accepted into Heaven—they just occupied a different realm than the angels. Today, however, I wasn't interested in finding any old seer and sorcerer. I needed help from special ones who were comfortable embracing the dark.

I stopped in front of a stall where a female spirit was polishing her crystal ball. "You."

"What do you want?" she barked, not looking up.

"I am in need of your services."

"Yeah? Well, who's asking?" She remained focused on the task with her head down.

I sighed. If Leviathan had simply gathered the seer and sorcerer like I requested, I wouldn't have to put up with this. He was usually reliable. Granted, I had given him other things to handle as well, but I absolutely hated interacting with spirits who didn't respect me.

When I leaned my hands on the edge of her table, she briefly stopped polishing and raised her head. A curtain of pale hair hid her face. She must not have recognized me because she took my hands in her grasp. Once again, big mistake. The Hellfire latched onto her, scorching her skin.

I pulled back, releasing her hands before too much damage occurred. She seemed unfazed by the pain, however. The only change was that she finally stood to address me.

"Sir, I am terribly sorry, I didn't know it was you. You typically don't grace us with your presence in these parts."

"Indeed." I took in her figure. Her long, scraggly hair hid most of her features, but I could tell she was blind. Although I couldn't see her face, I could sense she was much younger than I expected.

"How can I be of assistance?"

"You'll find out in time," I said. "Now, come with me."

Obliging, she followed close behind as I continued on my journey through Envy.

"Do you know of any good sorcerers?" I asked over my shoulder.

"Tabitha's pretty good."

"Do you work well with her?"

"I suppose. We *are* sisters. I'm Astrid, by the way."

The fact she felt compelled to tell me her name was amusing. I didn't really care who she was, I only needed her skills.

"Can you take me to Tabitha?"

"Of course." She led the way.

Following Astrid was a poor decision. Not only was she blind, and therefore kept drawing unnecessary attention as she bumped shoulders with strangers, she also took the most convoluted route through alleyways and backstreets. At one point, she even walked through a solid wall before realizing I didn't possess the same skill. In the end, she led us back to exactly where we started.

"Astrid," I demanded.

· 135 ·

THE GENESIS OF SEVEN

"What?"

"You were supposed to take me to Tabitha. Where is she?"

"I'm right here," a figure said, popping up from under the table that held the crystal ball. She was much older than Astrid, her long, scraggly hair gray where her sister's was blonde, but her voice was smooth and strong. "Been here the whole time. I just needed a moment to prepare myself for your services. You king types usually require the most mysterious ingredients, so I had to scour my entire cabinet to find the most unusual and peculiar things."

Peering over the table, I realized there was a door that led to a cellar, presumably where Tabitha kept her magical objects.

"I'm not in the mood for games!" I barked.

"Neither are we, dearie," she challenged.

"Yeah! What's in it for us if we help you?" Astrid asked loudly, donning a fake bravado that didn't match her character.

These spirits were smarter than they appeared. "I haven't thought about it. What would you like?"

"Coin!" Astrid exclaimed.

"How much?"

"Two hundred thousand," Tabitha demanded.

"Fine."

"Really?" Astrid dropped the fake persona. She clearly thought I would be a much more challenging negotiator.

The truth was, I would have agreed to any amount. I desperately needed their services, and the currency system itself was something of a hoax, created as a way for residents of Hell to buy and exchange goods. In reality, it regulated the system and fooled many into thinking they needed money, which essentially forced them to work. Outside of Hell, spirit coin and demon cash didn't exist. It was quite laughable, actually.

"What are you smiling about?" Tabitha asked.

My smirk was erased. "You dare speak to me in that way?"

Recoiling, Tabitha whispered, "I'm sorry, sir."

"Good. Now, come with me."

"Where are we going?"

"To my quarters," I told them, retracing my steps back to Cerberus's cave.

"In the Royal City," Astrid said dreamily, using Elysium's nickname, as she and her sister followed behind.

"Would you shut it? We need him to take us seriously," Tabitha chastised.

Leave it to me to find the two chattiest spirits…

I stayed ahead of them, and we arrived at Cerberus's cave before they could drag me back into conversation. As we entered the cavern, the two of them fell into silence.

When the growling started, Tabitha demanded, "Where are we?"

Cerberus's three heads snarled in her face, eliciting screams of fright from both Tabitha and Astrid.

"Cerberus," I said calmly.

The dog turned to look at me.

"They're friends."

He whined as if to tell me it was forbidden for spirits to leave the city.

"I need them upstairs," I told him, "so their departure is sanctioned. They have a special job to complete, and Leviathan knows this."

At the mention of his master's name, Cerberus backed off, allowing the sisters through. Once we neared the precipice of the cave, their fear returned.

"Why are you taking us to The Pit?" Tabitha demanded, halting in her tracks. "Is this some kind of trick?"

"The Pit!" Astrid exclaimed in fright.

"Calm down," I commanded. "The easiest way to get to my quarters is to fly up there."

Tabitha stepped closer to the edge to determine how far we had to go. "I'm not sure we can travel that far. As spirits, we have the ability to fly but not long distances."

They were beginning to infuriate me. "Do you want your coin, or not?" I snapped.

"Tabitha, stop asking questions," Astrid pleaded. "We need that money."

"Fine. Lead the way, Your Highness," Tabitha said sarcastically.

Spreading my wings, I launched into the air, not having the patience to wait for them.

In a few seconds, I had traveled the short distance back to the throne room entrance. As I stepped on the familiar stone floor, my wings automatically folded themselves behind my back. I turned to look down into The Pit, but Tabitha and Astrid were nowhere in sight. With a sigh, I hoped I would not have to go rescue them.

Then, two gray orbs appeared through the dark. Their ascent was slow, and I was forced to wait as they floated up over the edge.

"I told you it was too far," Tabitha complained, breathless.

"Sister, shh. Look where we are!" Dreaminess entered Astrid's voice again.

"Astrid, you can't see."

"Yes, but I can imagine its beauty," she sang, twirling around.

With a skeptical look, Tabitha took in the entirety of the room and did not seem impressed. I couldn't blame her. It was just an enormous rocky cave that held a large stone chair, the throne.

"Yeah, it's absolutely breathtaking," Tabitha snorted.

I couldn't help but smile at her sarcasm. She was lucky I had a sense of humor.

"Come with me," I said, leading them out of the throne room.

We entered the hallway that connected the throne room to my private quarters. Ahead of us stood the archway to my rooms.

"Ooh, what's in here?" Astrid wondered, moving to walk through.

Tabitha must have sensed my sudden tension because she grabbed her sister by the arm and said, "Astrid, don't go in there."

Stepping in front of them, I turned to the right and strode down the hall. At the far end was another archway leading to another cave. Gesturing with my arm, I signaled that they could enter. Tabitha pulled Astrid into the small space, and I followed behind.

"This is where you wanted to take us?" Tabitha asked. "What for?"

"I know I can't see, but it doesn't seem very pretty in here," Astrid said.

"This is my portal room, formerly the place where I fell."

This got their attention.

Walking around the room, I admired the three invisible gateways made of divine light. They were archways like in all the other caves, but each had its own capability and resembled the barrier He had used to trap me in this very cavern. When I broke the original one with Hellfire, it left behind small bits of residue, which I had collected and analyzed in the hopes of reusing and modifying.

In the middle of the space, there was a large stone table where I conducted my studies. It had taken many attempts to recreate the barrier, but I finally succeeded after consulting the expertise of Haborym, one of my fallen angels who had worked on similar barriers in Heaven. After she helped me recreate the original gateway, I used the skills she had taught me to create new ones that were capable of imprisoning beings and granting me a passage to the human world. During my journeys back and forth between realms, I had amassed a collection of books, which I now stored on shelves carved into the stone wall opposite the three gateways.

I halted my admiration of the room and turned to face the sisters. "Through this gateway," I said, indicating the one directly ahead, "is where I found the fallen forces when we first arrived. Now, it leads to Elysium."

Tabitha peered at the invisible surface separating us from the metropolis.

"Through that gateway," I said, pointing to my right, "is nothing of concern to you, and you must ignore it at all costs."

Superstitiously, Tabitha and Astrid backed away.

"And through the final gateway," I said, turning to the left, "is where I previously journeyed to Earth."

The sisters gazed at me in disbelief.

I stepped up to the portal and placed a hand on my once greatest treasure. "It no longer works," I said solemnly. Dropping my hand, I faced Tabitha. "I want you both to find out why, and then I want you to fix it."

"Us?" Tabitha was incredulous. "How do you expect us to do that?"

"Well, I expect Astrid to find out what needs to be done."

"And how do you expect her to do that?"

"She is a seer, is she not?"

"Yes, but—"

"And you are a sorcerer, are you not?"

"Yes, but—"

"Then fix it!" I said within inches of her face.

"You don't understand," she protested. "Astrid's power is a gift. She cannot summon it on command."

A screeching gasp brought our attention to Astrid, who stood with one hand on the invisible portal. She was frozen in a trance, her body rigid and her hair blown away from her face, revealing two white, iridescent eyeballs clouded by blindness.

"I need paper and something to write with," Tabitha said. At my lack of movement, she ordered, "Now!"

The sight of Astrid was so striking, it took me a moment to process her words. I searched the room for parchment and a writing utensil, locating a quill and ink bottle on the workbench, and grabbed desperately at paper shoved between the pages of books. I delivered the objects to Tabitha, who anxiously awaited her sister's next move.

Another screeching gasp alerted us she was about to speak.

Trapped in a fiery Hell
Lord Satan suffers in where he fell
The bloodline causes this to be
Since blood ties are the key
You to her are bound forever
Until ties are dissevered

The descendant that walks the Earth
Is a force stronger than any other birth
The one that makes your imprisonment be
Must be vanquished for you to be truly free

A temporary fix I can see
As long as you listen to me

An amulet must be made
To grace the place where the cross once laid
Three things are needed for you to be freed
As stated in this creed

A feather black as night
A matching one that is white
Your blood shall seal the deed
When the dark moon bleeds

Vigorously, Tabitha recorded her sister's words on the parchment, committing the divination to memory, though the pronouncement was unforgettable.

Astrid's screeching gasp struck the air once more as she rushed toward me and placed her hands on my face. Before Tabitha or I could react, the Hellfire started burning her hands—but the seer did not take notice, her screeching voice filling the cave with another divination.

The one you think of is alive

Trapped for years by an angel's drive
Inside an orb is where she rests
Awaiting a fall from the blessed

The Triune imprisons her
Because they do not want her to stir
She is needed so you see
In order to fulfill the prophecy

Astrid released yet another screeching gasp as her hands fell away from my face. She stood still, bent at the waist, her hands smoking from the contact with my skin.

Unforgettable.

That was what I thought when Astrid placed her focus on me. Earlier, I associated the sentiment with something else. Or, rather, *someone* else.

Lilith.

I had to find her.

Tabitha finished writing down Astrid's divinations and then came to her sister's side. At her touch, Astrid stood straight once more, her hair covering her face again. The seer and the sorcerer knew they could do nothing for her burned hands but leave them to heal as well as they could on their own.

"What did I miss?" Astrid asked.

Tabitha read the words scribbled across the paper, and I quickly realized why they needed to record them. Astrid was never consciously aware of what she was saying when under a trance.

I, however, would be incessantly haunted by her words.

JORDAN

16

During our stay at Zadkiel's place, the three of us realized just how difficult it would be to get to the Gibson Desert. I located it on Zadkiel's laptop, but the map showed it was nearly impossible to find a direct route. On the bright side, I learned it was a nature reserve, which verified Gabriel and Zadkiel's suspicions it was Uriel living there.

The remoteness of the area still remained a problem.

After much discussion, Gabriel and Zadkiel decided we would fly into Perth and make our way to the reserve by car. It was roughly an eighteen-hour drive. Considering I had just survived a seventeen-hour plane ride, I didn't look forward to sitting in a car for even longer. I was beginning to understand why Gabriel was so frustrated when none of his brothers answered the call. If only Uriel had flown to New York, this whole situation could be avoided.

Then again, where was the adventure in that?

As we took off from the airport, I was really sad to leave England, wondering if I would ever be back. But now we were in Perth, and my mind was preoccupied with a new emotion: worry. I still didn't know exactly how we were going to find Uriel. I trusted the angels, but their plan seemed a little unreasonable. Maybe I felt this way because I was restless after being confined to a plane for hours on end.

After navigating the airport and going through the luggage retrieval process again—with two chests this time—we hailed a taxi that took us to our hotel.

"A bed never looked so welcoming before," I said, relishing in the luxury as we entered the two-bedroom suite.

While Gabriel and Zadkiel settled in, I dropped my bags and headed for the shower. Clean if not refreshed, I came out of the bathroom and collapsed on the bed.

A moment later, I felt someone nudging my arm.

"What?" I asked groggily.

"Jordan, you need to wake up. We have to leave soon."

It was Gabriel. Slowly opening my eyes, I peered at the bedside clock. It was seven a.m. already. We had landed in Perth around twelve p.m. yesterday and arrived at the hotel just before two.

"Did I seriously sleep that long?"

"Yes. You needed it. If you're still tired, you can sleep in the car, but for now, you need to get ready."

"On it," I said, getting out of bed.

As Gabriel walked out, I gathered the few things I had taken out of my duffel and went to the bathroom to freshen up. When I'd finished, I picked up my duffel and the backpack and headed out of the bedroom.

"Good morning," Zadkiel greeted me from the living room, where he was rearranging the books inside his chest.

"Morning," I replied. "Where's Gabriel?"

"He went down to the car to load his luggage."

"Should we meet him down there?"

"Only if you're ready."

"I'm ready."

"All right." Zadkiel secured the chest and handed me a foil wrapped burrito and a bottle of juice. "This is for you. It's not much, but Gabriel wanted you to have breakfast."

"That was nice of him to think of me. But why is he so worried about my well-being? He constantly makes sure I'm eating and sleeping, but I'm not a little kid. I know how to take care of myself."

"I know that. Gabriel does too. But since we do not eat or sleep, it's easy for us to forget others require such things in order to survive. He also feels responsible for you and wants to make sure you're taken care of. Essentially, it's Gabriel being Gabriel, so get used to it." Zadkiel chuckled. "If you think he's bad, wait until we find Chamuel…"

"What kind of angel is he?" I asked.

"You mean, what's his vocation?" Zadkiel clarified.

Remembering his comment about taking in information and being open-minded, I said, "Yes, that's what I meant."

"He is an angel of the home, so caring for others is something he excels at."

"I see. In other words, the nurturing and nourishing is only going to get worse?"

"Exactly," Zadkiel said, exiting the hotel room with his luggage.

I followed him as we made our way downstairs to the lobby. Through the glass doors of the hotel's main entrance, I saw Gabriel waiting by an SUV. We approached him and loaded in our bags.

"You have your food, right?" he asked.

"Yes." I held up the burrito and juice.

"Good." Gabriel strolled around to the driver's side, which was on the right side of the car, and I hopped into the back seat since Zadkiel was in the front.

After getting the GPS to work, Gabriel put the car in drive, and we were off. As we drove, I sat in the back seat in utter silence, staring through the window at the city. There were skyscrapers of various heights, much like New York, yet the main difference was the beautiful coastal surroundings. The sky was a clear light blue, the ocean a clear cerulean. I wished we could stop driving and spend a day at the beach, but unfortunately, we had a mission to accomplish.

Realizing this was a good time to jot down all the new angelic information, I reached for my duffel and pulled out my notebook. I made charts and lists, mainly of keywords that kept being thrown around, and when I was done, the digital clock on the dash revealed we were only one hour into the drive. I thought the task would have taken longer. Sitting in the quiet, I was already growing restless.

"Can we turn on the music or something?"

"Oh, you had to say it," Zadkiel complained.

"Say what?" I wondered, as Gabriel fiddled with the stations.

"Music. It will be our undoing."

"How so?"

Classical music sounded through the speakers.

"*That's* how so," Zadkiel groaned. "All he listens to is instrumentals."

"That's not entirely true," Gabriel defended. "I do prefer them over vocals though."

Staring up at the ceiling of the car, I wondered how long I could take Gabriel's music. Two hours into the ride, it was killing me.

"Can we turn it off now?" I asked.

"Please?" Zadkiel begged.

"Fine."

The car was thrown into silence once more.

"If we can't listen to music and no one is going to talk, what am I supposed to do?"

Zadkiel turned in his seat to face me. "There are some word puzzles and things to keep you busy," he said, indicating a plastic shopping bag on the floor next to me.

I looked inside to find word searches, mad libs, and adult coloring books with colored pencils. Thinking this was some kind of joke, I studied their faces in the rearview mirror. Nope. They were completely serious.

"Why don't we begin my training instead?" I suggested. I was not about to waste this opportunity with word puzzles when I had Zadkiel and Gabriel together without any distraction.

Zadkiel eyed me. "That depends."

"On what?"

"On the questions you are prepared to ask."

Wow, no pressure. I wracked my brain for the correct thing to say. "The Book of Prophecies," I said finally, recalling the name. "What is it, and why does Satan want it?"

Zadkiel smiled as if I had just won points in some normal game families played on road trips. "Ah…that's a good question. I see you want to cut right to the chase."

"Does that mean I passed?"

He laughed. "Yes. Are you ready?"

Hurriedly, I scrambled for my notepad and pencil. Pushing the top to release the lead, I poised my writing instrument over a clean sheet of white lined paper.

"As an angel of teaching," Zadkiel began, "I have access to most but not all of the divine wisdoms that reside in Heaven. The Book of Prophecies is considered one of those wisdoms. I have only seen the pages of the book once, and I was not allowed to read any of them because the book contains information so powerful it is restricted even to an angel of teaching."

"What kind of information?" I asked, writing this down.

"The book foretells things that could be. Things with the potential for enormous power that can match that of Father's and possibly overthrow it. However, unlike other prophecies, the prophecies in this book are things that *could* be, but that doesn't mean they *will* be."

"Where do these prophecies come from? How did they originate?"

Zadkiel was clearly impressed by my questions and nodded his head in approval. "They originated the way everything else originated."

"You mean, they were created by God?"

"No. I mean their origin was already set before the very fabric of this world was created."

"How is that possible?"

"That's something I cannot answer. All I can say is, they are called divine wisdoms for a reason. They involve many cultures and faiths."

"I see. And what does this all have to do with Satan?"

"Before the war in Heaven, objects went missing, the book being the first. In hindsight, it's understandable since this book held the knowledge to gain insurmountable power. No angels other than the angels of teaching were supposed to know about it. However, Satan— or Samael, as he was known then—did know about the book, and he also knew about the insurmountable power. Because of this, accusations were made, and Samael was one of the accused."

"Why?"

"Because not only did he know things he shouldn't," Gabriel inputted, "his disposition also changed. He was openly expressing his defiance against Father." His hands tightened on the steering wheel.

Zadkiel placed a hand on his shoulder as a gesture to calm him down. "What Gabriel said is true. Satan's disrespect for the order of things made him the most plausible suspect. The book wasn't the only thing missing. The Castle Key disappeared as well. It unlocked the castle tower in High Heaven, and the object residing in that tower is known as the Sovereign's Scepter. It's a required item for a particular prophecy."

"The one used to gain insurmountable power?"

"Yes."

"Before you go on," I said, "could I ask some clarifying questions?"

"Of course."

"High Heaven? What is that?"

"Heaven is divided into many realms. The one inhabited by angels is split into three: High Heaven, Middle Heaven, and Low Heaven. The First Choir dwells in High Heaven, the Second Choir in Middle Heaven, and the Third Choir in Low Heaven."

I nodded my head in understanding since Gabriel had already

explained this system to me. "So, the archangels live in Low Heaven?"

"Correct."

"All right. And since the book and Castle Key led to the scepter, and the scepter was needed for a specific prophecy that promised power, it was obvious Satan was the one behind all this?"

"That's what we thought at the time. The fact Satan himself went missing for a short period also acted as evidence."

"Where did he go?"

"We don't know. But his intentions were clear on his return, when he attacked High Heaven mercilessly in order to obtain the scepter."

I took notes as quickly as I could, so absorbed in writing that Zadkiel's next words surprised me.

"Satan wasn't really the one who started all this."

"What do you mean?"

"Before the worst of the war began, Gabriel discovered a fellow angel of music had stolen the book and Castle Key with the aim of going after the scepter. However, this angel was working for someone else, and his fear grew so strong he could not complete the final theft for her."

"For her?"

"For Lilith."

"Lilith? Isn't she some kind of demon or something?"

"Lilith is many things, but a demon isn't one of them," Gabriel said.

"Although, some would say she's demonic," Zadkiel added.

"If Lilith isn't a demon, what is she?"

"She was the serpent in Eden, and she knows many things because she presumably took from The Tree of Knowledge."

Gabriel scoffed. "She doesn't know many things. She knows *everything*."

"Very true, brother," Zadkiel agreed. "Yet Father never told us more than that, so there could be more to her story."

"Wait, wait, wait… The serpent who tempted Eve?"

"One and the same." Zadkiel nodded.

"How is she not a snake anymore?"

"That's where our story aligns itself. You see, as archangels on the council, we were given duties others were not. One of them was to check on Eden. The thirteen of us shared this responsibility equally, and when it was Satan's turn, he went but came back changed. Right after that, his defiance began."

"So, Lilith was to blame?"

"We believe so. She had the ability to tempt Eve—why not Satan too? It makes the most sense. There is only one thing that could have unleashed her from the form of a serpent."

"Which is…?"

"A holy weapon made from heavenly light in the Forge. Each angel of power is gifted such a thing. If Satan encountered Lilith in Eden, and she tried to attack him, it would be a natural response for him to defend himself. When he went on his excursions to the garden, he never went without his sword. Neither did Michael. Their swords had the ability to release her, and that's probably what happened—Satan struck her with the blade."

"Okay, that makes sense. But you said there was another angel behind the thefts. That would've been when Lilith was still a serpent?"

"Right. It would seem this other angel—Araziel was his name—was going to Eden as well," Zadkiel continued. "You must understand, the garden was unlike anything we had seen before. I'm sure the garden's allure drove him to visit even though he wasn't supposed to, and whether in the form of a serpent or not, Lilith has the ability to tempt. She likely persuaded Araziel to do her bidding."

"More than anything, I'm sure Lilith wanted to be released," Gabriel cut in, "and I believe she thought she could use the scepter for this purpose. However, when Satan released her instead by striking her with his sword, her ambition did not stop. She still wanted the scepter, presumably to harness its power. But unknown to her was the influence she had over Satan."

"It must have been strong," I mused.

Zadkiel nodded. "While she might have realized she'd polluted his mind, she didn't fully grasp the hold she had over him. He was so linked to her that her ambition became his, which is why he went after the scepter even though he hadn't stolen the other objects. But what you must learn about Satan is that he only acts for himself. When he sought the scepter, he too wanted to gain insurmountable power and overthrow Father."

"If they both were so close, what prevented it from happening?"

"Us," Gabriel said.

I wasn't expecting that. The two angels in front of me were not angels of power. The circumstances in Heaven must have been dire for them to join the battle.

"Well…us, and the fact Father hid the scepter away," Zadkiel added.

"Where did He put it?"

"We don't know. But when Satan discovered it wasn't in the tower, his anger overtook him, and Michael was able to capture him. With their leader out of the way and the fact Father arrived to enact punishment, the rest of the fallen submitted. As for Lilith... Well, Satan stole her thunder, so to speak. He went after the scepter before she could, but she didn't give up. She arrived on the battlefield and killed Araziel, the only angel to tie her to all these transgressions. However, the Seraphim captured her before she could escape. Father then sent Lilith to Hell with the rest of them."

"What happened after that?"

"I'm not entirely sure. All I know is, Satan and the fallen have grown too strong. We have no idea where Lilith is or what she is doing."

Zadkiel paused in his story to gaze out the window. I was glad for the break. All this information was hard to process.

I yawned and tried to fight against the sleepiness as I wrote everything down. "This is all so...interesting."

"You're tired," Gabriel said, glancing at me in the rearview mirror. "Rest now. There'll be time for more questions later."

I was about to protest and ask more, but the drowsiness of jetlag overtook me again, and quickly, my eyes were forced shut.

JORDAN

17

AUSTRALIA, PRESENT DAY

When I woke up, another two hours had gone by. I rubbed my eyes to focus my vision. It seemed we were driving through a more residential area now, passing row upon row of single-story homes. The GPS said we were in Merredin.

I reached over to retrieve my notebook and pencil, which had slid off my lap, then read through my notes, waking my mind from slumber.

When my brain was functioning properly, I asked, "What's the prophecy for insurmountable power called?"

Zadkiel jolted in his seat, not expecting me to be awake.

Gabriel chuckled. "Did you really think he would be quiet for long?"

"I'm sorry," I said. "Am I annoying you?"

Gabriel glanced in the mirror to determine my mood and smiled when he realized I was joking. "Of course not." He turned to his comrade. "Perhaps you should continue your story."

Zadkiel nodded. "The prophecy is called the Union of the Spheres."

I jotted down the title and listened as the angel of teaching continued.

"What I have not told you is that something else was required in addition to the scepter for the prophecy to come to fruition. That something is the Sovereign's Orb."

"Isn't that what they coronate kings or queens with? You know, the ball they hold in their hand? Don't they use a scepter too?"

"Both the orb and scepter are very similar to that, yes. While a coronation orb typically signifies power, the orb I'm referring to actually gives power to whoever wields it. A power that can destroy as well as create. A power that provides control and dominance. The Sovereign's Orb isn't easy to come by. There is a process involved, one Satan did not know about. However, I'm positive Lilith knew about it."

"Couldn't she have revealed it to Satan?"

"Perhaps, but Lilith reveals only what is needed for her to persuade others to her will."

"What he means is, she doesn't play all her cards at once," Gabriel said.

I nodded. "So, she's deceptive and manipulative."

They both looked amused at my summary.

"Yes," Zadkiel said.

"All right. What is this process, exactly?"

"Overall, the process is what it sounds like—the Union of the Spheres. Quite literally, the spheres are solid, round balls of stone about the size of a grapefruit. I'm sure you might have encountered something similar before. Humankind tends to sell such objects in gift shops and the like."

I nodded my head in recognition.

"There are thirteen spheres, each forged out of different gemstones."

"One for each council member?"

"Indeed. The spheres were created when the angels were created. We did not know Father initiated the council in order for us to control the spheres, but that was His intention. He assigned a particular gemstone to each of us." Zadkiel grabbed at his right hand and slid the ring he wore off his finger, holding it up.

I leaned forward in the back seat to see it.

"This ring signifies which gemstone I have control over. Each of us has one."

I glanced at Gabriel's right hand, and he raised it so I could inspect his ring. "You said the ring was able to locate the others because they were forged of the same fire."

"They were, but their connection goes far beyond that," Gabriel said. He returned his hand to the steering wheel, and Zadkiel put his ring back on.

"I see. And when the thirteen spheres come together, they make the Sovereign's Orb?"

"Actually, yes. The process of combining them together is based on the placement of the spheres as well as their location. I'm unsure of where the Union needs to happen because I have not read the prophecy, but as for the formation, the spheres need to be positioned in a certain shape known as Metatron's Cube. It's quite hard to describe. I will have to show you a diagram of it at a later time."

"That's fine. Who is Metatron?"

"Metatron is an archangel and Head of Council. He was not sent to Earth and still dwells in Heaven. He's an angel of teaching and quite a unique being. He sometimes has visions about the divine wisdoms, and the formation is something he saw in one of those visions. He committed the configuration to paper, and it has been known as Metatron's Cube ever since."

"I never knew that." Gabriel was surprised.

"Yes. It's something only Raziel and I knew about. Well, Father knew too, but He didn't want others to know. Metatron's gift is special and rare, so He didn't want anyone trying to manipulate it. He confided in Raziel and me to protect Metatron when he was in a trance. Anything that came from the visions, we shared with Father, then this knowledge was locked away in the Sanctuary of Teaching."

Gabriel nodded in understanding.

"Anyway," Zadkiel said, "getting back to the Union, I believe the formation and the location are the only components to the prophecy. However, I haven't seen the prophecy myself, so I could be wrong."

"Then how do you know so much about the process?"

"In the aftermath of the war, many things in Heaven changed. For instance, all of us were trained for battle. This luxury no longer pertained to only angels of power—every angel, no matter their vocation, was prepared for combat. Father didn't want any of us caught off-guard again, so He revealed all He could. That's how we learned about the Union of the Spheres, but out of concern for safety. He didn't divulge everything."

"What happened to them? The objects, I mean."

"They were hidden around Earth in various locations. While the objects pose a great threat to humanity, they are an even larger threat if they remain in Heaven. On Earth, they are much safer because they are spread apart, which serves as greater protection."

"I can understand that. But what if a human discovered one?"

"Then we have to rely on human ignorance. None of you know about them, and even if you did discover one, the rational part of your brain would create an inaccurate explanation for its existence."

"Or you would simply put it in a museum," Gabriel offered.

I realized I should take offense for the entire human race, but their words held truth. "So, what you're saying is, the objects from Heaven are here on Earth?"

"With certainty, I know the spheres are on Earth. As for the scepter and the book, I'm not completely sure, but if the book is in the backpack, then the scepter might be here too."

"All except for the Castle Key, of course," Gabriel said.

"The one that went missing?"

"Yes," Zadkiel said. "The Castle Key was destroyed after the war because Father did not want anything locked up in the castle anymore. Besides, if He sent the scepter to Earth, there was no need for the Castle Key any longer."

I stretched out my hand. It had grown numb from the intensity of pressing pencil to paper. The car slowed down, and I noticed we were stopping at a fuel station.

"I should fill the tank up," Gabriel said, "and you should go find some food."

I obeyed. I was getting kind of hungry, and I needed to stretch my legs.

Several minutes later, I came out of the service station with chips, a sandwich, and a bottle of water. I also grabbed some other snacks since I didn't know when we'd find food again.

"I take it you found some food," Zadkiel said from the front seat as I settled in the back.

"Yeah, and I went to the bathroom too. Figured I should get that over with before it became urgent."

Zadkiel nodded in agreement. After several moments, he said, "You did well today."

I glanced at him in the mirror. "Thanks. Are we going to start again?"

"Not now. I think that was enough for one day. I don't want to overload you."

"Good, because everything you told me requires some processing."

"Indeed."

Gabriel opened the driver's side door and took his place behind the wheel again. "Everyone ready?"

Zadkiel and I murmured our agreement.

He started the car and steered us back onto the road. I chowed down on my sandwich and felt both of them watching me. Their overprotectiveness was annoying, but I was sure I would get used to it. At least, I hoped I would.

To break the awkward moment, I asked, "How much longer?"

"Several hours," Zadkiel replied.

"We're on Highway 94, and we need to take this to Highway 49. After that, it's mainly back roads. I want to get to Warburton tonight. We can remain in the car until morning and then make our way to the reserve," Gabriel explained.

Realizing I needed to waste away more time before I could really sleep, I placed my notebook back in my duffel and took out the puzzle booklets. As night fell, I grew tired and closed my eyes, but I couldn't sleep fully since my biological clock was out of whack. Darkness surrounded us, and the car headlights were our only hope of seeing anything. After a short time, I realized we had stopped driving and must have made it to Warburton like Gabriel planned. Peering at the time on the dashboard, I saw it was almost two a.m. Instead of trying to force myself to sleep, I sat there with my eyes closed, hoping morning would come soon.

I must have dozed off again, because when I opened my eyes, sun was streaming in through the window. I sat up in the back seat.

"Where's Gabriel?" I asked Zadkiel, who now sat on the driver's side.

"He's in there." He pointed to the building we were parked in front of.

Outside the window, a sign read, "Warburton Roadhouse." Gabriel came out of the facility talking to some man who had short light brown hair, a brawny figure, and a fuller face with some facial hair scattered across his chin. They parted ways, and Gabriel headed for the car while the man walked to a parked pickup truck.

"He's hoping to find out how to get to the reserve," Zadkiel said.

"I thought we knew."

"We do, somewhat. It's off in that direction but it's not exactly open to visitors."

A wave of heat poured into the back seat as Gabriel got into the car. "Follow him," he said as he settled in the passenger seat.

"Who is he?" I asked.

"His name is Matthew. He works at the reserve. He can take us there."

"Does he know Uriel?" Zadkiel asked, steering the vehicle in the direction of the truck.

"Yes, he does, but he goes by Uri here."

Smirking, I asked, "Uri what?"

Gabriel shook his head at my amusement. "Uri Reed."

I chuckled. "Reed?"

"Clever," Zadkiel said.

"How?"

"Well, I simply created an anagram, but Uriel seems to use his Celtic tree sign as his last name," Zadkiel explained.

"Celtic tree sign?"

"What did I tell you about being open-minded?"

"I am! But what is that?"

"Remember when I told you about each of us having an affinity for certain things?" Gabriel piped up, keeping his eyes on the truck.

"Yeah."

"Well, each of us is also associated an astrological sign. In the Celtic culture, those take the form of trees rather than constellations. While a reed may not be a tree, it is still an object of nature."

"Okay, I can understand that. Are you associated with the constellations too? I mean, you must be, right, since each of you has the symbol tattooed on your wrist?"

"Yes," Zadkiel said.

The truck braked in front of us at a barricaded entrance. We waited as Matthew showed the guard his badge and pointed to our car. Then, the truck proceeded forward, and the guard waved us through.

We continued to follow the truck until it pulled into a small lot in front of a building, where we met Matthew by the entrance.

"So, you blokes are all looking for Uri? I didn't know he had any brothers. Let's go and see where he is," Matthew said, guiding us through the door and clocking in behind the main desk. Two women looked up from their work. "Sheila, Daisy, either of you know where Uri is?"

"Yeah, he's out checking on a vandalism incident. There was sign of a fire and debris left everywhere. He went out a while ago. Not sure how long it will take him."

Matthew looked at us. "Well, there's your answer."

"Do you mind if we wait here for him?" Gabriel asked. "There's been a family emergency, and we have no way to reach him."

"Sure, make yourself comfortable." Matthew pointed to some chairs.

"Thanks." Gabriel smiled as Matthew retreated to his office.

We all sat down next to each other. I reached for a magazine from the pile on the table and skimmed through it idly for several minutes before standing up to walk over to the wall of glass windows. Outside, the desert was a landscape I'd never encountered before. All I could see for miles was red dirt and low, brushy foliage. The temperature was unbearably hot, so I could only imagine what it was like at sunset when the landscape turned redder and started to cool off.

While I daydreamed, a burgundy Jeep Wrangler pulled in. A man hopped down from the vehicle and slammed the door shut, then strode toward the building with a purposeful step. He was quite short—at least, compared to Gabriel—and wore cargo pants and combat boots, with sunglasses covering his eyes and a baseball cap on his head. No one could miss the long red hair peeking out from underneath it.

Before I could announce his arrival, Uriel strode through the front door and went straight to the desk. "We definitely have a problem," he said in an Australian accent. "Whoever was here last night, they were illegal campers. Can you pull up any camera footage? Maybe we can see them somewhere along the perimeter."

"Sure thing, Uri, I'll get to work on that. You have some visitors," Sheila said, drawing his attention to us.

When Uriel turned and saw Gabriel and Zadkiel, he grimaced. "What are you doing here?"

"Coming to find you," Zadkiel said.

"Considering the message I received from you, I thought you'd be expecting my arrival," Gabriel said. "Then again, Zadkiel wasn't too keen to see me either."

Uriel strolled closer. "I take it he coaxed you into coming."

Zadkiel shrugged. "Yes, but I realize now that we are needed."

He sneered. "I can't understand how we're all of a sudden needed now, but we weren't needed yesterday or ten years ago. I'm not about to waste my time gallivanting all over with no purpose in sight. Now, please excuse me. I have work to do." With a shake of his head, Uriel returned to Sheila.

I was in no mood to put up with this. "You better wait just a minute," I said in my most intimidating tone.

Uriel turned to face us again.

"We flew seventeen hours to come find you, then drove another eighteen just to get out here in the middle of nowhere. And if that wasn't bad enough, we've got to repeat that trip to find the others, so we are *not* leaving this room without you."

Unfazed, Uriel tipped his head back slightly to take a hard look at me. "Who are you?"

"Jordan. The sign you've all apparently been waiting for."

Uriel eyed Gabriel.

"Let me explain," Gabriel said.

"Please do."

"Perhaps not in front of them?" He gestured to Sheila and Daisy.

"You're right. Follow me." Uriel led us down the hall and into an empty meeting room.

Zadkiel closed the door behind us once we were all inside. Then, Gabriel enlightened Uriel about everything that had happened.

He shook his head. "The Sacrarium never knows when to keep out of things that don't involve them." He eyed me in accusation.

"Hey, don't look at me. I'm not one of them." I paused. "Well, I might have been, but if I was, I didn't know."

"Uriel, Jordan is someone we can trust," Gabriel said.

"He was obviously someone they trusted too."

"Yes, but what's inside that bag has nothing to do with the Sacrarium and everything to do with us. I think Sister Helen used Jordan as her messenger because his lack of knowledge would essentially allow *us* to trust him. Her deepest regret in not training him actually turned out to be a saving grace."

Zadkiel nodded. "Now, we're able to teach him what he must know. The proper way," he emphasized, looking pointedly at Uriel.

"Hmm." He didn't seem convinced.

"Why do you distrust them?" I asked.

Uriel glared at me.

"Notice I said *them*, not *us*."

"It's not that I don't trust the Sacrarium, I just don't want to be associated with them. We have nothing to do with them," he explained, scrutinizing me. "Is that backpack the reason why you're here?"

"Yes," Zadkiel answered for me.

Uriel's jaw tightened, and he visibly swallowed, gearing himself up for the inevitable. "Fine. I'll come with you."

"Just like that?" I was stunned.

"You're obviously not going to leave without me. Besides, I understand I have a duty to fulfill."

Gabriel shook his head. "You're both readily agreeing to join me on this adventure now, yet when I called, every one of you refused to come."

"I think that's because we didn't realize the severity of the situation," Zadkiel said.

Uriel nodded in agreement. "Seeing the kid and feeling the energy of whatever is inside that backpack is certainly more compelling than a simple message to gather together."

Sensing slight tension, I stepped in. "Okay, now, let's not rehash the past. We have four more of you to find."

"Agreed," Zadkiel replied.

"You're right," Gabriel said.

"I suppose. But I'm not about to do all that driving. We're chartering a plane out of here and getting on our merry way." Uriel shook his head.

"We could have flown here?" I exclaimed.

"No, not you. But I have connections."

Uriel opened the door and left. We followed as he strode down the hall to speak to Sheila, telling her about our need for transport. She called for a small plane from one of the regional airports to come pick us up that afternoon and take us back to Perth.

"The plans have been put in place," Uriel said when he returned to where we stood aimlessly by. "Come with me, and I'll take you to the bungalow. You can relax there while I pack."

Well, this was going much better than I thought…

SATAN

18

"Let me see those papers again," Tabitha said. "I can't remember one of the lines."

Astrid searched the table for the divination parchment that rested next to her arm.

"What part could you possibly forget?" I asked. I'd memorized every line without glancing at the page once.

"Something or other about bleeding," Tabitha remarked.

"The moon bleeding," Astrid corrected.

"Right, the moon bleeding. What do you think it means?"

"I was going to ask you that."

I rolled my eyes. "A blood moon."

"Oh, a blood moon!" Astrid nodded. "Why didn't I think of that?"

"Because you're not as brilliant as you think," I mumbled.

"Hey!" Tabitha scowled and pointed a finger in my face. "You were the one who wanted our help. Now you have it, you better treat us properly."

"I don't know if I need your help anymore," I said. "I wasn't expecting the divination to be so easy. I thought we'd need more sorcery."

"None of this makes sense to either of us. What part of Astrid's divination is so *easy* to you?"

I stepped away and stared off into the distance. Cradling my hands together, my left finger absentmindedly stroked the area between my thumb and forefinger where the scar from Lilith's bite was permanently etched into my skin. The wound was from our first encounter in Eden.

"That's because it isn't about anything that pertains to either of you."

"Do you care to explain?"

Sighing, I gestured for her to take a seat at the table next to Astrid and explained the divination, line by line. If they knew what it meant, they might be able to help me repair my portal quicker.

"'Trapped in a fiery Hell, Lord Satan suffers in where he fell.' That obviously refers to me and my situation, the fact I'm unwillingly trapped down here."

"We knew that much," Tabitha said.

"Yeah, we're not stupid," Astrid added.

I glared at the two of them, and they fell silent. "The next verse, 'The bloodline causes this to be since blood ties are the key.' The bloodline, meaning the Son of God, who some refer to as Jesus, is what imprisons me here. I'm not entirely sure what 'blood ties are the key' means, other than that they're important."

Tabitha and Astrid nodded in agreement.

"Then, 'You to her are bound forever until ties are dissevered,' must signify the descendant is a female, and I'm bound to her and trapped in Hell until our connection is broken." Lost in thought, I continued on. "'The descendant that walks the Earth is a force stronger than any other birth.' I must not have the ability to journey to Earth because the descendant is stronger than any others who came before her. 'The one that makes your imprisonment be must be vanquished for you to be truly free.' This implies she must die in order for me to be liberated.

"The next part outlines what needs to be done to allow me to travel through the portal once more. 'A temporary fix I can see as long as you listen to me. An amulet must be made to grace the place where the cross once laid.' I must listen to Astrid's instructions and make an amulet, one that can hang around my neck where I used to wear the cross. 'Three things are needed for you to be freed as stated in this creed. A feather black as night. A matching one that is white. Your blood shall seal the deed when the dark moon bleeds.' These are ingredients—a black feather, a white feather, and my blood. I must combine them together to form the amulet when there is a dark blood moon."

I fell into silence, my explanation over.

"I guess that *is* simpler than we thought," Tabitha acknowledged.

"We always overthink things," Astrid said.

"Well, these ingredients won't be too hard to come by. You can supply the black feather and the blood. I'm not entirely sure how we go about finding a white feather though. It's not like your blessed brothers visit you much," Tabitha said.

"Don't worry about the white feather, I'll take care of it. What you need to focus on is finding out when the next dark blood moon will be."

She saluted me. "Aye, aye, Captain."

As Tabitha went to the bookshelf to peruse the titles, I turned to leave.

"What about the other divination?" Astrid asked. "You know, the one about your lady lover?"

I froze in my tracks and whipped around. "She's *not* my lady lover. She's a friend…an acquaintance."

"Whatever she is, she seems important."

"She is."

"Then what's the divination mean?"

"Astrid…" Tabitha warned. "It's none of your business."

She pouted. "But I want to know."

"Well, it's not for you to know," I said firmly.

Before either of them could voice any further complaint, a loud clap of thunder sounded off in the distance. Within seconds, one of the demon servants came hobbling in.

"Master, master."

"What is it?"

"The Six have returned. They're en route from Elysium."

"I'll meet them in the throne room."

"Yes, sir." The demon hobbled out of sight, back in the direction he came.

I looked at Tabitha and Astrid, who were hovering over a pile of books. "Find the answer about the blood moon. I'll be back soon." They glanced up at me. "And don't touch anything you're not supposed to."

"Roger, roger," they said in unison.

I shook my head at their strange quirks as I entered the hallway and braced for my visitors. I was leaving behind two inept spirits to face six disappointing angels.

Quietly entering the throne room, I scanned those within before they turned to see me. Lucifer was standing tall before the others, his lean muscular form ready to face my response. He stared through black eyes at my throne, short golden hair slightly mussed from the hood that was now pulled down and resting on his back. He was dressed in all-black and wore a plain t-shirt with jeans and boots in addition to his jacket.

At his side was Leviathan, who was shorter than Lucifer but still lean and muscular. He was ready to face my wrath as well and stood with arms crossed, in a black sweater, tight pants, and suede shoes. His hood was a separate garment he clutched in his hand. He had brown hair and black eyes. The black eyes were a feature of all the fallen, since evil had darkened our souls and taken the pigment out of our irises.

Turning my attention away from my two best soldiers, I analyzed the big, burly form of Beelzebub, whose bald head glistened with beads of sweat. He kept cracking his knuckles even though he knew it irritated me and wore a hideous yellow leather jacket that looked like it had been stitched back together several times. He'd matched it with distressed jeans, a cut-off button shirt, and laced-up boots.

Mammon stood next to him smoking a cigarette, another act I deplored. He had a hooked nose and a sour expression. He was the most frightening of The Six, his body covered with piercings and tattoos. Although all of us had ink, it was nothing compared to his. Mammon's stringy, long brown hair completed his appearance and was currently hidden by a hooded leather jacket. He wore black leather pants and a low-cut shirt that revealed a portion of his chest, also covered in tattoos.

Asmodeus loitered among their ranks, completely self-absorbed.

He was analyzing his cuticles, more concerned with his appearance than anything else. Tall and slender, with wavy, long dark brown hair that was shiny and perfectly groomed, he had a trimmed mustache and a goatee and wore tailored black trousers and a dress shirt. His patterned vest and pointy leather shoes looked expensive. He carried a hooded trench coat, which I presumed was his disguise.

Belphegor was the last among them, slumped against the wall of the cave. His brown hair looked unwashed and stuck up in every direction. He was the shortest and thinnest, but with a brain for technology, he could be very cunning—when motivated. At the moment, he was far too exhausted to live up to these talents. His jeans were ripped in several places, and various patches had been sewn onto his cut-off button shirt to cover the holes. Dirt and stains marred his leather jacket, which looked like it belonged in the trash rather than on his body.

Even though each of them presented themselves differently, identical fear lurked in their eyes, revealing their failure even before they spoke.

"I see you still don't have the bag," I declared, alerting them to my presence.

"No," Lucifer said.

"And why did it take you so long to return?"

"After the boy went into the apartment, we had to cover our tracks at the orphanage," Leviathan explained.

"We also tried waiting him out, but it didn't work," Lucifer said.

"And where is he now?"

"We don't know." He looked down. "We haven't been able to trail him."

"Why not?"

"None of us had a chance to place a tracker on him," Leviathan said.

"How old is this boy, exactly?"

"Eighteen," Lucifer replied.

I laughed. "None of you were able to outsmart an eighteen-year-old?"

"He's a weaselly one," Beelzebub said. "Slips right through your fingers."

"Yes, and he's extraordinarily lucky," Asmodeus added.

"I don't want excuses!" I yelled, my palpable fury silencing the six angels. "There is no reason the boy should have gotten away."

Beelzebub was defensive. "I had him."

"And you lost him," Lucifer clarified. "All because of a backpack doused in holy water. I thought you were stronger than that."

"I am," Beelzebub barked.

"Enough!" I stopped them. "Your childish bickering will not solve anything."

A hush fell over the room as I thought through the predicament. "He's only a boy. He couldn't have gone far."

Unease entered the air.

"What is it?"

"He's with *them*," Mammon said, knowing this news would further my outrage.

My entire body tensed. "How…is that…possible?" I tried to listen through my fury as Leviathan continued.

"We weren't able to breach the apartment building. Couldn't even get through the front door. There was an unmistakable sensation shrouding the place."

"A feeling of…sanctity," Lucifer elaborated. "One only associated with holy ground, meaning someone must have blessed the place. Since it was an apartment building and not a church, we think an archangel is behind the defense."

I sat in my throne fuming and took a brief moment to absorb their report. "You know what this means?" I asked.

"The boy and one of the archangels must have gone off in search of the others," Lucifer said.

I nodded. "How long has it been since you lost the boy?"

"Almost a week."

I grimaced. "That's too much time. The seven of them could be gathered together by now."

"Impossible," Belphegor said under his breath.

I stood from my seat and approached him. "Is there something you wish to say?"

"N-n-no," he stuttered. "It's just…it seems very unlikely they could have joined together so fast."

"Oh, I see." I grabbed him around the shoulder in a gesture of camaraderie, making sure not to touch his skin. "You think you know the workings of the archangels better than I do?" A red blaze ignited inside as I clamped my hand on the exposed skin of his neck.

"No!" Belphegor shouted as the pain seared through his body.

I waited a few long seconds before releasing him. Belphegor was always the stubborn, unruly, defiant one, constantly challenging my will, so he had to be disciplined more than the others.

"Now…" I stepped away and returned to my seat. "We need to know where they are. If they responded to the call, our time is short. But if they had to go find each other individually, our circumstances are better than I first thought. We could potentially attack them while they're still vulnerable."

"How do you propose we find them?" Lucifer asked.

"Leave that to me." I twirled my archangel ring around my finger. "What I want you to worry about is retrieving that bag."

"We don't even know what's inside it," Beelzebub remarked. "You only want it because the Sacrarium had it."

My face hardened, and I stood up once more. "You all think I don't know what's in the backpack. The blessed think I don't know any of their plans. But all of you are wrong. Never question my motives. I want that bag, so you will oblige and get it for me."

Prophecy.

The thought presented itself as if it had been whispered in my ear. A blank expression crossed my face as I thought about the Sovereign Orb and what I needed to do to get my hands on its power.

"Satan, are you all right?" Lucifer asked.

"I need that bag!" I commanded, thoughts of the orb consuming my mind.

"How do you suppose we get it if the bag's sealed and untouchable?" Beelzebub asked.

I rubbed my forehead at his senselessness. "I don't know," I said mockingly. "Did the idea of wearing the gloves I made ever cross your mind?"

"Oh…no. It didn't," Beelzebub said.

I sighed. Lilith's glove, the one she had left behind after I tried to stop her from leaving, had special capabilities. It acted as a barrier to my Hellfire and combatted the energy of any holy object. I'd given the glove to Haborym, and she was able to create similar pairs for The Six.

"But the lock…" Beelzebub continued.

"I will deal with the lock!" I shouted.

"All right. No need to get unreasonable," Beelzebub mumbled.

I clenched my hands into fists. "Any other questions?"

"What about the boy? What do you want us to do with him?" Mammon asked.

My anger subsided, and I leaned back in my throne. "Kill him."

JORDAN

19

AFRICA, PRESENT DAY

After chartering a plane and arriving back in Perth, the angels made the decision to fly next to Maun airport in Botswana, where they believed we would find Raphael. As an angel of healing, it made sense for him to be using his gift in an area that needed it. However, identifying his whereabouts would be difficult. Botswana was a big country, and there were several communities in need of medical aid.

For this reason, their plan was to arrive in the country and meet with the locals to inquire about any doctors in the area. It seemed like a time-waster, but we had no other option. So, that is what we did. Well, that is what Gabriel, Uriel, and Zadkiel did, since I was confined to the hotel, usually with at least one archangel to watch over me. Considering I hadn't been chased or attacked since New York, I figured I was safe, but as Uriel repeatedly told me, no one was safe from the fallen. This served to scare me rather than reassure me, but he seemed so genuine in his ominous warning, I didn't think he was fooling around, just being brutally honest.

"We've found him," Zadkiel announced on his and Gabriel's return to the room. They'd been gone for a few hours.

"You did?" I got up from the couch in excitement. "Where?"

"The Central Kalahari Game Reserve, or thereabouts."

At my confused look, Gabriel elaborated. "We met a man in town who said he knew about a doctor helping out the Bushmen native tribe. We think the doctor is Raphael because the man told us the natives regard him as a divine presence. Their land is on the Central Kalahari Game Reserve, and some of the tribe reside there. Others have been relocated outside of the reserve but they are still close by. Either way, this seems to be our best shot."

"Let's get moving then," Uriel said.

We jumped into action, repacking our things. I was finally able to journey outside with Zadkiel and Uriel while Gabriel checked us out of the hotel.

Zadkiel peered closely at a transport map. "There should be a bus arriving soon. We can take that to a town near the reserve."

"You can read that?" I asked, indicating the back of the pamphlet, which was written in an African language.

"Yes. We know all languages," he replied, still scrutinizing the map.

I turned to Uriel. He nodded his head in verification.

"You don't eat. You don't sleep. You know every language. You can drive. Yet it's almost impossible to get all of you together," I mused, bewildered. "Neither of you see the humor in that?"

"No," they answered in unison.

I smiled. These angels truly amazed me. Their seriousness in moments like these made me realize what was absurd to me was completely normal to them, and vice versa.

"Do you know what bus we need?" Gabriel asked, exiting the hotel and placing his storage chest at his feet. Zadkiel and Uriel had done the same.

I was curious to find out what each of them had inside their chests. It must be important if they were willing to drag them around the world.

"Yes, it should be here in a few minutes," Uriel said.

"Good." Gabriel sat down on his chest to wait.

I was astonished he continued to travel in his formal clothes even as we traversed deserts and the heat. Uriel had dressed accordingly for the occasion, the cargo attire suiting him. Zadkiel had even substituted his dress pants and a sports coat for jeans and a t-shirt. As I spent more time with the angels, I was learning each had their own personality with different quirks and dispositions.

The bus pulled up to the stop, and we headed over with all of our luggage. It was a miracle we found a seat since the space was small and crowded. Everyone had the windows open as there was no air conditioning.

"Get as comfortable as you can," Gabriel said from the seat next to mine. "We're on this bus for almost five hours."

My jaw dropped. "What?"

He smiled sympathetically. "I never said all this travel was going to be easy."

I turned my head to look out the window. We passed through the center of town and approached a short bridge that took us over the river running straight through Maun. Every so often, the driver stopped, and a flux of people came and went, so many passengers crowding the seats and aisle at one point it was impossible to move.

I was extremely nauseous, and there was no direct escape route if I happened to get sick. Closing my eyes, I tried to calm my queasy stomach and relax enough to sleep.

That didn't happen. Instead, I leaned my head against the window and watched the scenery move by. Hours passed in this state of nausea fueled by the gas fumes, bumpy roads, and reckless driving. When my queasiness was at its most intense and throwing up seemed imminent, Gabriel stood to indicate it was our stop. In times like these, I was thankful to be traveling with three celestial beings. Their presence commanded attention and made people move out of the way.

We collected our things and disembarked the bus, which had stopped near a fuel station. As soon as my feet hit the ground, I knelt down and took deep breaths of fresh air.

"That was torturous. I feel terrible." It occurred to me they probably never got nauseous since they never ate anything.

"Here." Zadkiel handed me some crackers.

"You had these all along?"

"Yes, but eating them on the bus would have only made you feel worse."

I took the crackers from him and nibbled on them. "Where are we?"

"Rakops," Uriel said.

"The reserve is that way." Gabriel pointed west.

"Are we walking the rest of the way?" I asked.

"Unless we find a car," he replied.

I continued to eat my crackers, hoping for a car to miraculously appear, while Uriel walked over to the fuel station behind us.

"Where are you going?" Zadkiel called.

"To see if we can get a ride down the road."

"We could have made decent progress by now," Gabriel complained uncharacteristically.

"Gabriel, don't be foolish. This heat is unbearable. *We* wouldn't have made it that far, let alone Jordan."

Gabriel rolled up his shirtsleeves—something I had yet to see him do—clearly indicating his discomfort. "It is warm."

"Yes, it is," Zadkiel replied. "And you're the first who'll suffer from heat stroke solely because you're too stubborn to dress properly."

Uriel came striding toward us. "We have a ride," he said, as a truck drove in our direction from behind the fuel station. "The owner is willing to take us to the reserve."

Sighing in a combination of relief and dread since I hadn't shed the full effect of the nauseating bus ride, I climbed into the bed of the pickup and sat down. The angels loaded their luggage and used their chests as makeshift seats. As the truck took off along the dusty paved road in haste, I braced myself against the side of the vehicle and tried to face forward in an attempt to avoid more queasiness.

Soon enough, the truck pulled up to the guarded entrance of the reserve. We all climbed out, and I was happy to be on my own two feet again. While Uriel thanked the driver, Gabriel walked to the gate and began speaking to the guard in his native language. Soon, the truck turned around and sped off, issuing a cloud of dust that made me sneeze. Zadkiel and Uriel blessed me.

Gabriel waved us over. "They're letting us in and providing transport to Raphael's campsite."

The vehicle provided by the game reserve had no roof, so visitors could easily take pictures and see the animals, and an extended back seat capable of seating six. The ride was definitely more pleasant this time. We traveled through the reserve, spotting various types of wildlife: giraffes grazing on leaves from tall trees, elephants bathing in a watering hole, zebras walking the plains, and lions lounging lazily in the sun.

A campsite appeared in the distance. Natives eyed us in curiosity as we approached, and small children ran up in warm welcome. The vehicle came to a stop, and we clambered out dragging chests and duffels, which we left beneath a tall tree. I made sure to wear the backpack for safekeeping.

A young white woman in her thirties quickly approached. "Who are you?" she demanded.

"We're here to see Raphael," Gabriel said. "We're his brothers. There's been a family emergency."

Her eyes narrowed into slits. "Yeah, I don't believe that. I suggest you go back to wherever you came from. We don't want any trouble here." She stood her ground.

"We don't mean any harm, we just need to see Raphael," Gabriel said.

"Dr. Wolf is indisposed at the moment. I suggest you come back later."

This woman was far too overbearing.

"Who are you?" Zadkiel asked.

She turned her eyes to him. "I am Dr. Parr, a colleague of Raphael's."

"I see." Zadkiel stared as Uriel strode swiftly past her.

"Hey!" she shouted, going after him.

We followed.

Dr. Parr grabbed Uriel by the arm. "I'm talking to you," she demanded. "You aren't going anywhere!"

He twisted out of her hold and faced her.

"Intimidation won't work," she warned. But that was not Uriel's aim.

Reaching inside his pocket, he pulled out his wallet and took out some sort of photo ID card, which he handed to Dr. Parr. "Uri Reed," he said, "Wildlife Research Specialist."

She scanned the ID and looked up at him skeptically. "Is that supposed to impress me?"

He sighed. "No, it's supposed to show you we don't mean any harm."

She handed the ID back to him. "You still want me to believe you're here because of a family emergency?"

Exasperated, Uriel opened his mouth to argue, but Zadkiel spoke first. "Just because we don't look like Raphael doesn't mean we're not his family."

Clearly, his words struck something inside. Dr. Parr's face finally relaxed, and a look of empathy crossed her features. She remained silent for a moment, weighing up her options.

"He's inside the aid tent," she said finally. "I can take you there."

"Thank you," Gabriel said before she could change her mind.

Dr. Parr wove us through a maze of tents inside the camp. The natives continued to eye us in interest. I met eyes with an African woman standing in front of one of the medical tents. She held a baby and was surrounded by other young children. When she saw Dr. Parr, she smiled and stepped aside, making a clear path for us to enter.

My eyes adjusted to the dim interior as we ducked to walk in. A tall black man leaned over a boy, obviously distracting him, as the boy laughed and did not flinch when the doctor stuck a needle in his arm. He disposed of the instrument and placed a Band-Aid over the small wound. When he set the boy down from the table, the child ran off toward the woman outside.

The doctor went about tidying things up, his back still turned to us. Long black dreadlocks fell past his shoulders, some strands twisting into braids. I could tell he was extremely muscular just from the size of his arms and his broad chest.

"Raphael," Dr. Parr said. "Sorry to interrupt, but these men are here for you."

He froze mid-action. "I knew they would come for me sooner or later." He turned around to contemplate us with a steady gaze. "They are my brothers."

"Oh. They said that, but I didn't believe them." Dr. Parr clearly felt guilty.

A deep laugh rumbled out of Raphael's chest. "Understandably so." His smile brought attention to his full goatee and deep brown eyes.

"I'm sorry," she apologized.

"No worries," Gabriel said. "We all understand why you were being cautious."

She nodded. "Thanks. I should take over administering the shots in the other tent, give you all some space." With a smile, she dipped under the tent flap and left.

"Did she give you a hard time?" Raphael asked.

"That's putting it lightly," Uriel said.

"She is a feisty one," the doctor laughed. "I once saw her take on a man twice her size, and he had a gun."

"A gun?" I repeated, surprised.

Raphael studied me. "Yes, a gun. They were trying to steal drugs from us, medicines we use to treat our patients." He paused. "You must be Jordan."

I froze. "How do you know my name?"

"Because Sister Helen arranged for you to come here. She said I was to train you. She didn't elaborate much, but I imagine she meant that by coming here, you might hopefully gain some worldly experience and knowledge."

Through all our travels, I'd forgotten Sister Helen had arranged for me to go to one of the archangels in Africa. "How did she find you?" I asked.

"She told me she asked a friend of hers who worked for the Red Cross about potential locations for mission trips. This friend happened to be our medical supplier, so, naturally, he knew about my work. The next time we received a shipment from them, a letter from Sister Helen arrived as well."

"She didn't tell you anything else? Perhaps about this backpack?" I wondered.

Raphael shrugged. "No, but I can feel the energy of it. Feels similar to some object from Heaven, one of the gemstones perhaps. What's inside?"

"That's the million-dollar question," I replied.

Surprised, Raphael said, "What do you mean?"

"It's locked, and we don't have the key," Gabriel said.

Confusion replaced surprise as Raphael shook his head. "Well, I don't have the key."

I slipped the backpack off my shoulders, exhausted and dejected. "Why couldn't Sister Helen just explain things to me?"

"There was no time. You know that," Gabriel reminded me.

"I know, but it doesn't make it any less frustrating."

"You cannot let anger get the best of you." Raphael stared directly into my eyes. "I had a brother once who did that, and I'm sure you know where he is now. I can only imagine how it must feel to learn about us archangels and the many intricacies of our world, but I assure you, we will figure all this out together. Even the things unknown to us."

"Does that mean you're coming with us?" I asked.

Raphael hesitated. "I'm not sure."

"What do you mean?" Uriel said.

"I can't leave this place." Raphael looked around. "They need me here."

"Yes, but we need you too," Zadkiel said.

"I understand that. However, I'm in charge here."

"You can easily leave Dr. Parr in charge," Uriel suggested. "She seems highly capable of taking care of this place."

"And there are other doctors too. You have a whole team, don't you?" Gabriel asked.

"Yes, but—"

"But, what? We need you, Raphael." Uriel was insistent.

The angel of healing looked torn between his earthly duty and his heavenly one. I understood his dilemma. He was helping people in need here, and to leave them behind for some unknown object locked away inside a backpack didn't seem nearly as demanding.

He studied the bag at my feet. "I need time."

"Fine. But we leave by morning," Gabriel said.

Raphael nodded.

"Can we stay the night?" Zadkiel asked. "It's been a long trip, and Jordan needs rest."

"Of course. I'll show you where you can settle in."

Raphael escorted us to the middle of the camp, where a row of tents sat along the perimeter of the site.

"These are for the doctors. You can have mine," he said to me.

"Are you sure?"

"Positive." He showed me inside. "It's not much."

I didn't understand what he meant. Everything seemed so extraordinary. I ran my hand along a table where a map was spread out and took in the rest of my surroundings. There were all sorts of African masks and native decorations.

"The tribespeople give me these gifts in a display of their gratitude. Sometimes, the gifts are masks. Other times, they are woven bowls or dyed cloth," he explained.

Raphael also had a chest similar to those the others continued to lug around. There was a corner full of extra medical supplies, and an area with a sleeping cot. I was getting a taste of what my life would have been like if the fallen had never surfaced in New York, and I was loving every minute. I only wished we could spend more time here.

"Will it do for the night?" Raphael asked.

I nodded as I walked over to the cot. "Yes. Thank you." An object on the small table caught my eye. "What's this?" I asked, picking up the glass ball full of clear liquid.

He looked amused. "A holy water grenade. I was going through things the other day and found it. Jophiel invented them. I never found any use for mine. I was meaning to dispose of it, but now all of you are here, I'm sure someone will take it."

I placed it back on the table. "Jophiel? Does he always invent things?"

"Yes. He is an angel of art. He enjoys crafting things together."

"I see."

Gabriel stepped inside the tent with my duffel. "I thought you might want this," he said, placing it near the cot.

"Thanks. Are you all settled in?" I asked.

"We made camp right outside, by the tree." He pointed to an enormous tree in front of Raphael's tent.

"Wonderful…" I was still trying to come to terms with their constant vigilance.

After settling in, I went outside to stretch the stiff muscles in my neck and back. The horizon slowly turned pink as the sun became a giant orange orb in the sky, dropping low in an impressive sunset. In the distance, I saw the giraffes once more, their tall figures casting shadows and silhouettes. I walked over to the tree where the angels would keep their watch and ran my hand along the smooth bark. This was truly a surreal experience.

When darkness swept over the plains, we all gathered around to share a meal the doctors had prepared in our honor, together with the natives. The aroma of their cooking made my stomach growl. The angels didn't eat but expressed their gratitude. I finally realized why the natives regarded Raphael as a divine being. Of course, he didn't eat or sleep, and they obviously noticed. It was easier for the other angels to conceal their behavior since they weren't always in the company of a large group, but out here in an isolated camp, Raphael could not easily hide his differences.

I sat between two boys who were slightly younger than me. We ate in companionable silence and then laughed together when some of the children played practical jokes. After the meal, our night was full of dancing and singing.

"Are you enjoying yourself?" Raphael asked when I joined my friends under the tree.

"Yes, very much," I told him. "There's something I was meaning to ask you."

"What is it?"

"Earlier, you said you could feel the energy from the backpack. Something about it being similar to a heavenly object, like a gemstone. What did you mean by that?"

Raphael turned to Gabriel and Zadkiel. "I take it you haven't explained the Wonders and the Keys yet?"

Zadkiel shook his head. "We didn't have time to get that far."

I stared at them. "This sounds an awful lot like the birds and the bees."

"You humans and your silly expressions," Raphael chuckled. "The Wonders and the Keys have nothing to do with the birds and the bees."

I laughed. "Good, because that's a conversation I *don't* want to have."

"Me neither," Raphael agreed.

Ignoring us both, Zadkiel said, "The Wonders signify the Wonders of the World, and the Keys are items Father placed at the Wonders."

"And you know about them?" I asked.

"Yes."

"That means these items are the spheres then."

Zadkiel smiled his approval. "You're becoming an astute pupil, Jordan."

"Thanks." I glanced at Gabriel, hoping to take in his reaction, but he had a faraway look in his eye.

GABRIEL

20

"Zadkiel, we need to go."

He glanced up at me from the parchment he was reading. "Already? But I have had barely any time to study this document."

"Indeed. I have had barely any time to compose music with all this combat training we have to complete." I stared forlornly at my violin.

"It is only for the best after everything that happened."

"Do not remind me," I said sadly.

Zadkiel followed me out of our room, where we ascended the stairs to the top of the tower and flew to the one flanking it. We retrieved the keys that hung from our garments by a chain and inserted them into the appropriate keyholes.

The door swung open, and our comrades, the remaining members of the Council of Archangels, greeted us.

It took a while for Metatron to call the meeting to attention. He was distracted by the presence of Seraphiel, who was speaking to him seriously. When their conversation ended, Metatron clapped his hands and remained standing.

"Greetings, brothers and sisters. I would like to welcome you to this meeting. As you can see, we have a guest who has come to deliver a message from Father."

If this was any other time, I would have been surprised by Seraphiel's presence, but now, it felt natural. All angels in the hierarchy were interacting with each other more since the war. Though, the last time I saw Seraphiel was when she escorted the fallen to the edge of High Heaven.

I briefly looked over at the empty seat—a clear reminder of the brother we had lost.

"I was sent here because Father felt it was time for some explanations, starting with these." She reached for the wooden box Metatron was holding and opened the latch to reveal its contents.

Twelve round objects rested inside, the thirteenth noticeably missing just like our fallen brother. The interior of the box was covered in black velvet, and the spheres rested perfectly inside on small pedestals, each about four inches in diameter. They were made of precious gems and varied in color, from emerald to ruby to lapis lazuli and more.

"These objects are known as spheres," Seraphiel explained. "These spheres are needed for a powerful prophecy Satan was striving to fulfill." She said his name so nonchalantly it surprised several of us, especially Michael. Seraphiel took no notice. "Father knew these spheres were powerful, so He made sure there were beings He could trust to protect them."

"Us?" I asked.

She met my gaze and nodded.

"What?" Michael exploded.

"Michael," Metatron chastised. "Please, let her finish."

"Why? She is displaying the very objects we just had a war over!"

"I understand your distress," Seraphiel said, "but you should not worry. These objects are being separated. In order to hide and better protect them, seven will be sent to Earth, and five will remain here in Heaven. Father does not want another war over the spheres, so he thought the best course of action would be to divide them."

"Wait a moment," Zadkiel interrupted. "You just said we are to protect these objects. If seven are being sent to Earth, how can we?"

She looked at him solemnly. Seraphiel did not speak. Clearly, she was trying to choose her next words carefully.

Finally, she said, "Because seven of you will be sent down with them."

Outrage overcame us. My brothers and sisters flung questions left and right.

"What?" Chamuel cried.

"How is that possible?" Raziel asked.

"Who will you be sending?" Tzaphkiel wondered.

Seraphiel sighed. "The First Choir has debated the decision. Some feel you all should have a choice. Others believe Father should decide for you."

"Well, which is it?" Uriel demanded.

"Neither. There was another option, a compromise. Father has chosen seven of you, but you can refuse the request if you wish."

This was absurd. Even if Father gave us a choice, it was one we *really* could not refuse.

"Who has He chosen?" Metatron asked.

"Michael, Gabriel, Raphael, Uriel, Chamuel, Jophiel, and Zadkiel."

She paused slightly after every name, making this more like a punishment than a chance to express our freewill.

I gazed around the room at the other angels who had been chosen, realizing we were the ones who acted without council consent during the war. *Maybe this is a punishment after all...*

"Father chose the seven of you for a reason," Seraphiel clarified. "Your courage and bravery to act during the war when others could not is a sign you all can make tough decisions in difficult circumstances." Her words soothed my fears. "Now, Father has tasked you all with an equally challenging duty: sending you to Earth and bidding you not to interfere with the problems of humanity during your time there."

"You are saying we cannot act?" Michael spoke up. "What if something terrible goes wrong? Can we act then?"

"All Father said is that you are to watch and wait for a sign. This sign will indicate it is time to act."

"What sign? When will it come?" Jophiel asked.

"I do not know. He only told me what I have told you. For those of you chosen by Father, do you accept His request to be sent down?"

We did not answer right away, but eventually, there was a resounding, "Yes."

"Good. Let me explain how it will happen." She motioned with her hand to Metatron, who brought another wooden box to the table. Seraphiel slid it next to the first but did not open it. "Each of you were chosen to be on this council because Father deemed you all strong enough and capable enough to protect a sphere. He assigned a gemstone to each of you, and the rings you wear are an indication of this."

I glanced down at my danburite ring and then set my gaze on the open wooden box, where a danburite sphere could be seen among the rest.

"As you all now know," she continued, "these spheres can be united into one through a process known as the Union of the Spheres. Father has done everything in His power to make this process nearly impossible by creating a series of keys. The first key is known as the Classic Key. These keys are already in your possession."

Metatron demonstrated by laying his metal key in front of him on the table, the same one that opened the door to the council room.

"The second key is known as the Gemstone Key." Seraphiel opened the second wooden box to reveal a set of twelve gemstones. They were small enough to hold in the palm of one's hand, and each had a unique shape. She selected a Gemstone Key and placed it in front of Metatron. The stone now sat next to the metal key. Seraphiel then reached into the first wooden box and pulled out a matching sphere, which she also placed in front of him.

"All of these objects are necessary to complete the Union. For the angels remaining in Heaven, I will now distribute them to you." She went about the room, placing the small gemstones and spheres in front of Ariel, Raziel, Tzaphkiel, and Sandalphon. "I expect you all to protect these items and keep them in a safe place."

The four of them and Metatron nodded.

"As for those who will be traveling to Earth, your items will be hidden away in specific locations. I need you all to hand over your Classic Keys so they can be hidden as well."

Alarmed, Zadkiel asked, "How are we supposed to enter the council room?"

Seraphiel looked at him. "After this meeting, you will not need to enter the council room."

"We are being sent down so soon?" Raphael asked.

"Yes."

Voiceless, we struggled to come to terms with the magnitude of this. I reached for the key hanging at my side and took it off its chain, then passed it reluctantly to Seraphiel before standing back to watch the others do the same.

"Will we know the locations of the keys and the spheres?" I asked when everyone was seated.

She nodded. "Yes. The Classic Keys will be hidden at the Ancient Wonders of the World, the Gemstone Keys at the Natural Wonders of the World, and the spheres at the Modern Wonders of the World. Exact locations will be revealed to each of you individually as you depart. These precautions have been put in place for safety measures. All of you knowing the locations would be dangerous."

"Why?" Raziel asked.

"Because there is always the possibility someone might stray from the path."

We all knew what she was trying to say. The empty chair at the table was a sad reminder.

"What about *his* keys and sphere?" Michael wondered, staring at the empty seat.

"They have been hidden in a similar manner, entrusted to others for protection. You should not concern yourself with them. Father has made sure anything heavenly associated with Satan is renounced. All that matters is we hide his keys and sphere."

It made sense now why Seraphiel had demanded Samael return his council room key before he was cast out of Heaven. The object was a significant piece in an intricate puzzle, one that could not fall into the wrong hands. Everyone remained quiet, but I knew each of us was thinking about the immeasurable impact of Seraphiel's words.

"That is all I have to say," she concluded. "The seven of you to be sent down may go and collect your things. Once you are finished, please come to the castle in High Heaven for your departure."

With that, she left the tower.

We sat unmoving in the heavy silence.

Metatron finally cleared his throat. "I believe this meeting is adjourned." He paused. "I will miss all seven of you, and I wish you luck on your journey."

There was a chorus of well-wishes from the angels who were staying behind as the seven of us stood and walked out of the council room together. With appreciative nods and glances, we all went our separate ways and prepared as best we could for our fate.

JORDAN

AFRICA, PRESENT DAY

21

Gabriel still had that faraway look in his eye as Zadkiel finished explaining the Wonders and the Keys. I didn't want to dwell on the subject too much since it was obviously hard for him to relive the moment, but there were questions I needed answers to.

"Has Satan retrieved his keys and sphere?"

"We don't know. Ever since he managed to escape Hell and travel to Earth, all our prior assumptions about him have been challenged. Retrieving his keys might not be impossible after all." Zadkiel looked dejected.

I understood that feeling. The magnitude of the fallen's strength certainly left me dejected too. But I had other another thought.

"How is all this possible? I thought there were only seven Ancient Wonders."

"History has done a good job of erasing anything linked to Satan when he fell, which is no coincidence," Zadkiel said. "Anything associated with Satan was either disavowed entirely or was completely reinterpreted to signify something evil. For instance, the raven didn't always have dark connotations, but now, many consider them to be a sign of evil or death."

"The raven is Satan's bird?" I thought back to the time at Gabriel's apartment when the angels' birds landed on his balcony.

"Correct. My point is, there were Eight Wonders of the World at some point, but the eighth no longer exists. Or, it might still exist but is no longer considered a Wonder."

"Weren't the Wonders of the World destroyed?" I asked as the realization dawned.

"The Ancient ones, yes, for the most part. Many of them were either attacked, destroyed, or severely damaged by humans and natural occurrences. We had to extract the Classic Keys when this happened, so now they are safe with us at all times, locked away in our chests, which only open at our hand. The Gemstone Keys and spheres remain at the other Wonders. All that matters is the keys and spheres are safe."

"For now," Gabriel amended.

I stared at my notebook and realized by the time this was all over, I would have numerous journals chronicling everything I learned from the angels.

Uriel came to join us under the tree.

"Where have you been?" I asked.

"Trying to evade Dr. Parr. She's been trying to get me to dance ever since the festivities started."

"I take it you don't dance?"

Uriel stared at me, unamused.

Raphael elbowed me in the side and said, "She must have taken a liking to him."

As I smiled at his joke, a group of children ran over and picked up Gabriel's violin, gesturing for him to play. This small act was exactly the distraction he needed. The angel immediately retreated from his thoughts and stood to accept the instrument. Satisfied, the children ran off again to keep dancing.

The rest of us remained quiet as we sat under the tree watching the festivities and basking in the spirit of the moment. Gabriel played his violin, the African men continued to drum, and the women sang, but the melody had a different pace and a magical quality. Gabriel strung out notes with ease, perfectly combining his sound with that of the tribespeople to create a symphony of music that was evocative and unlike anything I'd heard before. I finally understood why he was an angel of music. There was an effortlessness to the beautiful rhythm, and his melody held the attention of every person around—though he didn't seem to notice as he lost himself in the act of playing.

When the music and celebration ended, I retired to the tent, placing the backpack under the cot with my duffel before settling in to sleep. After such a pleasant evening, I didn't expect my dreams to be filled with nightmares, but there was screaming and shouting, an explosion of fire, someone yelling my name…

The next thing I knew, I was suffocating.

My eyes flashed open, and a skull tattoo met my gaze. Automatically, I grasped at my neck in a futile attempt to pry free the powerful hands that were gripping it. Losing oxygen fast, my vision blurred as I stared up at the menacing face and bottomless black eyes. My hands refused to keep up the fight, and my attacker leered down, recognizing the signs of life creeping away.

I didn't want to die. My body went lax, and my brain refused to work. My eyes were beginning to close when a voice inside my head yelled, *Run.*

Remembering Sister Helen's plea, I struggled with all my might to get free.

The man lifted a hand from my throat to restrain me.

Think, Jordan…

And then the fence scene flashed before my eyes, the moment I was miraculously released thanks to holy water.

The grenade.

I fumbled along the bedside table, feeling for the glass ball. When my hand closed around it, instinct kicked in, and I slammed it against the fallen angel's face.

"Argh!"

Glass sliced my hand. The tension around my neck eased. The man erupted into screams of agony while I choked for air.

My lungs burned. Finally, I could breathe again, and my vision slowly returned. But I wasn't safe yet. Stumbling, I gripped the table and advanced toward the front of the tent.

The second I tasted fresh air on my lips, I was dragged back to the ground.

My attacker had regained his composure but half of his face was burned. As he pulled me back by the ankle, I gripped the tent pole with both hands, smearing blood over the metal and pushing the glass remnants deeper.

"Help!" I cried out, hoping the angels would hear. "Let go of me!"

When I kicked my feet in defense, he slammed his fist into my face. Everything went black for a moment, dots coloring my vision.

That was when an arrow came whizzing through the tent and landed in the fallen angel's chest. The force of the weapon propelled him backward, and he released my foot.

Once again, I tried to stand, but my ankle was twisted. Off-balance, I managed to stumble out of the tent and into a scene of chaos.

"Jordan!"

Uriel came running to my side, a crossbow in his hand. He threw my arm over his shoulders so I could brace against him and make a fast getaway. We hobbled through the camp as fire blazed around us. Screams could be heard in the smoky distance.

A lone figure emerged from the noise and smoke. It was Zadkiel, holding a hand axe. He rushed forward to support my right side.

"We need to get out of here!" he shouted.

Uriel's eyes were wide. "What about the others?"

"They'll take care of it."

"No. We leave together."

"Jordan is our top priority right now. We need to get him to safety."

That was about all I heard as everything went black again.

I felt the distinct sensation of flying. I couldn't tell if it was my condition and the head trauma, or if Uriel and Zadkiel made their escape by taking to the sky. In either case, I regained consciousness in the back of a speeding vehicle. Raphael was looming over me, treating my injuries. We were surrounded by haphazardly thrown luggage. Two others sat up front.

I stared up at the night sky. The car had no roof. Small pinpricks of pain struck my hand. A bird seemed to be flying overhead, its wings spread wide. Blinking, I followed its flight as it grew larger, realizing it wasn't a bird at all.

Gabriel descended upon the car, grasping the exposed roll bar to right himself. He held the backpack in his other hand and gave it to whoever was in the passenger seat. Lowering his wings, he jumped down from the bar and crouched next to Raphael.

"How is he?"

"Not well. He has a concussion. I'm trying to pry these glass bits out of his hand, but they're lodged in pretty deep. Gave him some meds for the pain and some antibiotics so he doesn't get an infection. He's awake and hasn't said a word, so I hope they're working."

Concern was plastered across Gabriel's face.

"How did you manage to get the backpack?" Zadkiel asked.

"Force."

"Did you take any of them down?" Uriel asked.

"No, didn't have time." Gabriel glanced at Raphael. "I'm sorry about what happened."

"You needn't apologize. If this was anyone's fault, it was mine. If I'd agreed to leave with you sooner, none of this would have happened."

"We all made mistakes tonight, Raphael." Gabriel focused on me. "I just hope we can rectify them."

The small pinpricks turned numb as the pain medicine took over. I closed my eyes and faded into unconsciousness.

The next time I woke up, I was lying in a bed, and morning light was streaming in through a curtained window. I blinked several times to get my bearings. My head pounded, and my throat was sore. I shifted my body and groaned at the ache in my right ankle from where the fallen angel had gripped my foot. Lifting my arm, I went to rub my eyes and discovered a bandage around my right hand.

Trying not to panic, I put my arm back down and lay there, not knowing where I was or who I was with. It looked like a hotel room.

I opened my mouth to speak, but my dry throat kept me mute.

When the bedroom door opened, letting in more light, I was able to distinguish Gabriel entering the room. He approached the bed as I attempted to sit up.

"You're awake," he said in apparent surprise, reaching out to help me sit straight against the pillows.

I nodded, which triggered a crashing headache. With a grimace, I lifted my hand to my head. "Where are we?" I croaked out.

"Johannesburg." Gabriel reached for a glass of water on the bedside table. He gave it to me, and I took a few sips.

Swallowing hurt too.

Gabriel left my side briefly and went to the door. "Raphael, he's awake."

The other angel entered the room. "How are you feeling?"

I eyed him skeptically. "Terrible. But I'll survive."

"That's what I like to hear." He unraveled the bandage and inspected my hand, applying some medicine and a fresh compress. When he went to touch my face, I stopped him.

"What's wrong with my face?"

"That punch caused some damage. Bruising, a black eye, and a deep cut."

I chuckled. "Is that why it hurts so much?"

"You're lucky to be alive," Gabriel said.

"Please, don't start with that again. I understand now why you were all surprised when I escaped them the first time."

"That's not what I meant—"

I cut him off. "How long have I been out?"

"A few days," Raphael answered.

I sighed. "We're behind. We need to find the others." I moved to get out of bed.

"Where do you think you're going?" Raphael halted my efforts.

"We need to leave."

"You're not going anywhere yet," Gabriel said.

"Fine." I gave in, struggling to think through the horrible headache. "What exactly happened?"

"Ambush," Uriel said from the doorway.

"The Six attacked with a crew of demons," Zadkiel clarified, entering the room with him.

"The demons set fire to the camp as a distraction," Uriel said. "Raphael, Zadkiel, and I went to deal with them."

"I stayed behind," Gabriel explained, "to guard you. But The Six attacked me all at once. One of them managed to retrieve the backpack, and when that happened, they took to the sky. I followed, thinking you would be safe since the bag was no longer in your possession." He shook his head. "I was wrong. I should have realized I was only chasing five."

"Gabriel, it's not your fault. Even you can't be in two places at once," I said.

"But it is my fault. And I swear, it will never happen again."

"How were they able to touch the bag?" I thought back to the holy water.

"They had gloves on…some special kind," Gabriel said.

I reached for the cross hanging around my neck. "Is that why this didn't hurt him when he choked me?"

"Yes."

"And the tribespeople? What happened to them?"

Raphael looked away, unable to answer.

"A handful were killed in the attack. They tried to help us fight the demons. Most of them made it to safety though," Uriel said.

As this information sank in, so too did the shock. "And the doctors?"

"All of them made it out except one. Dr. Reynolds took on one of the demons to save a child. I'm not sure you met her," Uriel said solemnly.

"And Dr. Parr?"

"She's fine. Raphael left her in charge. She was more than willing to fill the role," Uriel explained.

"Raphael, I'm so sorry." I set my eyes on the dejected angel.

He shook his head. "It's not your fault. I should have left with you. Instead, I put the natives and my team in danger."

"But you can't blame yourself. How were we supposed to know the fallen were closing in?"

"I see your point, Jordan, but it doesn't change the way I feel. If anything, I'm more invested in my duty now than I was before, as I must put a stop to the evil that took my earthly friends."

We all fell to silence at the gravity of Raphael's words.

"What now?" I asked eventually.

Gabriel sighed and paced. "I don't know. We have three cities left, but I'm not so sure this is the right thing to do anymore."

"Why not?"

"Jordan, look at yourself. You're injured and incapacitated. You expect me to continue on like nothing happened, when in reality, you were nearly killed?"

"Gabriel, listen. I understood the consequences of our journey well before we left New York. Perhaps I wasn't expecting anything nearly this life-threatening, but I know better now, and I'm telling you, we are continuing on," I insisted. "I'm not about to let them frighten me into inactivity, nor am I going to let you treat me like a child. We make mistakes. We learn from them. We move on. Now, when are we leaving for Tokyo?"

They stared in admiration and amazement.

"You really are the sign we were waiting for," Raphael remarked.

"I knew I would make a believer out of you."

They all burst into laughter.

After sipping some soup, I rested a bit longer. When I awoke, later in the afternoon, the angels decided we would leave for Tokyo tomorrow.

With some help, I managed to get to my feet and I slowly hobbled to the bathroom, eager to take a shower and see myself in the mirror. All four watched me as I turned to close the door.

"I'll be fine."

My reassurance didn't seem to convince them.

I shuffled over to the mirror to check my reflection. *Wow, that guy did a doozy on me.* The entire right side of my face was bruised, already turning an ugly shade of greenish yellow. My right eye was purple and swollen, and my cheek had a deep cut that had been neatly sutured. Even my neck was marked, the hands of my attacker clearly imprinted among the shades of purple.

A knock at the door interrupted my inspection. I opened it to find Raphael holding a plastic bag.

"You need to put this over your hand," he directed. "Your bandage can't get wet."

I took the bag from him with a bleak smile.

Stepping into the shower, I let the water pour over my head and wash away all the grime and pain. I knew evading the fallen wasn't easy work. I just hoped it didn't get any harder.

SATAN

22

HELL, PRESENT DAY

We were getting close. The time was almost nigh for the blood moon to rise and my freedom to be restored. I was desperate to travel to Earth. The Six's attempts at retrieving the bag had ended in disappointment, and now disaster.

Mammon's screams could be heard through the entry cave into Greed. Pushing past the hellhound that guarded the cavern, I entered the city and spread my wings, taking to the air to make my way to his dwelling quicker. Upon my arrival, I found my five remaining angels anxiously waiting.

"What happened?" I yelled.

They all jumped.

"We failed you," Leviathan stated the obvious.

"I know that. But how?"

"I'm not sure," he confessed. "We had them outnumbered. The ambush was flawless. We even had the bag in our possession."

"And what happened?"

"Gabriel happened," Beelzebub said.

"Gabriel?"

"Yes. I've never seen him fight like that before." Beelzebub was clearly astonished.

"You're telling me *Gabriel*, the angel of music, single-handedly fought off five of you and took the bag out of your hands?"

"Yes," Leviathan whispered.

"Well, either you all are getting rusty, or Gabriel has stepped up his game. I've never known him to be a fighter."

"Neither did we," Belphegor added.

"What happened to Mammon?"

"The boy," Asmodeus said.

I glanced at the fallen angel writhing in pain. "The boy did this?"

"Yes. Mammon's greed got the better of him. He desperately wanted to take the boy out. I thought the five of us were more than enough to fight off the others. I was wrong," Lucifer said.

"What did the boy do?"

"Burned him with holy water, right in the face. Then Uriel shot an arrow into him," Asmodeus said.

"That was after Mammon did damage to the boy." Belphegor was anxious to point out.

"He's a weasel. Still managed to get away," Beelzebub added.

"The boy's *still* alive?" I was dumbfounded.

"Unfortunately, yes," Lucifer said. "At least, as far as we know."

"What do you mean?"

"Mammon put a tracker on his duffel bag. I suspect if the boy died, the angels wouldn't still be carrying it around," Lucifer explained.

"Are you hearing yourself?"

"You think they'd keep his stuff?"

"I don't know, and I don't care. All that matters is we know where they are and where they're going, so I don't have to do that ring trick again."

"It seemed difficult," Leviathan remarked.

"It was. I was drawing too much on my past."

"Well, now the tracker is in place, you won't have to do it anymore." I nodded.

"What's our next course of action?" Lucifer wondered.

I smiled. "Another attack."

"What? Why? It didn't work this time, and now they'll be expecting us."

"Right, but they won't be expecting me."

"*You?*" Belphegor repeated.

"Yes, me."

"How are you going to manage that? I thought you were stuck down here?"

"While the six of you were disappointing me on Earth, I was working on fixing that problem. As of tonight, my capabilities will be restored."

"How?" Lucifer asked.

"That's my business."

"The seer and the sorcerer." Realization flashed across Leviathan's face. "I completely forgot. I'm sorry."

"No matter. I took care of it myself."

"You did? Who did you find?"

"Astrid and Tabitha."

"Astrid and Tabitha!" Leviathan was outraged. "But they're the least competent!"

"You say that, but they delivered."

"You're satisfied with their performance? They can be very disrespectful."

"My problem isn't with disrespect, Leviathan, it's with defiance. Astrid and Tabitha are disrespectful to me with their strange quirks and snide remarks, but I simply need them as a means to an end. Now, if they were to act on that disrespect and try to betray me, then we would have a problem. But I don't think they're capable of doing such a thing."

The five of them stared, not expecting such a tirade.

"So, I don't need to find you another seer and sorcerer?" Leviathan was still disbelieving.

"No. Now, I expect all of you to formulate an attack plan and discover the whereabouts of the archangels."

"Yes, sir," they said in unison.

"And make sure Mammon is a part of it."

They nodded.

I turned on them and began the short journey back to my quarters, where I went to check on Tabitha and Astrid. The sight upon entering the portal room was not a welcome one. The seer and sorcerer were standing in front of the invisible barrier I ordered them to stay away from.

"What are you doing?" I demanded.

They both jumped. The fact this was the second time this had happened today made me realize they feared me more than I thought.

"Nothing." Tabitha tugged on Astrid's arm and stepped away from the barrier.

"It's just…there was lots of noise and banging," Astrid confessed.

I glanced at the invisible surface. "And why should that concern you?"

"It doesn't," Tabitha clarified.

Astrid, however, remained silent as a dreamlike quality overcame her. She approached the barrier with her hand stretched out.

"Astrid, don't!" Tabitha pleaded.

Before I realized what she was doing, it was too late.

Her palm rested on the barrier, and her hair flew back, revealing her white eyes. Before any words could escape her mouth, Tabitha grabbed her hand and pulled it away. She must have seen I was about to do so myself, and that would have led to the Hellfire consuming her again.

"Astrid?" Tabitha shook her sister's shoulders.

"Fourteenth sphere," she mumbled incoherently.

I approached her. "What did you say?"

"Fourteenth sphere. There's a fourteenth sphere," she continued to mumble.

Tabitha shook her sister forcibly, concern palpable in her voice. "Astrid!"

Astrid finally regained control and demanded, "What's in there?"

"Astrid," her sister chastised.

I stared at the seer, who seemed to challenge me with her blind gaze. "None of your business."

Her countenance clouded again as she whispered, "Fourteenth sphere. An angel's drive in the fourteenth sphere."

I ignored her ramblings and asked Tabitha, "Is everything in place for tonight?"

"Of course," she replied, her attention still on her sister. "You know what she's talking about."

It wasn't a question. Of course I knew what Astrid was talking about. At least, I had assumed the existence of a fourteenth sphere. Astrid's words only validated my assumption.

"I will say this once and only once. You and your sister had better reign yourselves in, otherwise I'll send you straight to the rivers."

Tabitha gasped. "That's worse than being incinerated by your Hellfire."

"Yes," I threatened, "because it's painful like the Hellfire but for all eternity."

Tabitha nodded and held on to Astrid, who was oblivious to our conversation.

"Now, is everything in place for tonight?" I repeated.

"Yes. Got my potion bowl and everything." She indicated the utensils on the table.

"Good."

"You have the coins we were promised?" Astrid asked, once again present.

"Astrid!"

I sneered. "Yes, I have your money."

"Good," the seer replied.

I left them then and retreated to my private quarters, where I sat at my desk and gazed around the room. There were bookcases on the far right wall filled with books and all sorts of objects—statues, coins, old helmets, and weapons. Anything I liked during my travels to Earth, I would bring back as trophies and put on my shelves.

Opposite, the entire left side of the room was my personal arsenal, where I kept all sorts of weapons. Rows of swords and knifes were neatly mounted to the wall, ready whenever I needed them. Behind my desk were enormous maps of the world so I could plan attacks and know the whereabouts of the things most important to me, such as the beings I kept alliance with. I had used these maps to track the Sacrarium as well, but my attempts at locating them over the years were unsuccessful.

I busied myself by polishing my swords and analyzing the maps, but the remainder of the day passed slowly in my desperate anticipation of the night. At some point, Lucifer came to present his plans. It seemed Gabriel and his horde were currently in Johannesburg. Lucifer wanted to wait to strike until we knew their exact location because he suspected they would start to travel again soon.

"I think that's a good decision," I replied absentmindedly. "Sorry, I'm a little preoccupied."

"I can tell."

I glared at him.

"Which is why I will take my leave. You have more important things to take care of tonight," Lucifer said.

Far too anxious to sit idly by, I stood up and went to find Tabitha.

"What's your progress?" I demanded as I entered the portal room.

"Progressing nicely," she said, bent over some sort of magical telescope.

"Whatever's in there isn't too happy." Astrid pointed to the gateway across the room.

"Astrid! What did I say?" Tabitha implored.

"That he was going to throw us in the rivers if we didn't behave."

"Yes, so behave."

"All right." She sighed. "But it's true. Whatever's in there isn't happy."

"I suspect they aren't," I murmured.

Tabitha returned to the telescope and peered through. "It's almost time." She glanced at me. "Did you get the feather?"

I held up the pure white object and set it beside a bowl on the table.

She returned to the telescope and said, "It's time. Are you ready?"

"Yes."

Tabitha released the telescope and reached over to pluck a feather from my wings, making sure not to touch my skin, then placed the black feather in the bowl.

"You could have been more ceremonious than that," Astrid commented.

I glared at her even though she couldn't see me. She must have sensed my irritation because she stopped speaking.

Placing the white feather on top of the black one, Tabitha slid a knife across the table to me. I picked it up and slashed my palm across the middle. Blood began to ooze to the surface, and I turned it over so the drops landed on the feathers. When there was a decent amount of blood, Tabitha started to chant in a rasping voice.

Astrid took up the same chant, though her hair remained covering her face.

I squeezed my hand again, eliciting another stream of blood. When I looked into the bowl, a smoky haze shrouded its contents. Something was happening.

A loud banging on the other side of the room pulled my attention to the gateway. I glared at the invisible barrier and turned back to Tabitha, who was undisturbed by the noise. Her chanting grew louder, and the smoke grew thicker. Her voice took on a mesmerizing rhythm. When it abruptly stopped, and Tabitha fell to the floor, I realized I had closed my eyes.

Astrid went to her sister's rescue, bending down and tending to Tabitha, who lay unconscious.

I was far more interested in what lay inside the bowl. Waving the smoke away with my hand, I reached down and touched something metallic. Pulling it out, I saw I was holding the chain of an amulet.

Raising the object to eye-level, I examined it. The amulet was comprised of two interlocking diamond shapes, one black and one white, overlapping each other in the middle. The pieces were smooth and polished and felt like they were fashioned from bone.

Forgetting about Tabitha and Astrid and the wound on my hand that was already healing, I placed the amulet over my head and let the metal slide down my shirt.

Fortified, I reached into my pocket and pulled out a pouch of coins, which I threw on the ground next to Astrid as Tabitha stirred and sat up.

"Your payment, ladies."

Astrid grabbed the pouch before I could touch it again and helped her sister to stand.

"It's been a pleasure working with you," I said.

Without a word, they floated from the room.

The banging at the barrier started up again. I smiled and strode closer. The noise continued until I stood directly in front of it.

"You can fight all you want," I said, pulling out the amulet and stroking it, "but nothing is going to stop me now. Before long, I'll not only have my sphere...I'll have yours as well."

JORDAN

23

JOHANNESBURG, PRESENT DAY

The next morning, I woke early, around five a.m. I'd slept so much in the past few days, it was understandable why I didn't want to do it anymore.

"You're up early." Zadkiel looked up from the newspaper he was reading.

"I'm just eager to get going again."

"How do you feel?" Gabriel asked.

"Better than yesterday. Still slightly achy, but I'll manage."

"Sit," Raphael demanded. "I want to see your hand."

I went over to the kitchen table. Medical supplies surrounded him as he restocked his bag. I sat down in the chair next to him and gave him my hand. Raphael took the bandage off and examined the wound. Since this was the first time I had seen it, I gasped.

"That's pretty nasty."

"I know. I've been worrying about it, but it will be fine now, as long as we treat it." He spread some antibiotic cream over my hand and wrapped a new bandage around it.

I noticed the sizeable knife jutting out from behind his medical bag. "Wait a minute, you all had weapons. Where did they come from?" I remembered Uriel shot the fallen angel and Zadkiel had brandished a hand axe.

"You think we've been traveling around unarmed?" Uriel replied.

"You mean, you've had them on you?"

Zadkiel raised the leg of his pants to reveal the portable axe. Uriel reached inside his carry-on and took out the small crossbow. Raphael grabbed the knife in its leather sheath and set it in front of me.

I turned to Gabriel.

"Why do you think I insist on wearing this?" he said, indicating his shirtsleeves and vest. He reached behind his back and retrieved a hand sickle.

My eyes widened. "You've all been armed this whole time? How has nobody noticed?"

"They're holy, sanctified weapons," Uriel said. "They don't show up on human radar."

"Like the backpack?" I recalled Gabriel's comment from our time in Heathrow.

"Yes," Gabriel said.

"So, are these the weapons you battled with in Heaven?"

"No. We consider these to be portable weapons," Zadkiel explained.

"For larger battle, we have others," Raphael added.

"Is that what you keep in the chests?"

"Among other things," Gabriel said. "I keep my violin in there too. Zadkiel keeps books. We all use them differently."

To me, this was not normal. Angels weren't weapon-wielders. But this fact only made them ten times cooler.

"When do we have to leave?" I asked.

"Not for a few hours. I suggest you relax now because it's another long flight, and I know how restless you get," Gabriel said.

I smiled. We had only known each other for a short time, but he had already caught on to my quirks. I had him somewhat figured out too, like how he paced in times of contemplation, decision-making, or frustration.

When it was time to go, we made our way down to the lobby.

"Whose car were we in the night the fallen attacked?" I asked.

"Mine," Raphael answered. He approached the hotel footman and explained that we needed a large SUV or perhaps a van.

"We ditched the Land Rover when we arrived. The Six saw us in it, so we don't want them to track us," Uriel explained.

Gabriel joined us outside as a large van pulled up to drive us to the airport. "Put these on," he said, handing me sunglasses.

I took them from him. "Why?"

"Your face is drawing attention. The less of that we have, the better."

"All right." I placed the dark shades over my eyes. "Do you have something to cover my neck too?"

He handed me a travel pillow. "When you can't use this, I suggest you wear a hoodie." He handed me a black pullover with the word "Johannesburg" printed across the chest.

"You think of everything, don't you?"

"I try. None of this is guaranteed to distract people from staring, but at least it will minimize it."

Our hustle and haste through the airport was a result of the angels' overprotectiveness. After being attacked, the four of them were on high alert. Since I was slightly woozy from the pain medication, I didn't mind their behavior much. Besides, being escorted to the first class cabin by four intimidating angels made me feel like someone important. It also prevented anyone with curious minds and prying eyes from asking questions.

Settling into my seat, I pulled my hood over my head and placed the travel pillow behind my neck. Although I insisted on continuing our journey, I had to admit to myself—if no one else—that I was still in pain. For that reason, I curled up against the window, shut my eyes, and fell into oblivion, needing sleep once more.

Gabriel gently nudged me awake when we landed for our layover. We had the perfect amount of time to stretch our legs and for me to eat. When we finally arrived in Tokyo, I felt much better.

We waited in line at customs, and when the attendee called for the next traveler, I strode up to the desk and handed the officer my passport. As I slipped my hood down, he peered at the picture, then looked at me.

"Glasses," he said, indicating I needed to take them off.

I removed the sunglasses and bared my wounded face to the man. His eyes widened.

"How did you get those injuries?"

I certainly didn't anticipate that question. Out of the corner of my eye, I could see the angels had successfully cleared customs. Having noticed my hold-up, they were visibly anxious.

Not wanting to cause a scene, I blurted out the first thing that came to mind. "I'm a fighter."

The attendant stared at me. "Like UFC?"

"Yes," I lied.

"Those are some bad bruises," he remarked, stamping my passport and sliding it back.

"You should see the other guy." I grabbed it from him fast, and the officer laughed as I walked through the partial gateway.

"Everything all right?" Gabriel asked.

I slid the sunglasses back on. "Yep."

They all relaxed, and we continued on our way. When we arrived at the hotel, we all reconvened in the living space of our suite once we'd settled in.

"So, who do you think is located here?" I asked, making myself comfortable on the couch.

"We think it might be Jophiel," Gabriel said, handing me the room service menu.

"He is an angel of art," Gabriel continued. "It makes sense for him to utilize his skill here, since Tokyo is one of the largest cultural art centers of the world."

"True, but what about Rome?" I asked.

"Jophiel's skill and specialization would be best placed here in Asia rather than Europe," Raphael said.

"Fair enough. Where should we go to search for him?"

"That's the problem. There are many museums and archives within the city," he explained.

"We'll have to ask around again," Zadkiel said. "Or we visit the largest museums and see if he's there."

"That will take time." Gabriel shook his head. "Something we don't have much of. I don't want to be caught off-guard again, and wandering around Tokyo will certainly alert the fallen to our presence."

"Gabriel, we can't stop taking chances now," Uriel said.

"I know," he replied. "But, Jordan—"

"Oh, here we go," I said, placing the menu on the coffee table. "What are you worried about now?"

"We can't have you out in the open."

"You're confining me to the hotel room? That doesn't make any sense. Besides, don't you think Satan will have to regroup before he sends his henchmen to come find us again?"

"Most likely." Gabriel nodded.

"Then stop worrying," I said. "I'm going to be fine. I'm also going with you. There's no way I'm about to be holed up in here."

Gabriel opened his mouth to protest.

"If I'm not around, which one of you will wear the backpack?" My question was met with silence. "Exactly. And how are you supposed to convince Jophiel to come with us if I, the sign you've all been waiting for, am not there?"

"He has a point," Zadkiel said.

"I know he does." Gabriel was agitated, yet he knew my words were true. "Fine," he said with a sigh. "But at the first sign of trouble, you're back here, confined to the hotel room."

"Okay." I said with a grin.

After eating my meal, the angels decided we should rest for the day and start looking for Jophiel tomorrow. When the morning arrived, we hit the streets of Tokyo and began to travel about the city from one museum to another. By the afternoon, we had already been to four locations with no luck.

"Are you sure it's Jophiel we need to be looking for?" I wondered.

They all glanced at me skeptically, as if telling me they knew best. I'd never met Jophiel before, but angels weren't always right. At least, I didn't think they were.

"What about the Archives?" Zadkiel asked. "It's one of the largest cultural buildings in the entire city."

"We can try it," Gabriel said.

We walked to the National Archives of Japan since a cab was too small to fit us. On our excursion, we passed lots of people hurrying to and fro about their day. The aromas of different Japanese foods floated on the air, and we heard the occasional honk of a horn and caught snippets of conversation from passersby. About thirty minutes into our walk, I realized the Archives were further than expected. I struggled to keep up with the angels, and since we didn't seem threatened by The Six at the moment, I was unsure why Gabriel set such a quick pace. Every part of my feet hurt, no matter how I adjusted my stride, and my ankle was throbbing again since I obviously hadn't given it enough time to heal. I slowed down when I felt myself start to limp. Bracing against the side of a random building, I took a rest.

The angels continued up the street, not noticing I'd stopped.

Though I was getting sick of wearing the backpack, I cherished it now as it propped me up against the concrete wall. Lowering my head, I sighed because I knew I had to move to catch up.

Suddenly, a glint of silver streaked past my head and landed with a crack in the wall behind me. Eyes wide, I looked up to find a metal throwing discus with razor-sharp edges lodged in the place where my head would have been.

What the...?

Across the street, an incoming horde of what I presumed to be demons scrambled down the sidewalk. Cursing the monstrous little creatures, I dragged myself up and full-out sprinted.

JORDAN

24

TOKYO, PRESENT DAY

"Run!" I yelled as I approached the angels.

Abruptly, they turned around, weapons at the ready. I ran through the middle of their ranks and kept going. They held their ground.

"What are you doing?"

"Killing these bastards," Uriel shouted. He made the sign of the cross and sought forgiveness for his "swear" word. Then, he produced his small crossbow from some hidden holster concealed by his jacket and reached down to pull three bolts out of his boot. Quickly, he loaded the weapon and launched arrows into the amassing horde, hitting his mark.

"Jordan, listen to me," Gabriel said, approaching my side. "You need to get to the Archives. We'll be right behind you, but we have to hold them off to give you a head start."

"It won't be a big one," Raphael said.

"Why not?" Gabriel turned to his brother.

"That's why." Zadkiel pointed to the figure emerging from the horde.

Gabriel stiffened. Grabbing me by the shoulders, he pushed me on. "Go!" he shouted.

I didn't hesitate and started running in the direction of the Archives. I'd never seen any of them so tense before, and the sudden change frightened me.

The building loomed ahead. I ran out in the middle of the road, dodging cars and shouting my apology to drivers who cursed in Japanese and honked their horns. These people didn't understand the gravity of the situation, and I was sure if they knew Satan had just graced the Earth, they'd be running in front of cars too. At least, I presumed it was Satan. Nothing else would set the angels on edge like that.

Having crossed to the other side of the street, I realized the Archives were situated at the back of a park. Weaving around people on the sidewalk, I finally made it to the entrance and approached the automatic doors. They slid open, and I ran in toward the information desk.

"I'm looking for Jophiel," I blurted in a rush.

The woman at the front desk frowned, clearly not recognizing the name.

Realizing my mistake, I tried again. "Sorry. I'm looking for someone by the name Jo—" I paused, not sure what name to give.

"You mean, Mr. Crane?" the woman asked. "Jo Crane?"

"Yes," I said. "It's a family emergency."

Screams erupted from outside. Curious, the woman ignored me and went to the front door to peer through the glass. With alarm, she came running back to her desk, picking up the phone and speaking quickly in Japanese. After hanging up, she and some security guards began to secure the doors and windows.

"Wait, wait!" I shouted as they approached the front door. "What are you doing?"

"Lockdown," the woman replied.

"No!" I tried to stop her.

The security guards drew their batons.

I raised my hands in the air. "I mean no harm. I just need to find Jo, and I can't be locked in here," I explained.

The guards did not back off.

Hands still raised, I glanced over my shoulder. Outside, a battle raged on the street in front of the Archives. My four angelic friends were fighting the demons, slaying them easily and quickly. The wicked beasts were merely a distraction as The Six closed in. Each of my friends took on two at a time, effortlessly fighting them like pros.

However, a lone figure advanced toward the doors.

I had never seen him before. From a distance, I could tell that he was dressed in all-black, from the boots on his feet to his long jacket. Underneath, he wore a pair of dress pants and a button-up shirt, the top few buttons open to reveal the small red scar below his collarbone and the glint of a chain. I could clearly see the skulls tattooed on his hands and the rings on his fingers. His hair was dark as well, and he was taller than Gabriel, if that was even possible.

Deep down, I knew he was Satan. What I didn't know was how we were going to get out of here, all of us, alive.

"Put your arms behind your back," the guards demanded.

Turning my attention away from the door, I faced them. "Please, just wait. They could make it inside." After the words came out, I realized I was hoping for the angels to advance closer so they could enter the building before it was locked down. That way, we would all be inside safe, away from the fallen.

The guards weren't tolerating me anymore. One moved closer, his baton prepared to strike. I closed my eyes and braced for the impact.

"Stop!" someone shouted.

I opened my eyes and saw an Asian man advancing toward us. He had black hair and light brown eyes, and a goatee covered his face. His height seemed comparable to Zadkiel's.

"Jophiel?" I said hesitantly.

"How do you know my name?"

"Gabriel told me. I'm Jordan—I was sent to find you. Please, they need your help."

"I know. That's why I came down." He strode past me, through the door, and joined in the fray, wielding a pair of handheld weapons with three metal prongs coming out from each hilt.

The guards stared pointedly. Dropping my hands, I went to leave, but the woman stopped me by placing a hand on my arm.

"You should stay inside. It's not safe out there."

Her offer was tempting. I had no idea how this would end. But I knew I couldn't leave the angels alone, so I smiled at her kindness and walked through the door.

Immediately, they were locked and secured.

Not entirely sure what to do, I ran over to a pillar and hid behind it. I was trying to think of a plan when things grew eerily quiet. Peeking around my stone shield, I saw Gabriel restrained by two of the fallen as Satan held a sword to his throat.

"No!" I shouted, leaping out from behind the pillar.

"Ah, there's the boy," Satan remarked. "Give me the bag, or he dies."

"Jordan, don't listen to him," Gabriel pleaded.

Satan put more pressure on the blade, issuing a small stream of blood from his throat. Gabriel grimaced but remained unmoved by the threat.

I stepped forward, not entirely sure what to do but knowing I had to perform some action so Gabriel wasn't vanquished right before my eyes.

Satan smiled. "Good boy."

"I'm not a dog, you know?" I responded, slowly advancing toward them.

"I know."

"Then stop treating me like one."

"Well," he conceded, "then I guess I should treat you like the vermin you are." He moved so fast I had no time to react. A glint of metal sped through the air, a dagger closing the distance between us until it met its mark and lodged itself in my right shoulder.

Winded, I fell on the pavement and remained in a kneeling position with my left hand braced in front of me. Pain seared through my arm, and I gasped in shock.

"Does that feel better?" Satan teased.

Gabriel struggled against his captors.

"Oh, we made him angry," Satan jested.

"Samael, you rotten—"

"Don't call me that!"

Everything happened in slow-motion. Satan's henchmen pushed Gabriel to the ground. They retreated into the background as Satan raised his sword to strike. The blade made its sweeping arc downward. There was a swift breeze and a rustle of feathers. The resounding clang of metal against metal tore reality back into real time.

A kneeling figure pushed forward against the shield that had rescued Gabriel, sending Satan backward. Before the devil could advance, a longsword came flying at him, wielded by a blond-haired, blue-eyed angel I had yet to meet. He matched Satan in height and conveyed a strength yet to be seen by any of the others. While they were all deft fighters, this one looked like he was created for it.

The demons and The Six were distracted by the sudden appearance of this new angel, so the others managed to free themselves from their captors, resuming the fight against the fallen as Gabriel made his way to me. I could tell the arrival of the mysterious figure meant something, since the demon horde retreated, and Satan was clearly taken aback.

"Retreat!" one of the fallen shouted.

Loud claps like the sound of thunder filled the air. Instantly, the fallen forces vanished into the Earth.

Sudden silence filled our surroundings. From my kneeling position, I kicked my legs out in front of me and sat down. Gabriel was saying something, but his words were muted. I clutched my shoulder and groaned in pain. The ringing in my ears wouldn't stop.

The others joined us.

Aggravated and uncomfortable, I released my arms from the backpack and cried out since the weapon was still lodged in my shoulder. Raphael assisted in taking the backpack off and handed it to Uriel, who slipped it onto his back. Tearing at my hoodie, he ripped off strips of cloth to tie around my wound, securing the blade in place and easing the flow of blood.

I tore the sunglasses off with my good arm and tried to focus on

THE GENESIS OF SEVEN

what they were saying, but the ringing in my ears grew worse, and I did my best to indicate this was the problem.

Gabriel nudged Raphael aside and placed his hands over my ears, closing his eyes.

The image of a violin came to mind, and suddenly, a high-strung crescendo crashed through my senses. Disoriented, I found myself yelling—in agony or frustration, I wasn't sure. I realized Gabriel had found his way into my head, and I could hear again.

"What happened?" I asked.

"It's all right, Jordan." Gabriel placed a hand on my good shoulder. "The fallen claps of thunder can hinder human senses. You needed the sounds of the blessed to restore your hearing."

"You went inside my head?"

"Yes, I have the ability to convey messages that way."

I leaned my head back and groaned. "This type of thing would be good to know about before you do it."

"Sorry."

Jophiel started to ask questions, but I wasn't paying attention. The unknown angel, our rescuer, was striding toward us with his shield and sword in hand.

Gabriel noticed his presence without turning to look. "It's about time you showed up."

"A simple thank-you would suffice," the angel bantered, sheathing his sword and placing the shield at his feet.

Gabriel beamed and stood to face him. They grasped forearms in a sign of brotherhood, camaraderie, and welcome.

"Thank you," Gabriel said with great intensity.

The angel shrugged it off. "I'm glad to help." He looked directly at me. "You've got yourself in a mess of trouble, Conway."

"You know who I am?"

"Yes. I'm a private investigator. Did some research on you before I arrived."

I stared at him. What he said was slightly disturbing. How did he get my name in the first place? But, I reminded myself, angels had ways of knowing things I would never figure out. It was pretty cool he was a private investigator. I mean, secret agent-style spy work was the only missing element in this crazy adventure.

"I would have thought the angel of power would be a soldier," Gabriel said.

The new angel shook his head. "That would mean involving myself in the problems of humanity. Besides, I don't like taking orders."

Gabriel chuckled.

My curiosity got the better of me. "Who are you?"

"You know him," Gabriel said. When I looked puzzled, he clarified. "Well...his name, at least."

It took a minute to figure out. Then, Sister Helen's words struck me. "Michael?"

He grinned. "Nice to meet you."

I understood now why she had hoped he was the angel in New York. The fallen feared him.

JORDAN

25

"We need to get him out of here," Raphael interrupted Michael's introduction.

Police sirens sounded in the distance, and the last thing we wanted was to get tangled up with the authorities.

"Of course," Gabriel replied. "Let's get him back to the hotel."

"No, you can't take him back there," Michael said.

"Why not?"

"They're tracking you. I'm not sure how, but they are."

Even though I was in pain and definitely not at my best, I knew "they" were the fallen.

"You can come to my apartment," Jophiel offered. "The boy can be treated there, and you can all explain to me what's going on."

Raphael gripped my arm to lift me up, but I refused to move. "Wait. What about our stuff at the hotel? I can't leave my duffel behind."

Gabriel understood the concern on my face. I was not about to lose my parents' possessions.

"A few of us will go back for our things," he reassured me. "For now, we need to get you off the street."

With my mind at ease, I let Raphael lift me up. He gently grasped my right arm, while Zadkiel came to my left.

"How far away is it?" Uriel asked.

"Not far. Just a few blocks that way," Jophiel replied.

It was a slow journey since I was still limping from my sore ankle, but in a short time, we were outside Jophiel's building.

"What are we waiting for?"

"They're going to check the place before we take you up there," Raphael explained.

Michael, Gabriel, Uriel, and Jophiel disappeared into the building. When Gabriel came back down and gave us the all-clear, we approached the door.

"How far up is it?" Zadkiel asked.

"All the way to the top."

"He's not going to make that. He can barely stand," Raphael said.

"Can you all please stop talking about me like I'm not here? I might be a physical wreck, but I'm not unconscious."

Zadkiel grinned at my boldness and released my left arm. Raphael then lifted me into his.

"What are you doing?"

We flew through the opening in the middle of the staircase and landed at the top in seconds. Raphael strode forward through the open apartment door, wings no longer visible. Gabriel and Zadkiel were on our heels, and I realized they must have flown up too.

Inside, the long dining table had been cleared off, and Raphael laid me on top of it. I stared up at six angelic faces and smirked.

"Why is it the wing appearances always happen when I'm not in a proper state of mind? For all I know, I'm hallucinating."

No one replied, but I could tell I'd amused them.

"We're going back to the hotel," Uriel said.

"Be careful," Michael warned.

He left with Gabriel and Zadkiel to retrieve our things, while Raphael cut away my t-shirt and hoodie to get better access to my shoulder. Jophiel came over with as many medical supplies as he could muster, and Raphael slipped on gloves. The angel of healing inspected the dagger in my shoulder, deciding how to pull it out.

"This is going to hurt, isn't it?"

"Afraid so," he said, grasping the weapon and pulling quickly.

I winced, trying to ignore the discomfort. The pain subsided slowly, and I jerked my eyes over to the wound. Dark lines had spread from the injury, snaking down my arm and through my veins. My eyes widened as panic set in.

"Holy water!" Raphael yelled. "I need holy water!"

Michael came close and stood behind my head. "Look at me," he said.

My eyes tore away from the wound, and I stared up at him.

"You're going to get through this," he reassured me, leaning forward to place his hand firmly on my chest in restraint.

"What are you—?"

My words were cut off as Raphael poured the liquid over my shoulder. I thought the dagger was bad enough, but it was nothing compared to this. I screamed out, again and again, as pain seared through my body. The holy water washed over the wound, combatting whatever infected it.

Eventually, either the pain subsided or my shoulder became numb to it. I was in and out of consciousness, but I knew Raphael was stitching up the wound as I could feel the small pinch of the needle every time it entered my skin.

When I opened my eyes, I was on the couch. My shoulder was bandaged, and I had no shirt on. Peering at the door, I took in the sight of four chests and realized the others had returned with the luggage. I groaned as I sat up.

Raphael came over to me. "How are you?"

"Fine, I guess. I'm still alive, which counts for something."

He smiled. "You're a fighter, that's for sure. You have some pain meds and antibiotics in you, which is why you're probably feeling better."

I nodded slowly and stood up, light-headed. Wanting to find a hoodie from my bag, I walked carefully over to the pile of luggage, catching my reflection in a mirror as I did.

I froze. I looked a hot mess, my hair standing up in every direction. My chin had a little scruff on it as I hadn't shaved in a few days. My bruised face and neck were a wicked shade of purple, and my shoulder was covered by a large bandage. The black lines running down my arm had turned red, as if whatever was coursing through my system had been burned out of me.

Taking my eyes away from the mirror, I returned my attention to the pile of luggage. My duffel was nowhere in sight.

"Where's my bag?" I asked.

"Right here," Gabriel said.

I turned around to find all of them staring at it on the dining table.

"Is there a problem?"

"Not anymore," Michael replied.

"What do you mean?" I moved toward them.

"Your bag had a tracker attached to it," Uriel explained.

"How is that possible?"

"We're not sure. The fallen typically don't dabble with technology, but Satan will resort to any means necessary to keep tabs on someone," Gabriel said.

I peered at the tiny crushed device that lay next to my bag. "This was it?"

"Yes. It was black, to blend in with your duffel," Uriel said.

"And it was in the shape of a fly, to avoid suspicion," Zadkiel added.

"Where would they get such technology?" I asked, picking up the device to analyze it.

"That's what we've been wondering." Jophiel's forehead crinkled with concern.

"I guess they filled you in on everything," I said.

"Yes, and there's no need to convince me. I'm ready to leave with all of you once you're recovered. Seeing the fallen today, especially Satan, made this situation all the more real. Add to that your bravery and whatever is in that backpack…I'm more than prepared to fulfill my duty." He looked at Gabriel. "I'm sorry I didn't come when you called."

"It's all right. No one answered. I was frustrated, but now I recognize we all simply fell into mundane routines that were hard to turn away from until the truth faced us."

They nodded their heads somberly.

"I have to ask, what exactly was going on with my arm?"

Jophiel brightened at my question. "I was hoping you'd bring that up. Follow me."

I grabbed a zip-up hoodie from my duffel and followed him to a room concealed by a large door. Jophiel slid it open. The others joined us and gathered around a long table in the center of the space, where the dagger lay amidst beakers, vials, and other chemicals. I remained in the doorway, taken aback by my surroundings.

It seemed we had stepped into an artist's studio crossed with a laboratory. Art supplies of all kinds could be found on the left side of the room; scientific objects like those of an inventor could be seen on the right. There were paintings, completed and unfinished, stacked along the far wall, and an entire counter full of artifacts in the process of preservation.

"What exactly is it that you do?" I asked, finally joining the others around the table.

"It's quite hard to summarize in one word," Jophiel said. "I've been called an art historian, an anthropologist, an archeologist, an archivist, an artist, and an inventor. I do all these things, but if I had to label myself, it would be an angel of art."

I smiled. The room was a testament to this.

"Are those the holy water grenades?" I asked, pointing to a line of balls along the back wall filled with clear liquid.

"Yes, the newly mastered model."

"How are they newly mastered?" Zadkiel asked.

"Well, they're no longer made of glass but plastic, so they don't crack and injure the wielder. Also, you can now press down on the top and throw them like an actual grenade since they explode on impact," Jophiel explained.

"That would have been helpful in my case…" I raised my bandaged hand.

Jophiel looked puzzled.

"He used the last one of mine," Raphael supplied.

Jophiel grimaced and nodded in understanding.

"What did you want to tell Jordan about the dagger?" Michael reminded him.

"Right. So, you might not know this yet, but there is more to these weapons than meets the eye. In fact, there is more to the fallen forces too," he said, glancing at his brothers standing around the table.

I followed his gaze and settled on Gabriel. The memory of whatever they were about to tell me played across his face like a movie.

GABRIEL

26

HEAVEN, AFTER THE FALL

I flew alone to High Heaven and landed gracefully on the expanse of clouds encircling the castle. I walked the remaining distance to the entrance, carrying the chest that held all the belongings I presumed I might need on Earth.

Since the war, the castle had been restored to its original beauty, but the memories still lurked within the walls. Memories of evil, darkness, destruction, and treachery. I entered the tower and climbed the spiral stairs, knowing what waited for me at the top was different this time. An open entranceway led to a circular chamber, where Seraphiel stood with Jophiel. My surprise at his presence was soon replaced with curiosity as I realized the entire right side of the chamber was open to the clouds. I set down my chest and stepped over to the ledge, gazing down into nothing but white.

"This is where you will descend," Seraphiel said.

I turned to face her. "But how will I control the descent? The drop is so sudden, my speed will accelerate quickly. Not to mention, I cannot see anything."

"What you are looking into right now is an illusion," she replied, walking away from me to the opposite side of the chamber. "A shield, I believe you call them."

Jophiel nodded.

I didn't understand what she was saying, and she immediately recognized that. "Father tasked Jophiel with conducting some experiments."

"Experiments?"

"Would you care to explain?" she asked.

Jophiel stepped forward. "Father wanted the angels of art to investigate two things: heavenly light, and divine light. He gave us samples of each to conduct our studies. The weapons created in the Forge are infused with heavenly light. These weapons are lethal to all of us, since angels both blessed and fallen originate from the same source."

I nodded my head in understanding.

"We were entrusted to test the samples of heavenly light for lethality. Father wanted to know what kind of damage could be done, not only to beings like us but also to humankind. We did not conduct these studies on ourselves or on humans but on synthetic materials Father created for us. There were many findings, but the most significant was the discovery of what we now term Hellfire."

"Hellfire? What is that?"

"It was an accidental result of an experiment. One of my comrades mistook the divine light for heavenly light and mixed together excessive amounts of each. There was so much light matter in the sample it started combatting with itself, and this aggressive behavior turned the material into dark matter. We termed it Hellfire. This all occurred right before the Seventh Day Gathering. Father immediately took the substance from us before it got into the wrong hands."

"That makes sense," Seraphiel said.

Jophiel and I looked at her.

"Father sent down the Hellfire with the fallen. He did not want it to remain here. It is now the fire that burns in Hell. He also turned it into Satan's punishment by having it physically reside inside him."

Jophiel was alarmed. "Do you understand what kind of punishment that is? We did not have much time with the Hellfire, but it was in our presence long enough to know exposure causes immeasurable agony. It is the most lethal type of matter."

Seraphiel was solemn. "He knew."

Outrage welled inside me, and it took everything in my power to quell it. I believed the fallen deserved to be punished for what they had done, but this punishment was severe. So severe I would *never* wish it on anyone, not even Satan.

Jophiel was shaken up too.

At his lack of response, Seraphiel said, "Please continue your explanation."

He nodded grudgingly. "Our studies of the divine light had a similar purpose. Father wanted us to figure out its capabilities and potential. After a series of short experiments, it was apparent this light could be manipulated to do things."

"Like what?" I wondered.

"It could transport, barricade, and cloak things. We have since termed the capabilities portals, barriers, and shields. The way they work is quite hard to explain because they are made of divine light and are invisible. We were still conducting our studies when Father used them."

I was confused. "When did He use them?"

"When He barricaded the fallen in High Heaven and sent them to Hell," Seraphiel said.

Recognition dawned on my face.

"After that," Jophiel continued, "we realized how easy it is to hybridize them by taking qualities from each and combining them together. Father barricaded the fallen, sent them to Hell, and allowed the Seraphim to walk in and out of the barrier before the fallen departed."

"And you are still conducting studies now?" I asked.

"Yes, although the majority of them have been completed."

I fell silent and looked at my feet. The magnitude of secrets they had kept was overwhelming.

"Is there anything else Gabriel should know?" Seraphiel wondered.

My head popped up from its downcast position. "I certainly hope not."

Jophiel shook his head. "There's nothing else...other than my warning."

"What do you mean?"

Seraphiel elaborated. "Father wishes for all of you who are being sent to Earth to have a complete knowledge of the fallen and what they are capable of."

"What are they capable of?"

"Some angels of art fell with Satan," Jophiel answered. "That means the fallen have the potential to manipulate all these substances since they were sent down to Hell."

"The First Choir believes this will not happen because Father put barriers in place to stop them," Seraphiel said.

Jophiel scoffed. "You only need one of them to be set free before they are all freed. If that happens, they have the potential to create weapons just as powerful as our own. They also have the potential to manipulate and hybridize the divine light like we have done in Heaven."

"I understand, Jophiel," Seraphiel continued, "which is why we have acknowledged your warning and are now informing your comrades so that they are prepared to deal with the fallen."

Jophiel did not challenge her further.

"I believe it is now time for you to leave." Seraphiel moved to lead him out, but not before he took in my presence one last time. Neither of us knew if we would see each other again.

I gave a faint smile. Before I could say goodbye, he was escorted out of the chamber.

When Seraphiel returned, I picked up my chest and stepped back over to the ledge. "So, if what lies below is some portal, my drop is not as far as it seems?" I asked.

"Correct. In fact, the portal does not lie down there." She placed a finger under my chin and lifted it. "It lies in front of you."

Briefly, I set the chest down and slowly placed my hand in front of me. Sure enough, I could feel the divine light.

"Are you ready?" she asked.

I nodded. "Where am I going? And where will my keys be located?"

Seraphiel explained all. Then, I stepped into the clouds and made my descent.

JORDAN

27

TOKYO, PRESENT DAY

None of the information in Jophiel's story seemed new to the other angels, but I had a ton of questions. One thought in particular crossed my mind.

"You mean, you guys can be killed by dark *and* light weapons?"

"Yes," Jophiel said. "The same goes for the fallen. The weapons wielded by the fallen and the blessed are sanctified in either dark or light matter, and since this matter is similar to the energy we are created of, they have the ability to harm us."

"What about regular human weapons?"

"Those cannot harm us. They can draw blood, but the wound will heal instantly. Except in the case of a gunshot, where the bullet would need to be removed first."

I paused to think this over. "You said God wanted to know how lethal these weapons could be to humans. Well, what damage *can* they cause?"

"Any type of weapon can harm humans," Jophiel said. "If they're wounded by a dark weapon, the dark matter infects the injury. If not taken care of quickly and properly, the dark matter takes over the person, turning them dark and even leading to possession."

My eyes widened. "That was happening to me?"

"Yes, but Raphael took care of it. Typically, the only way to do so is to cleanse the wound with holy water and lots of it. It's a difficult and painful process. Essentially, the dark matter must be burned out of the person."

I glanced down at the red marks streaking my arm. "How long does it take for the dark matter to take over?"

"It depends upon the injury. Usually, it's whenever it reaches one's heart. That's why the fallen never strike humans with a lethal shot. They would rather have them suffer and turn into malevolent beings they can control than strike them directly in the heart, which would kill them instantly."

"That's really messed up," I said. "What happens if a light weapon injures a human?"

None of them answered.

"Does it not happen?"

"No, it happens," Zadkiel said. "The person would be killed instantly because light energy is lethal to humans.

When I gasped, Michael said quickly, "But we make sure it doesn't happen."

"Yes." Zadkiel nodded. "That's part of the reason we don't go around showing our true selves. The human eye cannot handle the light we radiate. When we reveal our wings, energy is released but in a harmless amount. As members of the Third Choir, our light is weaker than those of the First and Second. We can control how much light we emit, so we keep our true iridescent light at bay."

"But sometimes, we have no choice in the matter," Raphael said solemnly.

"Why not?"

"Because those transformed by dark matter are still humans even though they are turned. To protect the innocent, we must deal with them," Uriel explained.

"I see. So, dark beings are humans that are infected with dark matter but are still alive, while demons are humans that were infected with dark matter but are now dead?"

"Yes," Michael said. "And then there are also the damned, which are deceased spirits condemned to Hell."

"I didn't know there was such a hierarchy," I said.

"There's a hierarchy to everything, even Heaven and Hell," Michael remarked.

"Interesting. I imagine the blessed can't wield dark weapons, and the fallen can't wield light weapons? I mean, you can't touch them, right?"

"Correct," Jophiel said.

"And if demons were once humans, why do they look like monsters?"

"Once a dark being is killed, two things can happen. If they are truly evil, they transform into a demon since darkness has consumed the soul," Jophiel explained. "However, if the dark being is truly pure of heart and was forced into evil intent, their soul is freed, and they are at peace in death."

"Oh. I didn't realize there was so much to learn about the fallen. But it makes sense since there's a lot to learn about the blessed too."

"You'll get used to it," Zadkiel assured me.

I nodded in agreement. "And what about what happened at the

Archives? When the fallen retreated, it looked like they went into the ground. Was that a portal?"

"Yes," Jophiel said. "My fear that the fallen would escape their bonds in Hell and manipulate the materials down there came true. Not only did they use the Hellfire to forge weapons of dark matter, they also know how to use the portals, barriers, and shields."

"Which are made from divine light?" I clarified.

Jophiel nodded.

"And divine light comes from God?"

He nodded again. "The light that comes from angels is heavenly light, whereas the light that comes from Father is divine light."

"All right. And the fallen can also hybridize the portals, barriers, and shields?"

"Essentially, yes. I'm sure the angels of art who fell must have shown Satan how to do so. There's a central portal somewhere in Hell that demons and other fallen angels use to travel to Earth. When these portals open, a thunderous noise follows. It's known as the fallen claps of thunder since the fallen are the only ones who use portals."

"Don't angels use them?" I asked.

"No. We're not allowed to travel to Earth unless it is sanctioned by Father," Gabriel said.

"All right…" I tried to wrap my head around all of this. "How do the fallen summon these portals?"

"If they're going to Hell, they must place their hand to the ground and say 'inferos,' which is Latin for Hell. To travel to Earth, they must place their hand on the portal and say 'terra' followed by the location. For example, 'terra New York,'" Michael explained.

"That's it? That's far too easy! They can go anywhere then." I was outraged.

"Exactly, which is why they're uncontrollable," Raphael said.

My thoughts were racing in so many directions. I blurted out another question. "You all said Satan was locked in Hell. Does that mean he can't use any of the portals?"

"That *was* true, though he has apparently remedied that," Zadkiel said.

"How?"

The angels were quiet. None of them knew the answer.

"What do we do with this thing?" I wondered, looking at the dagger.

"This is my favorite part," Jophiel said. He went to the counter and returned with a large jar of clear liquid. Unscrewing the lid, he placed thick gloves on his hands and picked up the dagger, submerging it in the jar before quickly twisting the lid back on.

Inside, the weapon began to disintegrate slowly.

"When it's destroyed, we'll throw the remaining water in a fire, obliterating it completely," he clarified.

"That's holy water?"

"Yes."

"Where did you get so much of it?" I asked.

"It's quite easy, actually," Zadkiel said. "We can make any water holy by sanctifying it."

"The purified kind in jugs is better though. It's more potent," Jophiel added.

"Okay, can we all get back on track?" Michael urged.

"He's right." Gabriel nodded. "Our work isn't done yet. We still need to find Chamuel."

"Then I guess we need to make our way to Italy," Zadkiel said. "I imagine that's where he is."

"Yes," Michael confirmed. "I was in Brazil."

"Let's not be too hasty," Raphael interjected. "Jordan needs rest."

"What Jordan needs," I said, "is to find Chamuel so that we can finally settle in one place and complete my training."

As the others exchanged glances, Michael shrugged. "I guess he has a point."

JORDAN

ROME, PRESENT DAY

28

Licking chocolate gelato from the cone I held, I followed at a leisurely pace behind Gabriel and Michael, who were determined to track down Chamuel by strolling around the streets of Rome. I didn't mind their method much. It gave me the chance to sightsee.

I'd never been out of the country before this grand tour with the archangels, but of everything we'd done so far, getting to see the Vatican was my favorite. It was also nice I didn't have to wear the backpack anymore. Since my shoulder injury, Uriel had silently accepted the position. I could tell he wasn't too keen about it though. Every so often, he kept readjusting the bag on his shoulders.

Abruptly, our group came to a halt as Gabriel asked a passerby in Italian for any information about Chamuel. The six angels had brainstormed that since he was an angel of the home, Chamuel must be performing a related role in society, so they were asking if the locals knew of any peculiar persons working in the culinary arts or interior design.

"How do you eat that stuff?" Zadkiel eyed the gelato.

"By licking it." I grinned.

He shook his head. "I meant, it seems unpleasant because it's sticky and cold."

"Exactly the opposite. It's delicious."

"I've never understood a human's fetish for sweets," Uriel remarked.

"That's because you've never tasted them." I slurped a drip of gelato and bit into the cone clumsily, forced to hold it in my left hand instead of my right.

When the local man departed, the angels joined Gabriel and Michael for further brainstorming since their conversation hadn't resulted in any leads. I stayed within a good distance and admired the scene around me—the whizzing cars and motorbikes, the various restaurants, and the sounds of chatter. Across the street, an advertisement attached to the bus stop drew my attention.

I maneuvered around the two cars passing by to get a better look. Immediately, the angels became distressed, shouting my name and following after me. It took them only a second to appear at my side.

"Jordan, what are you doing?" Michael demanded.

"You said Chamuel was an angel of the home, right?"

"Yeah."

"Well, what about being a chef?" I pointed to the advertisement. It promoted the opening of a new restaurant with a picture of the chef outside the building. The tall man had long, wavy blond hair pulled back in a loose bun and the most piercing blue eyes I'd ever seen, so light in hue they seemed almost white. Almost…angelic.

Jophiel was surprised. "How did you know that was Chamuel?"

"I don't, but I'm getting used to your terrible aliases." I pointed at the chef's name. *Cam Angel.* "See what I mean? Not very creative."

Michael grabbed a map from his back pocket and searched for the restaurant's address. "He's not far off either," he said, looking up at the street sign.

Gabriel peered over his shoulder to look.

I shoved the last bite of gelato cone into my mouth and wiped my hands with a napkin. They all stared.

"What?"

No one responded. Instead, they discussed the best way to make it to the Spanish Steps since the restaurant was close by.

Fortunately, we were able to hail a taxi van that comfortably fit all of us. Unfortunately, the driver was absolutely crazy, zooming about the streets of Rome, squeezing down alleys, and not giving a care to pedestrians. When we arrived unscathed, I breathed a sigh of relief and tried to keep the gelato down as my stomach twisted in queasy knots.

"Are you okay?" Gabriel must have noticed my face turning a pale green.

I nodded. It was unsafe to speak, my stomach was so unsettled.

Michael strode down the Spanish Steps and past the metro station, map in hand. The other angels followed after him, and I lagged behind with Raphael, taking my time to trek down the famous stairs. When we regrouped at the bottom, Michael already knew where we had to go. Effortlessly, he led us through the streets, glancing at the map only once.

Eventually, we entered a square lined with restaurants. In the middle, there was a medium-sized fountain with marble figures shooting water out of their mouths. I stopped briefly to marvel at the sculpture and how above, people sat out on their balconies watching the activity below.

"Jordan," Raphael said, "we should keep moving."

I moved forward with him and caught up with the others, who had stopped in front of a restaurant. They perused the menu while the maître d' stood by awaiting their decision.

"What are you doing?" I whispered.

"Pretending we're interested in the food," Jophiel whispered back.

"Why? Just ask to meet the chef."

"I don't know. They have some kind of plan." He gestured to Michael and Gabriel.

Screw the plan. "Excuse me," I said, stepping away from the group.

The maître d' looked over at me. "Si?"

"Can we meet the chef? The food looks delicious. I would love to compliment him."

"Wouldn't you like to try some first?" the man asked, his Italian accent thick but his skepticism more so.

"Well, you see, we know him. He's family," I replied.

The man eyed me. "I'm sure you do. But Chef Angel cannot be disturbed by such matters." He left us and moved on to the next customers.

Fine. I'd tried to avoid being rude, but he left me no choice. Defiantly, I strode through the outdoor dining area and into the restaurant, where I quickly found the entrance to the kitchen. Protests from outside meant I had little time, so I ran between tables and made my way through the swinging doors.

The sounds of pots and pans clanging jarred my senses as I trailed through the kitchen in search of Chamuel. The staff regarded me strangely, so when I met eyes with one woman, I asked, "Where is Chef Angel?"

She nodded to the left, not taking her hands away from chopping vegetables.

At that moment, the kitchen doors burst open, and the maître d' arrived in pursuit. I looked to the left and noticed a chef's cap. In a hurry, I darted over to Chamuel just as the maître d' caught up with me.

"Chamuel," I said as the man tugged my arm to take me back outside.

He looked up from his work. "Do I know you?" he asked in an Italian accent.

"No." I winced at the strong grasp on my injured shoulder. "Not yet anyway."

More tugging ensued, and the pain became unbearable.

"Gabriel sent me," I said, no longer able to resist. "The others are waiting for you outside!" I yelled as I was dragged out of the kitchen.

The maître d' walked me through the dining room and threw me back outside.

"Stay out!" the man barked.

I lost my balance and tumbled to the ground. Raphael rushed to my side. With his support, I limped over to the other angels, who had situated themselves on the low fountain wall.

"Thanks for the backup," I grumbled, cradling my arm and sitting down too.

"What happened? We thought you had him," Michael said.

"I did, but that guy was out to get me. You could have at least restrained him."

"I didn't think we would need to," Michael replied.

"And it's true—we didn't." Uriel gestured across the square.

Chamuel was in the outside seating area talking with the maître d'. When he looked over, the angel froze in place, taken aback by the presence of all his brothers. Slowly, he crossed the square to join us.

"You're here. All of you," he said in amazement. Then, he glanced at me. "I'm sorry if Umberto hurt you. He takes his job very seriously."

"Don't worry, I'm fine. Most of this is from Satan and his goons."

Alarmed, Chamuel sought explanation from the others.

"There's a lot to catch up on," Gabriel said.

"Satan is free?" Chamuel asked.

"Yes," Gabriel said. "If you come with us, we can explain."

"Where are you staying?"

"By the Vatican."

Chamuel nodded at Michael's answer, a gesture of approval. But the look on his face conveyed his concern.

"We can't stay here," Uriel said. "We have to keep moving."

"I know," Chamuel replied.

"Well, are you coming?" Zadkiel asked.

"Yes…I'm just not entirely sure what to do."

"Explain your dilemma," Gabriel said.

"I think we should stay together, but I need to get some things from my apartment, and I need to take care of things here too."

"You're worried about the restaurant?" Michael asked.

"No, but I need to tell them I'm not coming back. If I just disappear, they'll ask questions."

"Will it work for the others to head back to the hotel, and for me to stay behind with you? That way, you can tie up loose ends, and they can get Jordan back to the hotel," Gabriel suggested.

My shoulder was really hurting, and I had closed my eyes, focused on listening to the soothing sounds of the fountain. At the mention of my name, I snapped to attention. "Why do I need to go back to the hotel?"

"You aren't looking good. Raphael should check you out."

"Fine," I said, standing.

After another harrowing ride, I clambered out of the taxi in front of the hotel, glad to be back on solid ground. Together, the six of us entered the lobby and piled into the small elevator. The moment the doors opened and we arrived inside the hotel room, Raphael went to work.

"Sit," he commanded.

I took a seat at the table. Slowly, I eased my arms out of my shirt so he could examine my injuries. Raphael went to the bandage at my shoulder, and when he unraveled the gauze, concern marked his face.

"This is not healing," he said. "You're moving too much. We need to put a sling on it."

"A sling? It's hardly my fault. You should have seen how hard Umberto pulled my arm!"

Raphael stared. Umberto or no Umberto, he clearly thought I required a sling.

I sighed and lay my arm out in front of me so he could do what he needed. Once he had re-bandaged the wound, he fitted the sling across my shoulder.

"Are you comfortable?"

I frowned as I realized what the trade-off involved: greater comfort, but immobility.

"You'll get used to it eventually," Raphael insisted.

He then inspected my hand, face, and throat. When he was finished, I went to put my shirt back on but was struck with a dilemma.

"How exactly do I dress myself?"

"I should have made you put the shirt on before I fitted the sling," Raphael said, loosening the straps.

When my arm was freed, I reached for my t-shirt, but he stopped me.

"You shouldn't wear anything that requires you to raise your arms. Do you have something that buttons or zips in the front?"

"I only have hoodies."

"That will work."

I stood up to retrieve one, but Michael had already done so. "Thanks," I said, easing my arms into the sleeves and zipping it up.

Raphael fitted my arm in the sling again, making sure it was snug but not uncomfortable. When he placed a glass of water and two pills in front of me, I didn't hesitate and swallowed them down.

"I'm glad you're finally coming to your senses."

I rolled my eyes. "Just because I'm not questioning everything you do doesn't mean I've changed. It just means I trust you and I know you're right."

"Good." Raphael grinned. "It's about time you recognized that."

I smiled and stood up to move over to the couch. I was about to sit down when there was a knock at the door. All five angels went on high alert, reaching for hidden weapons and surrounding me in a protective circle.

Michael approached the door, knife drawn. He peered through

the peephole, then quickly sheathed his weapon, opening it up to welcome Gabriel and Chamuel inside.

"That didn't take long."

"Well, quitting my job isn't exactly something that requires much time," Chamuel said, placing his chest on the floor.

I realized he had changed out of his chef's attire and into a button-up denim shirt with khaki pants and suede lace-up shoes. His long hair was no longer pulled back, the wild mane now falling to his shoulders. He wore a ring on each hand, one of which must have been from Heaven, and several bracelets on his wrists.

"How much did Gabriel tell you?" Jophiel asked.

"Everything. Where's this backpack I've heard about?" Chamuel looked around.

I pointed at where Uriel had thrown it on the table the minute we got back to the hotel.

Chamuel approached the bag. Without even touching it, he said, "There's something important in there all right." He paused. "Now, what do we do?"

"We go to Brazil," I announced.

They all looked at me.

"Michael needs his stuff, right?"

"I do," the angel said. "But there's no point in everyone coming to Brazil. You all should get to a safe location. I can go back to Brazil alone."

"A safe location? Where might that be?" I wondered.

Gabriel was the first to speak. "I think we should return to my apartment in New York."

"Why should we go there?"

"Foremost, because it's in America. You don't have a visa, so we need to get you back."

"But the fallen chased me to your apartment. That means they know about it," I said.

"I know, but we don't have many options at the moment. Besides, they might know the location, but they could never enter. I sanctified the whole building."

I didn't ask when he had done that since it must have been before our paths crossed. Instead, I said, "Is it really safe to split up though?" The question was bugging me.

Michael chuckled. "I'm more than capable of taking care of myself."

I knew that, but I was still worried about him going alone. I had to remind myself, he was the one who had rescued us.

"If we're all in agreement, I'll go about making the travel arrangements," Gabriel said.

Everyone nodded their approval.

MICHAEL

29

It felt like just yesterday I was here, yet in reality, much more time had passed. As a private investigator, I was my own boss, and that feeling was freeing. But now, I had a new purpose—an old one, really—that needed to be fulfilled. More than ever, I could see the life I had been living was a façade, one to keep my past at bay. That wouldn't be the case any longer.

As my feet landed on the ground, the feeling that enveloped me made me feel more alive and more myself. Gabriel had chastised me before I left that flying to Brazil instead of taking a plane was an uncivilized way to travel, especially since I could be detected. I really didn't care. Humans these days blamed anything suspicious in the sky on aliens. Besides, I enjoyed flying. It was faster, and I rarely had the chance to do it anymore.

Walking out of the back alley, I grabbed my keys from my leather jacket and unlocked the main door. As I strode up the steps, I passed offices and other businesses that operated out of this building. On the top floor, I unlocked the door that read, "Detective Michael Lyons – Private Investigator."

Bending down, I picked up the mail from the floor, sifting through it as I shut the door behind me.

"Took you long enough to get here."

My head snapped up at the voice. "What are you doing here?"

"Came for a chat," Satan said. He slipped his feet off my desk and got up out of my chair. "Love these maps, by the way. Very informative."

I glanced at the two large maps on the wall. I had hung them there to track two things: a client's investigation, and the possible whereabouts of the Sacrarium.

"You should really take the time to sanctify the place. If you did, I wouldn't be able to get in," he said.

"How long have you been here?" I asked to keep him talking. A glance out the window showed he hadn't come alone. Two of The Six were stationed on the roof of the building opposite. That meant the others were somewhere else.

That meant I was outnumbered.

Satan ignored my question and strolled about the room.

"Why did you retreat in Tokyo?" I tried instead, still searching outside.

"That wasn't my decision. Belphegor, the buffoon, felt we were outnumbered, and I couldn't possibly take you all on alone. Don't worry, I punished him for not following orders."

I was only half-listening as I neared the window. I disliked when he spoke so flippantly about hurting others. "Why couldn't you have taken us on? The angel I remember could have easily dispatched us, myself included."

Satan fiddled at something under his shirt, obviously a necklace of some kind, and mumbled, "I'm not the angel I once was."

Confused, I remained silent and continued my search of the perimeter.

"What these tell me," he said suddenly, pointing at the wall, "is that you're getting close."

"To what?" I looked at him.

"Finding the Sacrarium. I've been trying to locate them for years, but it's hard to decipher their pattern of movement. Though, it seems you were able to do far more than that." He smirked mischievously. "I suggest you back off now, before things get out of hand."

His words were an ominous warning. One I was not about to take.

"You know I'm not going to do that."

He chuckled. "Wouldn't expect anything else."

"You said you wanted to talk. What about?"

"The spheres. How many were made?"

"Thirteen, I suppose. One for each of us on the council."

He glared at me. "Don't lie. I know you know about *her*."

"Who?" I had no idea what he was talking about.

He scoffed. "Oh, Michael. Your attempts at deception are terrible. Is there a fourteenth sphere, or not?"

"I told you, I don't know. Stop presuming I do. Father created the spheres. How would I know if there's a fourteenth?"

Satan stared smugly. "For once, might I know something you don't?"

I stared back. "Apparently so."

He smirked in satisfaction. "Well, when are you going to tell *them* about this?" He pointed to the maps again.

"When the time's right. I haven't figured everything out yet."

"Really? Because from what I've seen, you have."

"What's that supposed to mean?"

"That I've been in your office much longer than you think."

My muscles tensed. I badly wanted to fight him, but I knew that would be a death wish.

"Why did you do this?" I demanded.

"Do what?"

"Change everything? Make everything so…complicated?"

He shook his head and leered. "You think I wanted to do this? You think I wanted to be thrown out of Heaven?"

"You had a choice."

"Did I?" he yelled, his features threatening to reveal more. "You were supposed to go to Eden that day. I covered for you!"

"I was sent a message from the First Choir to see Father. What did you expect me to do?"

"Send someone else," he retorted.

"You were more than fine with it at the time."

"Yes, until it changed everything!"

"What happened? In Eden…what happened?" I pleaded for the truth.

Satan rubbed the area between his thumb and forefinger. "I was bitten by a snake that revealed to me the knowledge in The Tree of Good and Evil."

Surprised he was confiding, I asked, "Why didn't you say something sooner? Father could have fixed it. We could have gone to him, as I suggested."

"Don't you think I tried?"

"What do you mean?"

"I went to Him to seek forgiveness, to seek help. But what I witnessed…" He shook his head. "It reaffirmed everything."

"You're not making sense. Tell me what happened. Did you go before the Seventh Day Gathering?"

"Of course I went before the Gathering! I went to Him right after the incident in Eden. But when I arrived, I witnessed two things that solidified everything I proposed during council…everything I learned from the snake bite."

"What did you witness?"

"Father's intention for the Son of God. We are His children, divine beings greater than man, yet He chose man over us to represent His incarnation on Earth. Obviously, we were not good enough for Him. He commanded us to do His bidding on Earth and in Heaven, but not in this endeavor. It just shows how expendable we are."

"Stop. Your talk is blasphemous."

He scoffed. "Oh, don't think you're so pure and innocent. You're the one who got me into this mess."

"How am I responsible?" My voice rose at his accusation.

"Because I also witnessed something known as necessary evil. Seraphiel revealed Lilith was an unstoppable force, and Father agreed she would do whatever it took to expose the truth and get her revenge. It was only a matter of time, so why not speed up the process and send down some bait?"

"No," I whispered.

"Oh yes, brother. Yes. However, they encountered a problem. You, their poster child, the high and mighty magnificent leader of the army, were to go to Eden next. They couldn't have that, you see, because you meant everything. So, He sent for you. And what was your response, since you never leave a duty unfulfilled?"

Distressed, I said, "I sent you instead."

"Bingo. They all decided I would be Lilith's bait. But they never expected things to get so out of hand. Can you blame me? When I found out, it gave me a hunger for revenge. How dare they decide *my* fate! So, after you declined to help, I gathered allies and told them of Father's injustices. They believed me—unlike you. But you and Gabriel betrayed me, forced me to seek refuge in Eden since I didn't know where else to go."

"I didn't—"

"Yes, you did! You sided with Gabriel over me! Don't deny it!"

His words silenced me.

"It didn't matter that I went to Eden because my plans for war were already in place. My absence worked to my advantage, made you suspect something would happen during the Gathering. Yet I told my troops to wait until the festivities were over to catch you off-guard. Causing a civil war was my main goal, but then, I realized, why not go after the scepter? Might as well obtain immense power to defeat Him while I was at it. Of course, you had to come in and save the day. When that happened, I knew all hope was lost."

"Why?"

"Because you're you, and I'm…" He started for the door. "We'll just leave it at that."

"I didn't want to fight you either, but you left me no choice," I defended.

He nodded. "I realize that now and have come to the same

conclusion. Stay out of my way, otherwise we'll both be forced to do things we don't want to do."

"What are you up to?" I asked. "What's your end game?"

"Well, I can't tell you that. But I'm going to find them."

"Who?" I called after his retreating figure.

Satan paused before walking out. "The Sacrarium. And then Lilith. I do appreciate your help in the first endeavor. That map was a wonderful source of information." With a dark laugh, he strode out the door and was gone.

The Manhattan cityscape could be seen from the plane window as we landed, and the trees in Central Park had turned orange in the November cold. It seemed it was going to be an early winter, but that didn't matter because I was home. It would be nice to finally settle down.

Once the seven of us got through the airport, we took a transit van to Gabriel's apartment. When we arrived, the footman helped us to unload our luggage onto a bellman's cart and steered it inside to the elevator.

"We might not all be able to fit," he said as he swiped his pass and pressed the button.

"That's all right, Benny. We can go up separately." Gabriel swiped his resident's pass on the other elevator. "It's the Penthouse floor," he told the others.

"It's good to have you back, Mr. Maestro. I hope you had a pleasant trip," Benny said.

"Thanks, it's good to be back. We had a very good trip."

"I see you have some visitors." Benny looked over his shoulder at all of us.

"Yes, these are my brothers. And this is Jordan," Gabriel said, placing his hand on my good shoulder.

"Nice to meet you, kid. Nice to meet all of you."

The elevators dinged as they both arrived. I stepped into the first with Gabriel, Benny, and the cart of luggage.

"Benny, don't you normally work in the garage?" Gabriel asked.

"Yeah, been watching that car of yours you never seem to use."

Gabriel smiled. "Thank you. If you don't mind me asking, what are you doing up here?"

"Oh, Carmine called out sick, so I'm covering for him. There are more than enough guys working the garage today."

"I see."

Their brief conversation ended as the elevator arrived at the Penthouse. When the doors opened, Benny steered the cart out into the hall and wheeled it into Gabriel's apartment when he unlocked the door.

"Talk about living in luxury," Uriel said as the others exited the elevator too.

Gabriel smirked. "You know I like nice things."

"Yes, I do, and I wouldn't have expected anything less."

The angels assisted Benny in emptying the luggage cart while I loitered by the door. Before he could leave, Gabriel reached into his jacket and handed Benny some money.

"Thanks, Benny, for all your help."

"No problem, Mr. Maestro," Benny said, grabbing the cart and guiding it into the hallway.

I closed the door after him, then turned to find the others quickly settling in.

Zadkiel had books spread all over the dining table.

Raphael was resupplying his medicine bag on the counter.

Uriel was taking in the view from the balcony.

Chamuel was analyzing the kitchen and cutlery.

Jophiel was looking at all the artwork that decorated the walls.

Seeing all of them in the apartment together, I realized this was quickly going to get claustrophobic. I had every intention of brainstorming our next move, but I needed a shower and a nap before any of that.

"I'm going to settle in and rest for a little while."

"Of course," Gabriel said.

"Is it all right if I take the guest room again?"

"Absolutely. None of them need it."

I smiled. "Thanks."

I had only slept in there one night, but seeing the room was a great comfort. After taking a shower, I fell to sleep the moment my head hit the pillow.

Several hours later, I woke up to find it was almost dark outside. I sat up in bed and thought for a few minutes about what I wanted to do. I knew the angels and I still had loose ends to tie up, and it wasn't like Satan and the fallen were going away anytime soon. Yet despite the daunting task that lay ahead, I couldn't get the idea of seeing Sophia out of my mind. I didn't know if she would have answers, but she might know where Sister Helen was. At least if I could find her, everything would be solved.

Besides, it would be nice just to see Sophia again.

I got out of bed with every intention of presenting my plan to the angels. But when I walked down the hall, Michael's presence distracted me.

"You're here?"

All seven pairs of eyes landed on me.

"Yeah, and I brought you some pizza," he said, patting the box on the counter.

The moment I stepped out of the bedroom, I had smelled something delicious. My stomach growled.

Michael chuckled. "I guess it was a good idea."

"Yeah, thank you," I said, sitting at the counter and opening the pizza box.

Chamuel cleared his throat when I reached in for a slice.

"What?"

"Do you have any manners?"

"What do you mean?"

"I mean," he said, opening the cabinet behind him, "use a plate." He picked one up and handed it to me.

"Sorry," I said, taking the plate and digging in.

He didn't seem too mad because he quickly resumed their conversation. "What did Satan want to talk about?"

I nearly choked on my pizza. "Who encountered Satan?"

"I did," Michael said. "In Brazil."

"I knew we shouldn't have split up."

Chamuel placed a glass of water in front of me.

"Thanks," I said.

He nodded, and Michael said, "It was no big deal. I handled it."

"Well, what did he want?" I wondered.

"He said he wanted to talk. I knew I had no chance of fighting him off. The Six were stationed outside."

"What did he want to talk about?"

"He interrogated me about the spheres, to see if I knew about a fourteenth."

"A fourteenth? How can there be a fourteenth? There are—*were*—only thirteen council members," Zadkiel said.

"I know. That's what I told him."

"If it exists, what does he want to do with it?" Jophiel asked.

"I'm not sure. We were asking each other questions, but neither of us received any answers. All I know is, he's going after two things."

"Which are…?" Gabriel asked.

"The Sacrarium and Lilith."

The first concerned me because it meant Sister Helen was in danger. The second alarmed Uriel.

"Lilith!" he exclaimed. "How is that she-devil not dead yet?"

Michael shook his head. "I don't know. I really have no answers to any of this. But the two of them together means devastation."

"Devastation?" I was surprised by Michael's words. "Is Lilith really that bad?"

"She can be. She's wanted revenge since the war in Heaven. Do you realize how long it's been since then? All that vengeance bottled up inside for so long changes people, especially her, who I'm sure must be hell-bent on fulfilling the prophecy. And if you think Satan is something to be feared, wait until she returns. Her influence over him has proven no good comes about when the two of them work together."

"Then we have to stop him from finding her," I said.

Michael nodded. "I'm afraid I might have led him to the Sacrarium."

"What do you mean?"

"I was investigating two cases. One was for a client. The other was a personal case to track the Sacrarium. I wanted to see if I could find them."

"Why?" Jophiel asked.

"Because they've obviously been keeping tabs on us, so I wanted to keep tabs on them."

"Why should that concern us? We have nothing to do with them," Uriel said. His unease about the Sacrarium could not be swayed.

"I know. I thought that too, but now, it seems we are involved with them since Sister Helen sent the backpack to us. Anyway, I've been mapping their location, and every so often, they move around as if they're trying to hide something. In hindsight, I realize they were trying to evade the fallen and keep the backpack safe."

We all knew that was true. Sister Helen said as much in her letter.

"This map," Michael continued, "I had it hanging in my office. I didn't think I was making any progress, but Satan seemed to think differently…like he knew where to find them."

At this, I was resigned to find Sophia. She was the only one who might know where Sister Helen was, and we needed to find Sister Helen because she was very much in danger.

Before I could tell them my idea, Michael said, "There's more I have to tell you. Not about the Sacrarium, but about something else I was working on."

We all waited for him to continue.

"This man came to me. He went by the name Allen Clark. I say that because I'm almost certain that's not his real name. I think he was undercover and desperately needed help. He gave me a bunch of documents and told me to take them to the authorities. He explained everything he could, but he said he was running out of time." Michael stopped, clearly upset by the memory. "I don't know what happened to Allen. I've tried searching for him, but it's like he disappeared. I'm unsure if his cover was blown, or if he was pulled out of the operation. All I know is, they were after him."

"Who are 'they?'" Gabriel asked.

Michael looked forlorn. "The Nephilim," he said.

Uriel exploded. "What do you mean, the Nephilim? They were eradicated centuries ago!"

"Not completely," Michael declared. "They found a way to survive, to hide…and to procreate."

MICHAEL

31

SÃO PAULO, TEN MONTHS AGO

I was sitting at my desk reading through the newspaper when I heard footsteps running up the stairs. Alarmed, I rose from my chair as the door to my office opened.

A man entered and slammed the door closed behind him. He was tall and muscular and had sunny blond hair with a beard and mustache.

"Can I help you?" I asked in Portuguese.

"I don't have time for pleasantries," he responded in English, breathing heavily. Given the man was lean and well-conditioned, I knew it wasn't only the run upstairs that had tired him out. He wore black medical scrubs and athletic shoes and was holding an enormous stack of files. "You're a private investigator, right?"

"Yes," I said.

He brushed past me and set the stack of files down on my desk. With his back turned, I noticed a gun shoved in the waistband of his pants.

"I suggest you start explaining why you're here before I call the cops," I warned.

He abruptly stopped shuffling through the files. "I don't mean you

• 278 •

any harm," he said, straightening to face me. "I need your help. A man is after me, and I'm running out of time."

It was strange, but every instinct told me to believe him. "All right." I strode to my desk to see what he had brought—financial statements, patient records, and appointment logs. Nothing made sense.

"I need you to take these documents to the authorities. Not here in Brazil, but New York."

I frowned. "Why?"

He was quick to respond. "Because the authorities here can't be trusted, but those in New York will know what to do."

I simply stared. Nothing about this encounter was normal, especially not with the way he was acting, but his belief in the New York authorities led me to believe he was working for them undercover. My gaze shifted slowly to land on the only piece of jewelry he wore, a St. Michael medallion. It could be pure coincidence, but I didn't believe in coincidences. To me, the necklace was a sign, and I naturally wanted to trust him.

"All right, but can I at least have your name and some sort of explanation?" I sat down in the chair behind my desk and offered him the seat in front of it.

He sank down. "My name is Allen Clark," he began. "I work for a company called Geneloom. They're a genetic testing company, and I have evidence they're conducting a secret experiment with one of their biggest partners." He glanced around as if to check we were safe. "I should have time to explain everything to you. Let me start at the beginning."

I gestured for him to go ahead. "Please do."

"Geneloom is based in New York, but they have smaller laboratories throughout the world, such as here, in São Paulo. On the surface, Geneloom is like any other genetic testing company. They sell kits for people to do mouth swabs at home and send them back in the mail to get their DNA results. They're one of the largest companies in their line of business and are financed through donations and sponsors—and of course, the revenue they make from selling the DNA kits. However, all of this is a front.

"One of Geneloom's biggest partners," Allen continued, "is Giant Heart Healing Center. They're a rehab center based in New York, though their reach is slowly growing throughout the United States. They take in troubled young men and women. This means young homeless people, runaways, teens trying to get out of the system. Giant Heart's access to these young individuals is the reason Geneloom partnered with them. Well, that and for extra funding."

"Can you tell me more?"

He nodded. "During the company's early years, Giant Heart admitted young individuals, age eighteen to twenty-five, into their rehab program. Giant Heart knew these individuals would be easier to manipulate as they were in a vulnerable state. On arrival, they had to undergo a series of DNA blood tests. This was phase one. Giant Heart justified these tests by saying they wanted to support the well-being of their patients, so knowing about any illnesses or addictions was vital to the healing process. The tests meant nothing for about ninety percent of patients, but the other ten percent had a target put on them because of their favorable genes."

"Favorable genes for what?"

"For phase two of their secret experiment. From that ten percent, Geneloom and Giant Heart narrowed the pool even further, selecting only a few candidates with no serious health issues, with the intent of using them to create some kind of extraordinary offspring."

"Wait, let me get this straight… Geneloom was conducting a secret experiment and was in cahoots with Giant Heart to use and manipulate their patients?" It sounded so absurd.

"Yes, but they only took patients eighteen and older since they could legally make their own decisions. The patients who gave consent willingly handed over their reproductive DNA. Some of the women even consented to be surrogates."

I couldn't believe what I was hearing. "Why were the patients agreeing to this?"

"Because Geneloom and Giant Heart were enticing them with money and luxury, the means for a better life."

"I know people do odd things when they're desperate, but this is going too far."

Allen shrugged. "You could say that. But for these patients, it made sense to go along with the experiment. What they had to do was quite harmless in exchange for their freedom and stability."

I shook my head in disbelief. "What about now? You keep talking about this like it happened in the past. Are the companies still working on this experiment? Are they still using these people?"

"No. They only performed three trials before something went terribly wrong. For years, they were prevented from going any further. Now, they're back to phase one, taking blood tests of all Giant Heart patients and using DNA results from Geneloom's customers without their knowing. Their intent is to run the DNA samples through sequences to mutate the genes."

"And if the sequences work, what happens?"

Allen shook his head. "I'm not sure. All their attempts have been unsuccessful. I imagine because whatever extraordinary offspring they're trying to create is unrealistic."

"And they do this all secretly, on the side?"

Allen nodded. "Yes. To the public, both Geneloom and Giant Heart operate normally. No one on the outside knows of their nefarious actions."

"Is there any foul play?"

Allen sighed. "I have no evidence of it, and if there is, it's hard to find. No one talks, and everything is covered up. I know they have a man who takes care of loose ends, only because he's currently after me."

"What do you know about this man?"

Allen grew silent. He clearly had a history with him as his whole demeanor changed. Before, a sense of justice filled his words. Now, it was sadness and revenge.

"I don't know his name. I really don't know anything about him. All I know is that they call him the Sentinel because he's always watching and always ready to take care of business when something goes wrong. In truth, he killed…" Allen stopped, torn up by his emotions. "He killed my brother. We were on a mission." He paused and looked at me, realizing he'd slipped up with his choice of words. "Mission" hinted at some sort of covert operation.

Instead of asking questions, I motioned for him to continue.

"We were on a mission when the Sentinel showed up," Allen said hesitantly. "He obviously found out about what we were doing. When he arrived, he took me off-guard and shot me twice. Once in the leg, once in the side. Then, he went after my brother and shot him square in the chest three times.

"I remember lying on the ground, trying to figure out what happened. All I saw was the brim of his fedora and his black half-face mask. When he realized I wasn't dead, he raised his gold-plated gun to shoot me again, and that was when I noticed his black ring with a gold double helix engraved on it. I shouldn't remember all these details, but when your life flashes before your eyes, you start to focus on the little things.

"Before another shot rang out, I rolled off the side of the cliff we were on and into the sea. Everyone says I shouldn't have survived. But I did, and I know it was for a reason. I have to avenge my brother." He shook his head. "No one supported me. No one listened to me. Some thought I was crazy, perhaps a little too obsessive. But I had four distinct features to help me find the Sentinel. Ever since, I've been following him, and he led me to all this because he secretly works for Geneloom."

A long silence ensued as I processed Allen's words.

Hurriedly, he stood up. "I've said too much, but now you know why you need to take this information to the authorities."

I stood too. "Why can't you?"

"Because I know too much, and the Sentinel is after me."

"Maybe you should stay here. I can watch out for you, and we can go to the authorities together," I suggested.

"No." Allen was adamant. "I cannot put you in harm. Besides, you're my only hope of stopping these people—and they need to be stopped."

"Why me? Why trust me?" I wondered.

"I don't know. My feet led me here, and you seem like a good man." He grabbed at his necklace. "Your name is Michael, and I pray to him all the time."

This was definitely a sign.

I looked down at the files. "This is all your evidence?"

"Yes. It took me a long time to get all of it. I grabbed the last documents this morning, so I haven't had time to go through them all. I'm sure you can figure it out."

I grabbed a pencil and a stack of sticky notes. "Which file haven't you gone through?"

"It was called 'Operation Pure Form.' I think it's essentially what I've told you, but it wouldn't hurt to look."

I jotted the name down and stuck it to the folders. "I know you have to go, but is there anything else I should know?" I asked.

Allen wracked his brain for any other information. "The only thing I haven't told you about is one reported incident of something that went wrong, but the documentation of it is incomplete, probably on purpose."

"What went wrong?"

"I'm not entirely sure. It was during the trial experiments, but I know whatever happened made them stop and change their operation. Jazema Grigori was in charge of Geneloom, and she needed a doctor for the trial experiments, so she hired Dr. Salma Amir, a reproductive geneticist. Parvati Irin, the owner of Giant Heart, approved of Grigori's choice, and so the secret experiment began. But Amir didn't know what Grigori and Irin intended. At the time, Giant Heart had a small number of patients. They only needed five willing participants, so this didn't matter, but something triggered Irin to eventually volunteer herself for the trial as well.

"By then, Amir had found out about what they were doing and planned to stop it. That was when something went terribly wrong. Like I said, the documentation is incomplete. All I know is, Amir and Irin died in a lab accident. After that, Grigori remained in charge of Geneloom and led it to where it is today. She recruited her sister, Penelope Grigori, to take charge of Giant Heart."

I was frozen in place. The names Grigori and Irin were far too coincidental—and I didn't believe in coincidences. Quickly, I searched through the files on my desk for the new one Allen had found: "Operation Pure Form." I opened the folder and briefly scanned through the top page until I saw four words I was dreading to find.

The Nephilim. The Watchers.

"Are you all right?" Allen asked.

I looked up at him. "Yes, it's just a lot to take in."

He nodded in agreement, then said quickly, "I'd better leave now."

"Wait." I strode over to him and plucked a jacket and a baseball cap from the coat rack. "Take these. They'll help draw less attention."

He put them on. "Thanks."

After he left, I stared at the door and tried so badly not to question Father's command not to act. But it was hard to follow such an order in times like these, when fate had brought Allen to me, and Allen had led me to the Nephilim and the Watchers.

JORDAN

32

New York City, Present Day

I gaped at Michael after he finished his story. I didn't know who the Nephilim and the Watchers were, but I knew what they were doing was dreadful. It must have been hard for Michael to carry the burden alone for so long.

"Did you send the papers to the authorities?" Gabriel asked.

"Yes, but I kept the last file to myself. No human would understand the information inside."

"Rightfully so," Uriel agreed. "I can't even comprehend how the Nephilim have survived, let alone a human trying to fathom what they are."

Michael nodded. "Without those names, Grigori and Irin, I wouldn't have suspected anything. But I know those are other names for the Watchers, which means the Nephilim have not only created fake identities but are using these names as a way to glorify their forefathers."

Quickly, I interrupted. "Wait! Can we stop for a second? I'm so confused." They were flinging around cryptic words in every sentence, and it was becoming impossible to keep up.

"Where would you like us to start?" Zadkiel asked.

"The Nephilim. What are they? What's their history?"

"The Nephilim are half-human, half-angel," Zadkiel supplied. "Their fathers were a group of angels called the Watchers who were sent to Earth to teach humans. Instead, they became infatuated with women and committed the most forbidden sin any angel could: reproducing with humanity. Father was so angry, He locked them out of Heaven and sent the Flood to destroy them. Apparently, it didn't work. Now, the Watchers and the Nephilim are considered fallen angels even though they didn't fall with Satan."

"That's the problem," Michael interrupted. "To our knowledge, Satan never fraternized with the Nephilim because he considered them beneath him. But I have evidence they're forming an alliance."

"What evidence?" Raphael asked.

"The papers Allen Clark gave to me. There were old appointment logs documenting Jazema Grigori's meetings. Twice a month, she met with a man named Luc Helton, and now, she only meets with him once a year. One log noted Mr. Helton acts on the behalf of Samuel Cross. When I saw that, I knew these men must be Satan and Lucifer. There were even financial records showing a connection, as technological assets from Geneloom were gifted to Mr. Cross, which might explain how Satan got hold of the tracker technology."

"Was there anything else you discovered?" Gabriel asked.

"Not really. I delivered Allen's papers to the authorities in New York shortly after he gave them to me, but they haven't been able to stop the Nephilim."

"Why not?" I asked.

"Well, they're superhuman for one, and not in a good way. The

Nephilim look like humans so they blend in, but they have the strength and aptitude of angels. This makes them super-efficient at evading human tactics. Publicly, they're not doing anything illegal, which makes it difficult for the authorities to investigate them."

"But surely all the evidence Allen gathered allowed them to make a case?" Uriel said.

Michael sighed. "It should have, but it went missing. Just like Allen. I imagine the Sentinel had something to do with that."

Sensing his brother's grief, Gabriel said, "Michael, there's not much more you could have done. You listened to Allen. You did what he asked. It's not your fault the Nephilim have some powerful, ruthless man working for them."

"I know," Michael said, "but I should have tried to stop him. The Sentinel, I mean."

"Stopping the Sentinel seems impossible unless you're prepared to do…well, you know, something you wouldn't normally do." Uriel was clearly hinting at some lethal act.

Outraged, Michael shot back, "You know I would never resort to such a thing."

"Exactly, so stop beating yourself up."

"Why would the Nephilim even start this operation in the first place?" I asked.

"Because they want to continue on their ancestors' legacy, which was to procreate with humans. With modern technology and medical procedures, they have been able to do so synthetically," Michael said.

"It's still atrocious," Chamuel cut in. "I know you said these patients gave consent, but it sounds like they were manipulated."

Michael nodded. "I agree."

"Surely not all the Nephilim are a part of this?" Raphael asked.

"No, but the majority of them. Those involved in this operation tell the tales of their ancestors and pass along the idea their duty is to achieve a pure form."

"What's that supposed to mean?" I asked.

"The Watchers were angels, meaning they were heavenly and created of light energy," Michael explained. "The Nephilim consider this a pure form because much of their species is now tainted by genetic abnormalities. For instance, they no longer have wings, and their angelic aptitudes are diminishing. The original Nephilim born of the Watchers all had angelic aptitudes because their fathers' blood was so potent, but the Nephilim's blood has been diluted over the years. That's why Geneloom has been studying genetics and mutating genes, to learn how to recreate the old genetic markers."

"I see." I was overwhelmed by all this information. "And the women in charge are Nephilim?"

"I believe so." Michael's jaw tightened at the thought. "Which means they will not stop until they get what they want."

"They obviously have doctors and scientists working for them, but how did they convince them to participate in their plan?" Jophiel asked.

"From what I can tell," Michael said, "most of the human doctors and scientists don't know about the operation's true intentions. However, Geneloom tries to use Nephilim doctors and scientists as much as possible. Like I told you, they have blended into society, so the twenty-year-olds are going to college like any normal human. They're learning the science and medicine they need in order to conduct these experiments."

"These papers," Jophiel said. "Do you still have them, other than the file you kept?"

"I gave the originals to the authorities and made copies for myself. In fact, I kept sending copies to the authorities, but they kept going missing, so I stopped. I have them with me now."

"Good. I want to take a look at their research. Maybe I can figure something out, like a way to eradicate them completely. I'm no scientist, but it's worth a try." Jophiel shrugged.

"Sure, you can take a look. But I already know they haven't been successful at finding a way to create their pure form."

"How do you know that?" Chamuel asked.

"Well, Allen told me so, but also because they're increasing their efforts to find the Watchers."

"Wait, I thought you said God sent the Flood to destroy them?" I cut in.

"He did, but it didn't work. The Flood eliminated all the Nephilim at the time and most of the Watchers, but three Watchers survived. I don't know how they made it through that deluge—they must have hidden themselves. Centuries after the Flood, they resurfaced and started reproducing again, which is how the Nephilim are still among us today. Now, the Nephilim idolize these three and believe them to be their most powerful forefathers.

"Several years ago, Father somehow found these three Watchers and imprisoned them, but He couldn't do anything about the Nephilim. Humankind was too far advanced, and another apocalyptic event would have sent the whole world back, so He had to let them be. I guess He thought they would eventually weaken since they keep mixing their genes with humans.

"Anyway, since their efforts with genetic testing are not proving successful, the Nephilim are trying to find the three remaining Watchers. They want to free them to restore their powerful legacy. I know they haven't come far in their search because they believe the Book of Prophecies can tell them the location of their forefathers."

"Does the Book of Prophecies contain such information?" Uriel asked. "I thought it only held prophecies."

Zadkiel sighed. "The Book of Prophecies is a complicated tome of divine wisdoms. Its primary purpose is to hold prophecies, but Father told us other information is also contained within. It's quite possible the location of the Watchers is documented in there."

"Is this where Satan comes in?" I asked. All this talk of power seemed similar to his aims.

"Not exactly. Satan isn't involved in their operation or their efforts to find the Watchers."

"Then, how did their relationship originate?" Gabriel asked.

"I'm not entirely sure. All I know is that since Satan has been trapped in Hell, he's needed someone to provide him with information. The Six can only do so much. They don't have the human connections the Nephilim do."

"You mean, the dark and crooked ones?" I confirmed.

Michael nodded.

"So, Satan is using the Nephilim to give him information?" Chamuel asked.

"Precisely."

"If Satan's getting information, what are the Nephilim getting in return?" Raphael asked.

Michael shrugged. "Favor…trust…even more power. Who really knows?"

"In essence, they're forming an alliance, much like Michael predicted," Zadkiel said.

"Yes, but for what?" Chamuel wondered. "I understand they can feed off one another, but to what gain?"

The conclusion seemed clear. "War." I stared blankly ahead as the word left my mouth.

They all focused on me.

"That backpack," I said, pointing to the tattered bag on top of the kitchen table, "is what everyone is chasing after. If the Book of Prophecies is in there, it's needed in order to fulfill everyone's end game. And Zadkiel said it caused a war once—why not start one again, but on Earth this time?"

"The kid has a point. They could be forming an alliance not only for what they can get from each other, but to create an army with even more power than the one that struck us in Heaven," Uriel said with a note of danger.

"What's our next move then?" Raphael asked.

"About that…" I said, grabbing the angels' attention. "I wanted to go find my friend. She's the only one who might know where Sister Helen is, and if we can somehow get in contact with her, we might be able to warn her about Satan and find out some more answers. Specifically, about the key to open the backpack."

"Jordan, I'm not sure that's the best plan. Sister Helen said in her letter not to go looking for her, and I'm sure she knows Satan is still a threat," Gabriel pointed out.

"I know, but how do you expect us to move on?" I realized "us" really meant "me." Sister Helen was like my mother. Sophia was like a sister. I hadn't heard from either of them in months, and it was driving me insane. Plus, knowing Sister Helen could be in danger meant I had to find her no matter what she wrote in that letter.

Before I could say anything else, Gabriel continued. "Besides, if you go to see your friend, you might unintentionally involve her in all this. The fallen are powerful. More powerful than any of us expected. There's no telling what danger that might put her in."

I opened my mouth to protest, but no words came out. I had no argument. I would never want to put Sophia in harm's way.

"I see your point," I managed eventually. "What *is* our next step then?"

"Opening that backpack," Michael said.

"How do you suggest we do that?" Zadkiel asked.

"By force," Uriel suggested, approaching the bag.

Jophiel was alarmed. "No! We can't jeopardize damaging the lock. Whatever is inside might be stuck in there forever if we do that."

"Then, what?" Uriel was exasperated.

"We find the key," Gabriel said calmly.

"How?" I asked.

"By going to your house."

"My house?" I didn't understand. "You mean, the orphanage? It burnt down, Gabriel."

"I mean the house your parents left you," he clarified.

I grew silent. Seven pairs of expectant eyes watched me, trying to determine my reaction.

"Why should we go there?" I asked quietly.

"Sister Helen knew you would be able to open the backpack, but she didn't give you the key. However, she did leave you the house key, so I wonder if she put the key to the lock there."

Gabriel had a point. I chewed on my lip as he went on.

"Second, I don't think we can stay here. There's not enough room."

"And the fallen don't know about your house, so they won't be able to find us," Michael said. "I know Gabriel sanctified this place, but that's not a foolproof plan."

"Is this why you all want me to rest so much? So you can devise plans and talk about me behind my back?" I was upset, and I had every right to be. I trusted the angels. The fact they were scheming behind my back, especially about this, felt like a betrayal.

"Jordan, be reasonable. You know that's not true," Gabriel said.

"Really? You should know how hard this is for me, Gabriel."

Quiet fell over the room. I wasn't entirely sure why I was so hesitant to go to my family home. Deep down, I suspected it had to do with the memories hidden there, a history I had never been a part of. The house was a living reminder of the parents I had never known. Going there meant facing the life I was supposed to have. A life I buried long ago.

There was also a great deal of guilt involved. I was the reason for my mother's death. I knew it was silly to blame myself, but I always had. As for my father, I had no idea how he died. All I knew was that my mother and I were robbed of his presence before I was even born.

Thinking about my parents made me realize how little I really knew about the beginning of my life. Most orphans at Holy Trinity had suffered from the same unknown, and in comparison, I was one of the fortunate ones. I had discovered who my parents were and now had access to all the things they had left behind. Going to the house might be uncomfortable, but it would deliver answers others weren't so fortunate to have.

Coming to terms with Gabriel's decision, I finally said, "Okay. We'll go there."

"You're sure?" Gabriel asked. "I don't want to upset you."

"Really, it's fine. I'm sorry for the way I reacted. It's a touchy subject, that's all. Besides, the sooner we settle in one place, the better off we'll be. Information is being thrown around everywhere, but if we just had time to think things through logically, we might get ahead of the fallen rather than being two steps behind."

"He has a point," Uriel said.

Everyone nodded in agreement.

"All right then. We'll leave the day after tomorrow," Gabriel decided.

"Why not tomorrow?" Zadkiel asked.

"Because my car only fits four, maybe five people. We'll need another vehicle to get us all to the house."

"Then, it's settled. Tomorrow, we'll find another suitable vehicle, and the day after, we'll leave for Jordan's house," Michael announced.

With the plans in place, the angels all found ways to keep busy—packing, cleaning up, watching the news, looking for places to buy a car. I retreated to the guest room before realizing I had absolutely no idea where my parents' house was.

"Gabriel, where exactly are we going?"

"New York State," he replied.

All my life, I'd never known I was so close to home.

JORDAN

33

NEW YORK STATE, PRESENT DAY

It was a four-hour drive from the city to my house. I sat in the backseat of Gabriel's Mercedes G-Class with Chamuel, and Zadkiel took the passenger seat. The others drove behind in a Ford Transit van that easily fit fifteen. Right now, it was full of luggage and four angels.

I was nervous and on-edge, struggling to hide my true emotions. Despite being grateful for everything, I still couldn't wrap my head around the fact I was going to my parents' house. It was located just outside Ithaca, New York, on Cayuga Lake. I didn't expect a gated lakeside mansion, but sure enough, when we arrived, that was what stood before us.

Gabriel stopped the car in front of the gate and lowered his window to peer at the intercom. "Do you have a code?" he asked.

I stared at him. "You know Sister Helen only left a house key. There was no code."

"Now what?" Chamuel asked with a sigh.

Gabriel reached out and pressed the large button, which apparently called the house. We all heard it ring. Tension was thick in the car as we waited for someone to answer.

The sound of a horn honking behind made me jump. I turned around to see the others clearly confused. It seemed Uriel's impatience had triggered the horn, as Michael was pushing his arm away from the steering wheel.

Finally, the ringing stopped, and a woman's breathless voice answered, "Hello? Can I help you?"

We were all so shocked, it took Gabriel a second to respond. "Yes… My name is Gabriel, and I have Jordan Conway here in the car with me. We were hoping you'd let us in."

Silence.

"Ma'am, are you still there?"

"Let me see him," came the abrupt reply.

When Gabriel gave me a look, I lowered my window and stuck my head out since we were obviously being watched by some hidden camera.

The call went dead.

"Excuse me? Hello?" he said into the intercom

A buzzing and the squeak of the front gates grabbed everyone's attention.

Gabriel closed his window and put the car into drive, entering through the gates and continuing up the driveway. The others followed. As the enormous house came into full view, he made a slight right where the driveway turned into a roundabout and parked the car.

The others began to get out of their vehicle, but I remained motionless as the angels left Gabriel's car. I stared through the window at the small decorative fountain in the center of the roundabout. No water ran through it because it was too cold. I fumbled the house key around in my coat pocket, unsure of how to proceed.

"Are we just going to stand here all evening?" I heard Uriel ask.

"Uriel, this is obviously very upsetting. He needs to do things at his own pace," Chamuel chastised.

"I understand, but it's freezing out here."

Nerves swallowing the sound of whatever they said next, I slowly opened my door and stepped out of the car. Gravel crunched under my feet as I approached the front door. The small pebbles of rock gave way to concrete when I entered the round portico, the door itself tall and wooden with a black knocker. I swallowed the massive lump in my throat and reached for it, yet the door swiftly opened before me.

An older woman, her hair completely gray and her eyes crystal blue, stood on the other side. She wore trousers and a blouse with a brilliant light blue sweater. Her warm face and kind smile seemed so familiar.

Before I could speak, she raised a hand to her mouth and said, with tears in her eyes, "You look so much like them."

"And you look like Sister Helen."

She laughed. "I guess I should. I am her sister."

I was shocked. "Sister Helen never told me she had a sister."

"I bet she didn't. Helen always was a secret-keeper." The woman reached out her hand and smiled. "I'm Martha, the housekeeper."

"Jordan," I said, shaking her hand. "But I think you know that."

She nodded and took a step back into the house. "Let's get you all in out of the cold so you can introduce me to your angel friends." When we all stopped, she added, "Oh, please. Helen might not tell me things, but I know enough."

I looked at the angels, who shrugged. Together, we entered the foyer, and I felt my parents' presence immediately. The interior was absolutely breathtaking. I could only imagine what the rest of the house looked like.

What I thought was a portico was actually a turret, and we were standing in the middle of its rounded shape. Looking up at the ceiling, I saw the roof topped off in a peak, and windows graced the uppermost section, allowing natural light to flow below. At my feet, three shades of marble joined together to create the design of a compass. A spacious hallway led to the back of the house, and to my right and left were more hallways leading further in. The banister on the grand spiraling staircase was ornately decorated, and paintings and artwork were placed all over.

"Welcome home," Martha said. "Please excuse the slight mess." She retrieved a feather duster from a table near the door. "And apologies for making you wait so long. I was doing some cleaning upstairs when you called, and the intercom phone is in the mudroom."

I gazed around, marveling at the grandness, but nothing seemed messy or unclean.

"Make yourselves comfortable. You can hang your coats by the door." Martha indicated a coat rack.

I shrugged off my jacket and hung it up.

"Oh, dear!" Martha was alarmed. "What happened to you?"

My injuries were healing, but it was a slow process. "The fallen," I told her.

"They did this to you? Oh, goodness me. I'd curse Satan right now, but given our present company, I'll refrain." She came closer to inspect the cut on my face.

Behind her, all the angels grinned, a sign they definitely approved of Martha.

"Who stitched you up?"

"Raphael," I said.

She took her attention away from me to look at him. "Nice work."

"Were you a doctor?" he asked.

"No, I was a nurse. As you can imagine, I've seen a lot."

"I bet. When did you change professions?"

"Gosh, well…a long time ago now. I was forty-five when I stopped nursing and took the position here. It's been eighteen years since then."

"You've worked here my entire life?" I asked.

"Yes, I have, and I won't stop until the day I die."

Her commitment was astonishing. "Thank you," I whispered.

She put a hand on my cheek. "You're welcome." Then, she turned back to the angels. "Now, who are the rest of you?"

They went about introducing themselves.

"It's a pleasure to meet you all. I guess I'll let you settle in. I can show you the house, if you want?"

"That would be great, Martha." Gabriel placed a hand on my shoulder. "We'll make sure all the luggage gets inside while you look around."

They retreated back outside.

I turned to Martha. "Would you mind if I looked around by myself?"

"Not at all. Let me know if you need anything." With a smile, she walked down the hall to my left and disappeared.

Alone, I let my feet take over. Following the direction Martha went, I passed through a formal sitting room adjacent to the foyer. From there, I discovered the living room, dining room, and eat-in kitchen, each branching off from the other.

In the kitchen, Martha was taking inventory of the pantry. I noticed there was a back staircase leading to the second floor, which would be great for late-night snacking or sneaking around. The living room boasted a sixty-inch flat-screen TV that could be hidden behind a painting at the touch of a button, and the dining room table could easily seat sixteen.

The entire right side of the house was designated as the library, a space so large and filled with so many books it spanned several rooms. Zadkiel would love it. I discovered another room attached to it, but it was locked, so I couldn't go in. I thought this was strange, but I kept moving.

From the library, I found another set of stairs and went down. The lower level had doors right out onto the back lawn and an incredible view of the lake and gardens. There was also a gym and another locked room on this floor, but I was so overwhelmed by everything else I didn't have the focus to wonder where it might lead.

Retracing my steps, and slightly concerned I could actually get lost in this labyrinth of a house, I reached the bottom of another set of stairs. I'd saved this part for last because I knew my parents' room must be up here as well as mine. Taking a deep breath, I went up.

The staircase brought me to a hallway with a series of doors that led to guest rooms, all lavishly comfortable but lacking a personal touch. All except for Martha's suite. Coming out of this hallway, I found myself in a common room with another entertainment setup. I gazed out the window at the front drive.

My internal compass registered I had just investigated the upper-left side of the house. If all the guest rooms were here, that meant the family rooms were on the right. Turning myself in that direction,

I stared down the hallway at a lone door. It struck me as odd that it was the only room in sight. I wondered if it was theirs, or mine.

Inching slowly down to the door, I placed my hand on the curved knob and dropped my forehead to the wood. I could no longer hold everything in. Tears streamed down my face.

Intuitively, from that brief touch of polished metal, I knew what stood beyond the door, and I wasn't prepared to face it. Not yet.

It was their room.

Releasing the knob, I backed away and brushed at my cheeks. Caught up in my own nerves, I hadn't seen the small set of spiral stairs winding up from the hallway. Placing my foot on the first step, I started up.

At the top of the short stairway was a wooden door with the letter "J" carved in it. Automatically, my fingers traced the swooping curve. I wasn't expecting a queen-size bed and furnishings for an adult, but this room was unmistakably mine. All the things I had ever wanted, wished, or dreamed for as a child had been magically placed inside the room: a bay window with a reading nook, a TV room attached in a small alcove, a private bathroom with a huge shower, all the books, movies, and music I'd ever been interested in. Everything my heart desired.

I knew this wasn't the work of my parents. This had Sister Helen and Martha written all over it.

A knock at the door drew me away from my thoughts.

"Sorry to interrupt," Gabriel said. "I figured you'd want this." He placed my duffel on the floor.

"Thanks. What about the backpack?"

"No longer your burden. Now we're here, Zadkiel is determined more than ever to open that thing. He already has Jophiel analyzing the lock."

"Good." A thought hit me. "I'm sorry. Did you all settle in? I kind of just left you."

"No worries. Martha helped us, and we settled in just fine. Zadkiel and Jophiel are holed away in the library, Chamuel is in the kitchen, Raphael is setting up an infirmary downstairs, Michael is inspecting the gym, and Uriel is exploring around outside."

I laughed. "I thought he was cold."

Gabriel smiled. "I think he wanted you to get on with facing your past."

"That sounds like Uriel. What about you?" I wondered. "Have you found a place for yourself?"

"Oh, yes. I find the sitting room quite nice. There's also a music room with a piano where I'll probably spend most of my time."

"There is? I guess I haven't seen everything."

Gabriel chuckled. "Well, it's hard to do in a house this big. By the way, we've claimed some bedrooms to store our things in, retreat to, and freshen up. I hope that's okay with you?"

"Of course. It's comforting to know I won't be up here alone."

Gabriel put a hand on my shoulder. "You'll get through this. And we'll be here, no matter what."

"I know." I smiled. "Thanks."

"Gabriel!" Zadkiel shouted. "Where are you?"

Gabriel dropped his hand and went down to the hall. I followed after him.

"What is it?"

"There's been a development with the lock."

"Did you open it?"

"No. It's hard to explain. Come see!"

JORDAN

NEW YORK STATE, PRESENT DAY

34

"The guys filled me in about the backpack. There was no way I was going to miss this," Martha said as we entered the library, where the others had all gathered.

Gabriel and I smiled and joined them around a wooden table strewn with books.

"What did you find?" I asked.

"At first glance," Jophiel began, "this device appears to be a normal lock. However, on closer inspection, I discovered this." He pressed his finger into the bottom of the lock, morphing it into a triangular shape.

"How did you do that?" Michael asked.

"Easy. What we thought was the keyhole is actually a button that, when pressed properly and with enough force, transforms the object into its rightful shape."

I drew closer to get a better look.

"What does this mean?" Uriel asked.

"It means the lock doesn't open with a traditional key," Raphael said.

I groaned. "I thought the key would be easy to find because it would look like this." I pulled the house key out of my pocket. "Now, it's some wacky, unique…impression thing?" I fumbled for the words because it was hard to describe exactly what we had to look for. The lock had completely flattened into a triangle. The device had an indentation with a sort of pattern on it, presumably where the key was to be inserted, but it seemed intricate.

"I said there had been a development. I didn't say it was a good one," Zadkiel said.

I sighed. "So, we're back to square one?"

"Pretty much," Jophiel said.

"Well, I see this as a good thing," Martha offered.

We all stared at her, dumbfounded.

"What? At least you know what key shape you're looking for now."

I embraced her optimism since it was all we had, but the fact she didn't know where the key was probably meant it wasn't in the house. "So, the key isn't here?" I asked her.

She shrugged. "I don't know. It could be. There are so many keys hidden in this house, it's a mystery it hasn't turned into a lock shop."

She chuckled at her own joke, but I was confused. "What do you mean?"

"I'm sure you found the locked rooms," she said.

I nodded, remembering the one downstairs and the door in this very library.

"I haven't found the keys for them yet. Your parents hid them so no one could get in."

"Why would they do that?" Michael asked, detecting suspicious behavior.

"I'm not entirely sure. All I know is, the room over there"—she pointed to the other side of the library—"was your father's office. The locked room downstairs was your mother's studio."

"Studio?" I asked.

"Yes, your mother was a painter. Not professionally, but she could have been. Most of the pictures in the house are hers."

I never knew my mother had such talent. The new knowledge brought a smile to my face.

"The only other room that was locked was the wine cellar," Martha continued, "but I managed to find that key. Believe me, it was no easy feat—step on this floorboard, touch this piece of paneling, and then, voila! A secret compartment popped out of the shelf. The only reason I managed that was because I got tangled up in the vacuum cord and nearly fell down." She chuckled at the memory.

We all stared as she told her bizarre story. A few of us couldn't help but laugh along.

"Anyway," she went on, "my point is, Helen likely wouldn't have hidden the key here because she knows how impossible it is to find the secret compartments."

I sighed, defeated.

"This shape seems so familiar," Gabriel interrupted.

"How so?" Zadkiel asked.

"The triangular form. It reminds me of something, but I can't figure out what."

"The shape is appropriate," Jophiel said. "I mean, Sister Helen must have put this lock on the bag if she wanted Jordan to open it, and the fact she worked at Holy Trinity brings to mind triangular symbolism."

I turned to Martha. "Do you know anything about this?"

"Not really. I'm not a member of the Sacrarium, though I know more than the average person. Helen never confided in me as a matter of protection, but you gather a little here and there from overheard conversations."

Gabriel nodded in understanding.

"There is a tiered ranking system within the Sacrarium to determine how much each member knows," she explained.

"Like a hierarchy?" Michael asked.

"Exactly," Martha responded. "The highest classification is Alpha, otherwise known as the Head of the Sacrarium. There is only one Alpha, and Helen is it. She distributes information to members and hardly tells anyone of her plans unless necessary. The second classification is Beta, and these members are typically the ones Helen interacts with the most, informing them of almost everything and giving them covert duties. The third classification is Gamma. They are informed on a need-to-know basis and are only called upon when needed.

"Finally, the lowest classification is Novice. A Novice is someone who has not yet taken the sacred oath to protect the bloodline. They are taught rudimentary information to prepare for their oath-taking. One must be a Novice for five years before they can take the oath. This ensures they are dedicated and trustworthy. The Sacrarium hardly ever gets Novices nowadays. Numbers have been dwindling over the years."

"All of this to say you don't know about the backpack?" Jophiel clarified.

"Yes." Martha nodded.

I let out a breath. "So, Sister Helen is in charge of the Sacrarium?"

She nodded again.

This didn't surprise me. Leadership was a natural trait of Sister Helen's.

Martha must have detected our low spirits. "I will do whatever I can to help you find the key. Who knows, Helen may have hidden it here. She certainly is not predictable and would resort to any means necessary to protect something so important."

"It's in this house, I know it," I said.

"Why do you think that?" Chamuel asked.

"Because…" It was hard to explain. "A gut feeling, I guess."

"Maybe you should look around your room," Martha suggested. "When Helen visits, she always makes sure to check on it."

"Why?"

"I think because she always thought you would come back here one day, so she wanted your room to be perfect."

"Well, if Sister Helen wanted me to find this key, and she was in my room, that's the place it's most likely to be."

I left everyone in the library and started back upstairs, but instead of going straight to my room, the lone door at the end of the hall seemed to call me toward it. I knew I had to find the key, but my curiosity got the better of me. Approaching my parents' door this time, I didn't hesitate to twist the knob and step inside.

Upon first inspection, it seemed like any other room, with a king-size bed, master bath, and a couple of dressers. It was the personal touches that made it unique to my parents. Trinket boxes, jewelry, and candles adorned the top of one dresser, while a pair of glasses, a watch, and other mementos covered the other. The four-poster bed was neatly made, with decorative pillows and an ornate bedspread.

Each end table had a clock, one modern and masculine, the other ornamental and feminine. A book sat beside each, bookmarks still in place. In the sitting area, a small table strewn with various magazines was flanked by lounge chairs and ottomans.

Stepping into the bathroom, I found two separate vanities containing the usual objects: toothbrushes, toothpaste, a razor, hairbrushes, cologne, and perfume. The closet was enormous, divided into two sides. Perusing through my father's side, I knew I'd inherited his organizational habits. His clothes were neatly hung and his shoes all in a line but with no clear organization. Opposite, my mother had color-coded her shoes and attire, even sorting items by tops and bottoms. Nothing was out of place.

I reached out each hand to touch my father's shirt and my mother's dress. This was the first time ever we were all in the same space, our energies mixing as one. At some point in my life, I would have to deal with moving their stuff, but right now, I just wanted to cherish everything. I didn't want to move the books or touch the trinkets on the dresser because that was the way they had left them, and I didn't want to give up this feeling of oneness, this feeling of finally belonging. It might be the only connection I would ever have to my parents.

Having relished in the feeling for a while, I ascended the stairs that led to my room and went straight to my duffel bag in search of the envelope. Grabbing at the plastic bag inside, I sat down on the area rug and pried it open.

I had to see their faces. I had to know who they were.

Shuffling through the pile of photographs, I found pictures of my parents' lives, from the time they took their first steps, to the lazy childhood summers and their graduation. It was apparent my mom and dad had known each other when they were young because many of the pictures featured them together as children. I realized they were high-school sweethearts.

The photos afforded me more than just a glimpse into their younger years. They also revealed my grandparents, aunts, and uncles. I didn't know if any of my parents' siblings were still alive but I guessed not, because if they were, I probably would have been sent to live with them instead of at the orphanage.

The next pile revealed my parents' college years. My dad had attended Harvard, and my mom went to Cornell. I was surprised since I would be attending the same school in two years' time. It was nice to know we shared something in common other than our DNA.

As I shuffled through the pictures, I eventually stumbled upon their wedding photo. The two gazed at each other with so much love and happiness in their eyes. Another series of photos featured them on their travels to various places throughout the U.S. and the world.

What halted my progress was a close-up of them sitting in the garden. I looked so much like my mother. I had her auburn hair, though mine was much darker and wavier rather than curly. My facial features were exactly like hers, especially when she smiled. I hadn't inherited her brown eyes though. I had my father's green ones, the intensity of the color an exact match to mine. He had dark blond hair and seemed quite tall even though he was sitting. I'd apparently inherited his height too, since I was almost six foot. His smile was just as happy and radiant as my mother's. You could tell they truly loved each other.

As this was the last picture in the pile, I stared at it for a little longer, absorbing more of the details. I noticed the ring my father wore, the one I now had and never took off, and I grabbed at the cross around my neck, discovering it was the one my mother had on in the photo. This offered me another sense of comfort, knowing I now possessed objects my parents had worn and touched every day.

Their jewelry made me think about the fleur-de-lis necklace. I reached for my duffel and pulled out the necklace, carefully examining the simple medium-sized pendant. I had worn this necklace almost my entire life and only taken it off when my ignorance put Sister Helen in danger. But she was the one who gave it to me in the first place, and discarding it so easily felt like a betrayal to her.

I rubbed my finger against the smooth metal as I tried to think like Sister Helen and figure out where she might have hidden the key. My fingers froze. There was nothing peculiar about the necklace. However, there was nothing peculiar about the lock at first glance either. It was only when Jophiel applied pressure that it morphed into its true form.

Opening the clasp, I slid the pendant off the chain and pressed down on the top point. Nothing happened. I applied more pressure. Again, nothing happened. I did the same on the two other ends and still, no results. I peered down at the pendant again. Pressing my thumb to the bottom of the fleur-de-lis, I applied as much force as I could.

Still nothing.

Maybe this isn't the key after all.

I brushed my finger over the smooth surface again. As my thumb grazed the straight bracket near the bottom of the fleur-de-lis, the metal moved inward slightly. I applied more pressure to the area and suddenly heard a metallic click as the pendant transformed into a triangle. Shocked, I stared at it in disbelief before realizing I had to go tell the others.

Jumping to my feet, I raced downstairs. "I did it! I found the key!"

The angels all turned as I entered the library.

"Where's Martha?"

"She went to the store for some groceries," Gabriel said slowly, his attention focused on the key in my hand.

I approached them. "Oh…well, I guess we can fill her in later."

"Where did you find that?" Zadkiel asked.

"I had it all along, I just didn't realize."

"What do you mean?" Jophiel stepped forward.

I looked at Gabriel. "The fleur-de-lis necklace. Sister Helen gave it to me when I was a kid. I never took it off until the fallen chased me in New York. I thought wearing it would cause more problems. But it was the key all along!"

Understanding dawned on Gabriel's face. "What made you figure that out?"

I told them about my parents' room, how exploring it had made me want to search through the pictures, and the pictures reminded me of the necklace from Sister Helen.

"At first, I thought I was wrong because I pressed on every end and nothing happened. But then I pushed in the middle bracket that runs across all three points, and it transformed into that," I said, indicating the triangular key piece Zadkiel now held.

"Don't you think it's time we open the backpack then?" Uriel asked.

Zadkiel glared at him. "You have no sense of what this will mean. The magnitude of it."

"Oh, trust me, I do," Uriel assured him. "I just can't take the suspense anymore."

"Me neither," Michael confessed.

Not delaying the inevitable any longer, Jophiel brought the backpack over to where we all stood and placed it on the table in front of Zadkiel. The angel of teaching picked up the transformed lock and ceremoniously fit the key into the grooves. A metallic click filled the room as the gears inside turned about. Ending in a resounding tick, the latch sprung open.

We all stood frozen and silent.

Zadkiel slowly took the lock in his hand and slid it out from the zippers. He carefully placed it on the table and brought his attention back to the bag. Grasping a zipper in each hand, he opened the backpack and placed his hands inside. We could all tell when he latched onto something because the muscles in his arms flexed as he drew the object out.

And then, there it was, right before our eyes.

The book was thick and old. A light shimmered about the gold-plated cover, revealing its divineness. There were symbols on the front, but I didn't know what they signified.

When I spied a latch on the side of it, I was disappointed, thinking it required another key, but when Zadkiel clicked the fastener, it opened.

My relief didn't last long.

Zadkiel fastened the latch once again and placed the book on the table, drawing his attention back to the bag.

"What are you doing?" I asked.

"There's something else inside." Reaching back into the very bottom of the backpack, he fumbled around until his hand caught onto a circular ball of black stone, about the size of a grapefruit.

"Is that what I think it is?" Chamuel asked.

I looked around at the angels, who had all grown quiet and fearful.

"The black onyx sphere," Jophiel whispered.

"That's a sphere?" I was surprised one of the all-powerful objects was in our possession.

They ignored me—not because they didn't want to validate my question, but because they were all so shocked at the sight of it.

I looked around the room at the rings they all wore, trying to figure out who this sphere belonged to. "Whose is it?"

"It's Satan's," Michael answered.

I did a double-take. "Excuse me? This is Satan's sphere?"

"Yes," Zadkiel confirmed.

"And I was carrying it around all this time? No wonder he wanted my head! I had his most valuable possession."

"It makes sense now why the energy radiating off the backpack was so peculiar," Jophiel said, analyzing the sphere from a distance.

"What do you mean?"

"Well, we all knew the book gave off a powerful energy, but the energy we sensed coming from the backpack was much more…potent."

"This can't be good," I said. "Right?"

"You're absolutely right, Jordan," Zadkiel said. "What worries me the most is that someone unearthed it with the intention for us to have it. The gravity of this situation is far more significant than we realized."

"There's only one thing that could mean," Uriel said.

I looked around at them. "Which is…?"

"Satan intends to perform the Union, and there are far more forces involved than we realized." Michael approached the table, eyeing the book but setting his sights on the sphere. He took it out of Zadkiel's hand. "We need to retrieve them…all of them, before he gets out of control."

"That will never happen," Raphael said. "Father put procedures in place to prevent Satan from getting to the spheres."

"Yes. The keys being one of them," Gabriel said.

"I understand." Michael's brow creased. "But Satan has outsmarted us." He paused. "And outsmarted Father for centuries."

"Meaning?" Chamuel asked.

"We need to prepare for war."

JORDAN
35
NEW YORK STATE, PRESENT DAY

I had come to the same conclusion at Gabriel's apartment, but hearing the words from Michael made the situation all the more real. He was an angel of power, one of Heaven's warriors. If he said war was coming, it was.

"Who would have unlocked Satan's sphere and given it to the Sacrarium?" I asked.

That gave them a moment of pause.

"I don't know. Unless there's another one of us from the council here on Earth," Gabriel suggested.

Michael scoffed. "I highly doubt that. None of them would come here unless it was under extreme—and I mean *extreme*—circumstances."

"Aren't these extreme enough?" I asked.

"No, trust me. Not for them," Michael assured me.

"Well then, who?" Gabriel wondered.

Michael hesitated. "I don't know."

"And for that reason, we need to figure out what's inside this book," Uriel said.

"Agreed. It may contain all the answers." Zadkiel reached for it.

I moved to get closer as the angels watched with grave expressions. They were afraid to open it. Afraid to reveal its secrets.

Zadkiel placed both hands on the book and opened the cover. As he carefully turned the pages, a hush fell over the room. "The Union of the Spheres," he read aloud, admiring the prophecy everyone sought.

I felt like I was on the inside of an angel sandwich as they all crowded around to peer closer at the single sheet of paper with the power to change their destinies. Their eyes darted back and forth over the prophecy. I couldn't read it, however, because it was in a language I didn't recognize. It didn't look like a human language at all—rather, one that was decipherable to them alone.

At their harmonious gasp, I knew they had figured out something important.

"What?" I asked.

"We must complete the Union no matter what," Zadkiel said.

"What do you mean?"

"We all knew the Union could grant the beholder immense power, but we didn't know the spheres must be united and then destroyed."

At my look of confusion, Zadkiel placed his finger upon the page and read the words aloud.

The Union of the Spheres
Grants power to the one who commandeers
Sovereign Orb and Scepter in hand
They can dominate any land

For thirteen spheres to unite

Components must be brought to light

According to an angel's vision
The Union must follow this precision
Sphere in circle, circle in sphere
Placed together during the twentieth year

Only the river can locate
The depths where the rocks await
Stone in stone they become one
The place hidden for all time by the Sun

Thirteen bound in blood by two
From ancient lines born anew
Both must live until blood is spilt
Afterward fighting hilt to hilt

Time will tell how events come to be
As the route to the spheres is hard to foresee
No matter the path, the Union is completed
Since the Orb and Scepter must be defeated

"That doesn't make any sense," I said, annoyed by all the cryptic meanings.

"It probably does, we just haven't studied it yet," Zadkiel replied, staring at the words.

"The first stanza is information we already know," Jophiel said.

"There are obviously several other components we did not know about though."

Zadkiel nodded. "The first stanza explains one can obtain immense power by uniting the spheres, and with the Sovereign Orb and Scepter, they are all-powerful. The next part clarifies how to do this by revealing the necessary components. This is where things start to get confusing, except for the angel's vision. It must be referring to what Metatron saw."

He left the table to rummage through a pile of books that were stacked neatly on a chair. These must have been the books he brought with him. When he found the one he was looking for, he approached us again.

"The thirteen spheres need to be placed in the formation of Metatron's Cube," he said. "That is what I was telling you about before, Jordan. This formation on paper is thirteen circles linked to each other. 'Sphere in circle, circle in sphere.'" Zadkiel pointed to the page in order for me to get a look at the mysterious formation. His description was accurate. Thirteen circles were depicted, with lines connecting them all together.

"Metatron drew this?" Michael peered at the page too.

Zadkiel nodded. "I'll explain later."

"It makes sense why the prophecy describes it as precise," Gabriel inputted, noting the intricacy of the design.

"What about the twentieth year?" I asked.

"I'm not sure. Metatron never mentioned anything about that." Zadkiel's brow furrowed in thought. "The fourth stanza about the river is trying to indicate the location where the Union needs to take place, but these words could have many meanings."

"All of this could have many meanings," Uriel said.

"I know, I know." Zadkiel shook his head in frustration. "The fifth stanza reveals blood from two individuals must be combined with the spheres. However, I am unsure who these two people are."

"One must be the holy bloodline," I said. "'Ancient lines born anew.' That's a pretty ancient bloodline, right?"

Zadkiel looked at me with admiration. "You're absolutely right, Jordan. That would make a lot of sense."

"What about the other one?" Chamuel asked.

"It must be Satan," Michael suggested. "He was born anew when he fell."

"And then they fight it out. The bloodline and Satan," I added, putting small pieces of the prophecy together.

"Apparently," Zadkiel said. "The last stanza indicates the Union must be completed so the Sovereign Orb and Scepter can be destroyed."

I nodded in agreement.

"I thought we had nothing to do with the bloodline," Uriel demanded.

"We don't," Gabriel said.

"Then, why are they involved in a prophecy that pertains to us?"

"This prophecy doesn't really pertain to us. We're only involved because of what happened in Heaven," Gabriel replied.

"Then, why are we supposed to protect it?" Uriel argued. "Why are the spheres assigned to us? Why are we the ones who must complete the Union?"

"Okay, okay, I see your point." Gabriel was exasperated.

"What do we do now?" Chamuel wondered.

Zadkiel rubbed a hand over his forehead. "I'm not sure. I don't know if we should locate the bloodline or recover the spheres."

"We go after the spheres," I said. "The Sacrarium is in charge of the bloodline. Let them do their part, and we'll do ours. Until we all need to come together, that is."

"That's a reasonable plan. We'll follow that unless something changes." Zadkiel glanced down at the book and grimaced. He leafed through a few pages until he came to a new section. "There's a page missing," he said, tracing his finger along the ripped edge.

"What?" My eyes darted to the book.

"What page?" Gabriel asked.

"I'm not sure," Zadkiel said quietly. "I've never been able to look at this book before." He inspected the other pages. "It seems this section is full of maps."

"Maps?" I wondered.

Michael pushed his way closer to look at the pages and let out a huge sigh.

"What's wrong?" Jophiel said, coming closer to assist in the inspection.

"The Nephilim believe this book contains the location of the Watchers," Michael explained.

We all nodded.

"Well, it seems they might be right," he said.

"How so?" Raphael asked.

Michael pointed to the book. "Whatever page was torn is the last one of this section. And the pages preceding it reveal where the Watchers were sent when they first came to teach humankind. It only makes sense the last page would contain information about what happened after, which is ultimately their imprisonment."

"Indeed," Zadkiel mused.

"But who would have taken it?" Chamuel asked. "The only beings who can touch this book are angels. The energy is too lethal."

At hearing this news, I stepped back.

"I don't have an answer for you, Chamuel," Zadkiel said. "It could have happened at any point, whether the book was in Heaven or on Earth."

Since there was no answer to Chamuel's question, I asked, "Is that the case with all heavenly objects? Humans can't touch them?"

"Yes and no," Zadkiel said. "All of our belongings are created in the Forge from heavenly light. Objects such as our rings and Gabriel's horn are not lethal to humans because they're infused with only a minuscule amount of heavenly light." To demonstrate, Zadkiel held up his hand, drawing his thumb and forefinger together to display the tiny amount of heavenly light contained in their rings and Gabriel's horn. "However," he continued, "objects such as our weapons, the book, the keys, and the spheres are lethal to humans because they're infused with large amounts of heavenly light." He extended his arms out wide in front of him to exhibit the difference. "That's another reason why it's time to retrieve the keys and the spheres. We have been lucky so far that a human has not stumbled upon them."

"So, when do we leave?" I asked.

"To where?" Michael said.

"I don't know. Wherever the Gemstone Keys are hidden."

"You think I'm about to let you journey around the world again before your injuries are healed?" Raphael raised an eyebrow.

"But don't we need to show some haste and get moving? I mean, it sounds like the world might be ending."

"The world is not ending," Gabriel said seriously. "But evil has grown too strong."

"Which should be cause for haste...no?"

"Jordan, I think we need to stay put for now," Zadkiel said.

"Yeah, and we really must start that training of yours," Michael added.

"Haven't I learned everything?"

Zadkiel shook his head. "Oh, no. There's far more you need to know."

"I wasn't referring to *that* training. I meant combat training," Michael clarified.

I stared at him. "Excuse me? *Combat* training? Why do I need to learn that?"

"Because you need to know how to fight and protect yourself. Maybe then you won't get hurt so much," Michael jested.

I didn't find this a laughing matter. "And *you're* going to train me? Satan fears your physical prowess. How do you think I feel?"

A great big belly laugh escaped Michael. The others joined in.

"I love how you all think this is so funny, but I'm not joking around here."

"Jordan, there's nothing to worry about." Michael chuckled. "I'll go easy on you."

"He needs time to heal and recuperate first," Raphael reminded him.

I realized the thought of sleeping in the same bed for longer than one or two nights was definitely appealing. For that reason, I kept my mouth shut and went along with whatever they had in store.

When the sound of the doorbell interrupted our conversation, we all froze in place.

"Who could that be?" I asked. "Martha has a key."

Michael drew his knife. "I don't know, but I'll go find out."

"Wait!" I said before he could leave. "This is my house. Let me get the door."

"Jordan, it might not be safe," Gabriel warned.

"Seriously? Who could possibly know we're here?"

I left the library and approached the front door, glancing through the window in the hallway to get a better glimpse of the person outside. All I could see was the figure of a girl. The angels followed, and when they saw the figure too, they backed off.

I walked into the turret, grabbed the knob, and opened the door.

The girl standing on the other side smiled at me and said, "Hi, I'm Naomi."

I gazed at her. She was about my age, with light brown skin, dark brown eyes, and curly black hair escaping from a bun at the back of her head. There were freckles all over her cheeks, and her smile was infectious.

"Hi," I greeted, smiling too. "Who are you?"

"Oh, right. Sorry." She drew her attention away from my injuries. "I'm your neighbor. I live over there." She pointed to the left. "Martha told my parents you were home, so my mom baked some muffins for you." She extended the basket she was holding toward me.

I took it from her. "Wow, thank you. How did you manage to get through the gate?"

"Martha gave my parents a keypad code for emergencies."

I smiled. "Well, I don't have any baked goods in the house, so this must be an emergency."

She laughed. "To my mom, it most definitely is."

"Well, tell her I said thank you."

"I will." She hesitated. "You're Jordan, right? Jordan Conway?"

I nodded. "Yeah, how did you know?"

She shrugged. "My parents were friends with your parents."

"Oh, really? That's cool." I knew the words sounded so silly, but I didn't know what else to say. I was nervous talking to Naomi, and I didn't know why.

"Anyway," she continued, "if you need anything, just let us know. We're not too far away."

"Thanks," I said again.

She headed down the walkway to the gate and the street beyond. I watched her retreating figure, slightly dazed.

"Jordan, are you all right?" Gabriel asked.

I jumped in surprise. "Yeah, why?"

"You've been standing there for quite a while."

"Oh." I closed the door. It really must have been a few minutes because a chill had seeped into the entryway. I noticed the other angels were lined up behind Gabriel and were all staring in curiosity. "What?" I asked.

"Someone has a crush," Michael jested.

"No!" I was quick to defend myself. "She's just a nice girl who lives next door."

"Textbook," Michael murmured with a smirk.

"Well, she must have spurred some feelings if she left you dumbfounded." Uriel grinned.

"I'm not dumbfounded! And there are no feelings," I argued.

They looked at me skeptically. My embarrassment must have conveyed some truth in their words. Honestly, I didn't know what I was feeling. All I could say was I'd never felt like it before.

"I'm back," Martha called from the kitchen.

We all left the entryway to help her carry in groceries, and I left the basket of muffins on the kitchen counter before I went out to the garage. Martha admired the baked goods as we toted in bags from the car.

Once everything was inside, Chamuel helped put things away, inspecting each item.

"Is there something wrong with that lettuce?" Martha asked.

"Not at all," Chamuel said. "I'm just thinking about all the recipes I can make."

She abruptly stopped what she was doing and went over to hug Chamuel. Unfamiliar with such affection, he lightly patted her back.

"Thank the Heavens they sent you!" she exclaimed. "I may be a housekeeper, but I cannot cook to save my life." She released Chamuel. "I thought poor Jordan here might have to suffer through my cooking."

Chamuel chuckled. "No need for that. I'm a chef and would be more than happy to cook for both of you."

"Oh, you don't have to worry about me. I'll get by," Martha said.

"But I insist, Martha. I can tell you're more than willing to help us, so let me do this one thing for you."

She smiled sheepishly. "All right. If you insist."

I could already tell these two were going to be fast friends.

JORDAN

36

NEW YORK STATE, PRESENT DAY

I sat on the floor of the gym breathing heavily and gulping down water. I'd just finished my training session with Michael, who hadn't even broken a sweat. We'd been working together for a few weeks now, and though I was better than when I first started out, I still had lots of progress to make.

"That's enough for today," Michael said, putting away hand weights. "We'll start again tomorrow with leg strengthening exercises."

I groaned. I dreaded leg day the most. The thought of it made my body feel ten times worse than it already did.

"All right," I replied, slowly getting to my feet.

I left the gym and made my way upstairs. It was a slow journey, the muscles in my legs already protesting every time I lifted them, so I headed straight for the shower, knowing the warm water would do wonders for my aching body. After I was done, I dressed in sweats and a t-shirt and went back down to the kitchen, where I knew Chamuel would have dinner ready.

But the usual aroma of his five-star cooking did not meet my nose. Instead, the angel sat at the counter peering over a cookbook, while Martha sat at his side cutting coupons.

"Is dinner not ready yet?"

Chamuel looked up at me. "Oh…not yet. I was just about to start it."

I glanced at the digital clock on the microwave. It was past six already, which was odd. Chamuel usually had dinner ready for six every night. In fact, he was acting weird in general, tapping his fingers against the counter in a nervous tic and pretending to read the cookbook.

Martha stared at him intently. I was going to watch some TV in the living room when she said, "Oh, I almost forgot, you had some mail arrive."

I approached the counter and filed through the stack of envelopes. My name was on all of them, but it was all junk.

"Thanks," I told her.

She nodded. "We got some of the neighbors' mail too. You might want to take it over to them." She handed me two envelopes.

The mail was for Naomi's family. At the thought of her, I smiled. It would be nice to see her again. She was so friendly, and we hadn't had the chance to connect since her visit. Besides, I never thanked her mom personally for the muffins.

With my mind set on delivering the mail, I walked back to the stairs.

"Where are you going?" Chamuel asked.

"To get some shoes and a coat," I replied.

The angel glanced at my clothes. "You might want to change too."

"I'm only going to drop off the mail."

He stared at me.

I sighed. Whenever the angels grew quiet and merely stared, I knew there was no arguing and that I had to listen. "Fine," I huffed.

When I was in my room again, I traded my sweats for a pair of jeans and left on the t-shirt. I slid my feet into my Converse and grabbed a coat from my closet, then strode back through the kitchen, grabbing the mail off the counter and waving goodbye to Chamuel and Martha.

Outside, I was immediately hit by cold air. Snow crunched under my feet as I walked down the driveway toward Naomi's house. The lights were all on inside, and I admired the meticulously hung Christmas lights out front.

Naomi stepped out as I approached her front door. "Dad, the lights are on!" she yelled, checking the exterior. Then, she noticed me. "Hey, Jordan!"

I waved and stepped forward. "Hi, Naomi!" Suddenly, my feet slipped on a batch of ice, and I careened to the ground, landing hard on my butt. *Great.* I cursed under my breath. The fall had my muscles aching all over again, but my embarrassment at making a complete fool of myself in front of Naomi was worse.

She approached to help as I scrambled to my feet. "Are you all right?" she asked, grabbing onto my arm.

"Yeah," I replied, steadying myself and trying to hide the red creeping into my cheeks.

She glanced at my feet. "Why aren't you wearing boots?"

I followed her gaze. "To be honest, I'm not sure. Stupid decision."

Naomi laughed. "Why don't you come in?"

I didn't answer since she was already tugging me to her door.

"You only just healed from your other injuries," she said as we entered the house.

Her words made me remember I was still sporting evidence of my injuries the first time we met. Now, I no longer had to wear the sling or a bandage on my hand, and the bruising on my neck and face had almost vanished.

She closed the door behind us. "Can I take your coat?"

I got a better look at her face under the warm light. There were those freckles again, and that curly black hair pulled back in a bun. A few tendrils hung loose about her face, and I thought she looked really pretty.

"Jordan?" Her dark brown eyes squinted in a quizzical expression.

I realized how dumb I must have looked, so caught up in her beauty I was rudely staring. *Pull yourself together.* "Sure," I said, slipping my coat off. My one sleeve got caught on my hand, which still gripped the mail. "Oh…these are for you." I handed the envelopes to her. "That's why I came. We got some of your mail."

She nodded and smiled, taking both envelopes and my coat. Naomi hung the garment on a hook near the door while I took my shoes off, then she strode down the hallway. I followed her into the living room.

"There you are. Are the lights on?" Naomi's dad asked from the kitchen, too focused on fixing a light-up reindeer to look up. He was tall, with blue eyes, blond hair, and pale skin.

"Yes, Dad. I said they were."

"Oh, must not have heard you." He looked up and noticed me. "Why didn't you say we had company?"

"Company?" Naomi's mom wondered, arriving in the kitchen from upstairs. She had curly black hair and brown skin, and when she saw me, she stopped in her tracks. "You must be Jordan," she whispered.

"Yes. Nice to meet you, Mrs.…" I didn't know their last name and couldn't recall what was listed on the mail.

"Barnes. But you can call me Deborah." She shook her head. "I can't believe how much you look like your mother."

"The resemblance is quite striking," Naomi's dad added. He strode toward me, hand outstretched. "Peter," he said, grasping mine. "And the pleasure's all mine."

Before I could respond, a timer chimed.

"Oh! That must be the chicken!" Deborah approached the oven and opened the door. A waft of herb-roasted chicken filled the air as she pulled it out and set it on the counter. "Would you like to stay for dinner, Jordan? There's plenty of food."

I glanced at Naomi for approval. She smiled and placed a hand on my shoulder.

"Of course he'll stay. It's the least we can do since he slipped on the ice outside our house."

Heat began to creep into my cheeks again, and she laughed. I started laughing too when I realized she was only teasing.

"Peter, I told you to put salt on it!" Deborah exclaimed.

"I was going to…then I found this and got distracted." He glanced at the reindeer.

"Would you put that away? We're about to eat."

Peter looked sheepish. "All right." He picked up the reindeer and headed for the garage.

Deborah transferred chicken, green beans, and mashed potatoes to serving dishes, her concern obvious when she asked, "Are you all right, dear? That fall must have hurt."

I glanced at Naomi, who was helping to set the table. She bit her lower lip to contain her amusement.

"I'm fine, really. I should have worn better shoes." I didn't think my trip to drop off mail would extend to a dinner invitation. If I'd known, I would have dressed differently. "Can I help with anything?" I offered.

"Oh, no. You just sit down," Deborah insisted.

I approached the table.

"You can sit here, next to me." Naomi indicated a chair. "What would you like to drink? We have all kinds of soda."

"A Coke would be great."

Just then, Peter came back in carrying all sorts of soda cans. "I wasn't sure what everyone wanted, so I brought a little of everything." He set them out on the counter as Deborah placed the food on the table.

Naomi went about making our drinks and then joined us all at the table. We piled food onto our plates and dug in.

"So, what brought you here tonight, Jordan?" Peter asked.

I swallowed a mouthful of chicken. "I got some of your mail at my house, so I wanted to return it to you."

Peter scrunched his face in confusion. "That's odd. The mailman knows our address. Doug hasn't misplaced our mail in years."

Deborah was quiet and looked down at her plate. Naomi stared at her mother.

"Mom, you didn't…"

She refused to meet her daughter's gaze. "I don't know what you're talking about, sweetheart."

Naomi shook her head and returned to her food.

Peter glanced at the two of them. "Am I missing something?"

"No, Peter," Deborah said, but he still looked puzzled. "I'll tell you later," she whispered.

I peeked a glance at Naomi and realized she was blushing. Since she was obviously uncomfortable, I asked instead, "Are you in school?"

She smiled. "Yeah, I go to Cornell."

"Really? I plan on going there too. I deferred my admission because I needed a year or two off, but I know it's a great school. I've heard the campus is beautiful."

"You haven't been there?" Peter interjected.

I shook my head. "No."

He dropped his fork. "You haven't been to Cornell! Naomi, you must take him to visit the campus."

"That's a splendid idea!" Deborah exclaimed.

"Stop! Both of you!" Naomi pleaded.

I took a sip of my drink and cleared my throat. "She doesn't have to."

"Oh, yes, she does. Your mother was a top student there. Plenty of faculty remember her and her family. Well, *your* family, I mean," Peter said.

"They were donors," Deborah explained.

"Big donors. The Sinclairs were very generous. Numerous times, they even donated anonymously because they felt the school had already given them enough recognition."

I sat there contemplating their words. As a future student, I wanted to see the campus in person because I was never able to do a school visit. Now, knowing my family history was rooted at the university and my mom had attended, I wanted to go even more.

"Wow, okay. Maybe it would be fun to visit," I said, then I looked at Naomi. "If you don't mind taking me."

Her eyes searched mine, trying to figure something out. When she finally found whatever she was looking for, she said, "Sure, we can do that. It would be fun. Let's go on Monday. Finals just ended, and the campus is nicer sometimes when people aren't there."

"And I can join you for lunch," Peter said. "I'll be at my office next week to grade papers—ow!" He stared at Deborah. Clearly, she had kicked him under the table.

"Don't you remember, you decided to grade from home that day?" she said pointedly.

"I did? Oh, I did!"

"You work there?" I asked to ease the tension.

"Yes. I'm an engineering professor. Your father was a great colleague of mine even though we taught different subjects."

"He taught there too?"

Peter nodded. "Yes, he was a history professor. It was convenient for him since the school is close to the house."

Wow, that was a tidbit I never knew. "You seem to have known my parents very well."

Peter and Deborah nodded, a faraway look entering their eyes.

"They were such dear friends," Peter said.

"How did you meet?" I asked.

"Well, through Deborah, really," he said.

Her eyes glistened with tears. "I met your mother in college. We were roommates freshman year, and we became best friends. Every year after that, we roomed together. I was maid of honor at her wedding."

I froze, not realizing their connection went so deep.

"Naturally, I knew all about your father. Your mother would agonize over him. They didn't attend the same university, and she was worried he would fall in love with someone else. He was a very handsome guy. I assured her it would never happen, and I was right. Anyway, I met him a few times when he came for the weekend. I was dating Peter, so all four of us would go on double dates. We became great friends, and that friendship continued into adulthood." Deborah stopped her story to dab at her eyes. "I was heartbroken when they died. So was Peter."

He leaned across and took her hand. "They were amazing people."

Deborah noticed my expression. "I'm sorry, I shouldn't be focusing on the sadness."

"It's okay," I assured her. "I enjoy hearing about them. It's nice to learn who they were."

She smiled. "They would be proud of you."

I looked away. For some reason, those words brought sentimental feelings to the surface, and I refused to get upset in front of Naomi and her parents. I had always wanted my parents' approval even though I never knew them. I wanted them to be proud of me, of who I was, since I would continue on their legacy.

Deborah and Peter began clearing plates, and I rose to take mine to the counter. Naomi stopped me by placing a hand on my wrist. We sat in our seats, and her eyes searched mine once more. She squeezed my arm, somehow detecting my sadness and reading my thoughts.

I smiled and mouthed, "Thank you."

She mouthed back, "You're welcome." Then, she took my plate to the sink.

Deborah returned and placed a cake on the table. "You have to stay for dessert. I tried out this new recipe," she told me.

My eyes widened in surprise at the sweet treat. It looked tasty. I remained seated as the family moved about the kitchen getting dishes, silverware, and drinks. It was nice to see the dynamic between the three of them—something I'd never experienced before.

When they all sat down again, I said, "Thank you for those muffins you baked. I realize it's been a few weeks, but they were delicious."

Deborah smiled. "That's the best compliment a baker could receive."

"Do you bake professionally?" I asked as she passed out plates full of cake.

"No, I'm just a hobbyist. I'm actually a lawyer, but the baking helps me relax."

I nodded as I took a bite of the cake along with Naomi and Peter. Deborah waited for our praise. There was a chorus of, "wonderful," "delicious," and "great."

As we ate our dessert, Deborah went to clean up the dishes.

"That's the thing," Naomi said. "She bakes but doesn't eat the results herself."

"I had a taste!" Deborah complained.

"Yeah, but we're the ones who have to finish it." Peter patted his stomach. The man was lean and in shape, but he winked at me. "Living with a baker can be deadly if you don't regularly work it off."

Naomi laughed, nodding her head in agreement.

Out of curiosity, I asked, "What do you study, Naomi?"

"Biomolecular engineering," she said.

I stopped mid-bite and stared at her. "That's hard-core science."

She nodded.

"I'm really bad at science."

She laughed. "It's not for everyone, and it's super male-dominated.

But I like a challenge." She said all this so nonchalantly it made me like her more. Naomi was fierce. "What do you want to study once you start at Cornell?" she asked.

"Not sure yet. I like helping people, so I hope to pursue a field that involves doing that."

After we finished our dessert, we talked some more about Naomi's two older sisters, Simone and Laila, who both lived in the city. She seemed close with them and got all excited when she talked about them.

When it was time to leave, she walked me to the door and handed me my coat.

"Thanks," I said, taking the coat from her after I laced up my shoes.

"No problem. Thank you for staying and enduring my parents."

I smiled. "I like them."

"They seem to like you too."

A moment of silence ensued as we stared at each other. My heart raced, and my hands felt clammy.

"I'll see you on Monday, around ten a.m. I'll come get you from your house," she said.

"Right. I'm looking forward to it."

"Me too." She opened the door. "Bye, Jordan."

"Bye, Naomi." I stepped out into the cold air.

"Watch out for the ice!" she called.

I pretended to trip again, and we both laughed.

When I arrived back at my house, Chamuel and Martha were still sitting in the kitchen reading the cookbook and cutting coupons even though hours had gone by.

"How was it?" Martha asked, snipping away at a piece of paper.

"Good. Great, actually. Naomi and I are meeting again on Monday," I told her.

Chamuel remained silent and continued to focus on the book. His behavior was strange tonight...like Naomi's parents. Suddenly, I realized what this was all about.

"You set me up!"

He looked up. "It was her idea! I just agreed."

I turned to Martha. "Care to explain yourself?"

She chuckled. "Deborah and I have known each other for quite some time. We ran into each other at the grocery store the other day and got to talking. Naomi is the only one of her girls without a boyfriend. I told her about you and what a wonderful boy you are. She insisted you come over for dinner to get to know Naomi better, but she needed an excuse for you to come. I took some of her mail and told her I would have you bring it to them, and the rest is history."

I turned to Chamuel. "And how do you fit into all this?"

"Martha insisted I skip making you dinner tonight. I didn't realize she was trying to set you up with Naomi until I told the others. When it became apparent what was going on, I didn't object since you seem to like Naomi. I'm sorry!" The words tumbled out of Chamuel's mouth like a confession. He clearly didn't enjoy lying.

"It's all right, Chamuel. I'm not mad. I really did enjoy myself tonight."

He sighed. "Good."

I turned to go upstairs and just as quickly froze. "You said the others. They were in on this too?"

He was silent.

"Chamuel…"

"I'm sorry! I had to let them know. I don't normally lie, and it was difficult, so I sought their advice. They all thought it was a good idea."

I turned away, completely mortified. I thought their overprotectiveness was bad, but it was nothing compared to this intrusion. Trudging up the stairs, I returned to my room knowing seven angels, a meddling mother, and a determined housekeeper had set me up.

But…maybe that wasn't so bad after all.

JORDAN

37

Πεw York State, Present Day

Months passed. Six in total since we arrived at the house. My body spent some of that time healing, and the majority conditioning. Michael was relentless in his training, teaching me all sorts of ways to defend myself. We started out in the gym but quickly moved to hand combat maneuvers, boxing, archery, and other weapon-wielding activities.

During our time in the house, I turned nineteen, got a new cell phone, grew about two more inches, and finally started developing some muscle. The latter was owed to Michael's intense training program. Being stronger was definitely a plus. I thought the damage imposed on me by the fallen would leave permanent injuries, but I only had a few scars.

Interspersed throughout this time were moments with Naomi, most of them virtual, either through text or video call. I really liked her, and I would definitely call her a friend. I knew there was potential for more, but I didn't know how she felt about me.

Combing my wet hair out of my face, I glanced in my bathroom mirror to make sure I looked presentable. My mornings were spent with Michael, and my afternoons were dedicated to Zadkiel. He didn't enjoy the sweaty odor that permeated my skin after a full morning of training, so every day after lunch, I would take a shower so I was ready to grace him with my presence and the fresh scent of shower gel and aftershave.

I descended the stairs to the main level and headed to the library. I was used to the layout of my parents' house now it had become our home. I felt their presence each and every day, and it was a great comfort. Planting myself in my usual seat, I watched Jophiel flip through papers in the corner of the room. I bet they were the documents Michael had given him about the Nephilim. The thought of those vile creatures still made my hair stand on end.

Zadkiel soon came sweeping in from another part of the library with a handful of books. He placed them in front of me, and my lesson began.

I was learning about history, religion, literature, art—anything and everything that could possibly pertain to angels. Zadkiel taught me various languages, Latin being our main study. He made me learn angelic script too, those foreign-looking symbols on just about everything the angels possessed.

Four hours into my lesson, Zadkiel announced, "I think that's enough for today. We'll continue tomorrow."

I was relieved. Four straight hours of concentration did a number on my brain.

On my way out to the kitchen, where Chamuel would no doubt have dinner waiting, I passed Michael. He was carrying more papers I presumed were for Jophiel. When a folded document slid out from his grasp and landed on the floor, I retrieved and unfolded it, startled by the handwriting.

"Where did you get this?" I demanded.

Zadkiel looked up when he heard the alarm in my voice.

When Michael saw the page in my hand, he tried to pry it out of my fingers. "It's nothing that should concern you," he said.

My grip tightened. "It *is* something that should concern me, Michael. Where did you get this?" My body language and voice exuded unease.

"Jordan, calm down," Michael said. "What is it about this letter that worries you?"

I swallowed the lump in my throat. "That's Sophia's handwriting. I'd know it anywhere."

"Wait... You know this Sophia?" Michael asked.

It was then I realized I'd never mentioned Sophia by name before in front of the angels. "Yes, I spent my entire life with her. I would recognize the way she writes."

"Have you been in contact with her?" Michael asked.

"No," I confessed. "Sophia is probably devastated she hasn't heard from me. She must think I forgot about her—which is the worst thing, because she has abandonment issues from when her mom left. I've wanted to go see her, but we've been a little busy. I don't remember her phone number either, otherwise I would have called her by now. She probably hates me."

"You have feelings for her?" Jophiel asked. He approached my side, reaching out to read the letter.

I scrunched my face in frustration. Their assumptions were getting annoying.

"Not in the way you're thinking," I said. "I love Sophia like a sister.

She's my best friend, and I'd do anything for her because we're all each other has ever had."

Naomi was a different story. I definitely liked her as more than a friend, but they didn't need to know that. Not yet.

"What exactly is your friend involved in?" Zadkiel asked, taking the letter from Jophiel.

"What do you mean?"

He passed the letter back to me. Although the correspondence was short, Sophia's looping script took up most of the page.

> *Aziza,*
>
> *I can't give you any information on the scepter pieces because I don't know where they are. Sister Helen isn't concerned about them. Still haven't located the fourteenth sphere yet. Will keep you updated on that front. If the Triune needs our help to find it, it must be important. I hope you and Yadira are all right. I haven't heard from either of you in a while… Any news on Kat? Please be in touch soon to let me know.*
>
> *Sophia*

I looked up and realized Zadkiel had gathered the other angels. Martha was out again, this time at her monthly book club. They gazed at me expectantly, so I read the letter aloud.

"The Triune. Why does that sound familiar?" I asked.

"Because I made you read about them a few days ago. The book about all the angel legends," Zadkiel said to jog my memory.

"Oh, right. They're the group of angels who assist in protecting the bloodline?"

"That's rumored to be one of their jobs, yes. It's also thought they were entrusted with certain objects from Heaven after the war ensued. Objects that were related to the bloodline."

"Like the scepter," I said.

"Yes, or the book and sphere. The Triune must have given them to Sister Helen."

"Which makes sense, because they are angels and would be able to touch those objects," Chamuel said.

"Indeed," Zadkiel agreed. "I wonder if the Triune was entrusted with Satan's keys."

"Why do you think that?" Michael asked.

"Well, when we were in Heaven and Seraphiel distributed our keys to us, you asked her what happened to Satan's keys."

Michael nodded. "Right. She said they were entrusted to others to protect them."

"Exactly, so why not the angels of the Triune?"

"I see your point. But what caused them to use the keys?"

Zadkiel rubbed his forehead. "I don't know. There's a lot to this puzzle we have yet to put in place."

While everything they said made sense, there was one thing that didn't add up: Sophia's involvement.

"When was this letter written? Where did you get it from?" I asked Michael.

"It was written about a year and a half ago. It was among the papers Allen Clark gave to me," he said.

I felt a sinking in my stomach. During that time, Sophia and I were seniors in high school, which must have meant she was keeping her involvement secret from me. Even worse was the mention of Allen Clark.

"Why was this letter with all those papers?"

Michael stared hard at me before saying, "Because Sophia is the bloodline, and the Nephilim have a theory that her DNA might be a way to achieve their pure form."

"What?" I exploded.

"Jordan, calm down," Michael pleaded.

"How do you expect me to do that? Sophia is in danger!"

"I understand, and we will protect her. But it's only a theory. It doesn't mean it's true."

I placed my hands on my head, grabbing at my hair as I tried to figure out what to do. Nothing could happen to Sophia. I would never forgive myself if it did.

"I need you to explain this to me," I said to Michael. "I need you to tell me whatever you know."

He nodded. "All right. Well, as I was going through 'Operation Pure Form,' the file Allen had not yet looked at, I stumbled upon some correspondence from the Sacrarium that confirmed there is indeed a bloodline. Don't ask me how the Nephilim have Sacrarium correspondence. I don't have a foolproof answer other than they somehow intercepted it."

"You mean, there's more than just this letter?" I asked.

"Yes, but this is the only one written by Sophia. The other correspondence is from Sister Helen to a woman named Emily, and it takes place over several years. I presumed the woman to be a member of the Sacrarium too. The first letter states ever since the child came to Holy Trinity, she has stood out among the others, but Sister Helen has tried to help her blend in. In another, Sister Helen describes how the child is progressing in her training. The last letter explains she is college bound to Harvard and will still be protected by the Sacrarium."

I winced at the mention of Harvard. That was the exact school Sophia was attending.

"The way they speak of the child in the letters made me assume she is the bloodline," Michael said. "Otherwise, that's all I know."

I shook my head in shock. The explanation was logical, but it made me question everything about my childhood. All those secrets. All those untruths. All of it happening right before me, and I never knew.

"I don't know anyone by the name of Emily," I said.

"You probably never met her." Michael paused. "I'm sorry about all this. I didn't realize you knew Sophia."

I didn't know how to respond. All of this was terrible. Not only did the Nephilim want Sophia, but if she was the bloodline, she would have to fight Satan to complete the prophecy. There was nothing I could do to help except offer my support, and what good was that when we were dealing with cosmic battles that determined the fate of the world? I wasn't even supporting her now. I'd left her for months without putting in the effort to get in contact. I was an awful friend, and I felt horrible about it.

Looking back, I realized all the little peculiarities from my childhood. Sister Helen would take Sophia to ballet lessons, and Sophia would come back exhausted and tired, always seeming to hate these lessons though she never quit. They weren't "ballet lessons" at all. She had been training, preparing for her destiny. They had probably taught her everything Zadkiel was teaching me now.

As I was trying to wrap my head around all of this, Gabriel broke the silence with an important question. "Why don't we know anything about a fourteenth sphere?"

Michael shook his head. "Probably because Father did not want us to know."

"Well, the fourteenth sphere obviously has to do with the Triune, which is most likely why He didn't tell us," Zadkiel said, reading the short letter again.

"What confuses me about this letter," Jophiel began, "is that it seems Sophia is acting as a messenger. Why would that be her role if she is the bloodline?"

"Because," Michael said, "the bloodline links the Triune and the Sacrarium together. She is their purpose. Why not make her the messenger between the two groups? Besides, I'm sure Sister Helen knows everything that is going on—she just can't implicate herself. As a sister, she has duties to the church to uphold, and I'm sure being a member of a covert group is not one of them. If anyone found out about her involvement, she could be divested. She needs an intermediary between the two groups to protect herself, and it seems Sophia is more than capable of handling the role."

Uriel brought up another point of contention. "When she says scepter *pieces*, what does that mean?"

"It seems to have been broken apart," Zadkiel said. "This has Father written all over it. I mean, He did everything in his power for the spheres to never be united. Why not the same with the scepter? Breaking it apart makes it even more difficult to find."

I rubbed a hand over my face. All of this was so complicated. But the thought of Sophia could not escape my mind.

"I'm going to see Sophia," I announced. "I don't care what arguments you all have about it, no one can stop me from going. I'm healed, I'm trained. Either you come with me, or you let me go alone."

Their silence left no doubt in my mind.

We were going to see Sophia.

Together.

JORDAN

38

Between my four-hour lesson with Zadkiel and now this shocking news about my best friend, I could feel a headache forming. I told the angels I would be back, but they followed me into the kitchen, talking with one another to figure out next steps. To them, it was obvious we had to go after the spheres. But I wouldn't let that happen until I saw Sophia.

Drowning out their voices, I grabbed a glass from the cabinet near the sink and went to the fridge for the pitcher of water. I had just finished pouring when Martha arrived back.

"Oh, hello," she said.

The angels stopped their conversation.

"Hi, Martha. How was your book club?"

"Great!" She set her purse and book on the counter. "What have you all been up to?"

That was such a loaded question, I didn't know how to answer her. The angels didn't know either. Thankfully, the ringing phone saved me from any further explanation.

Martha picked it up. "Hello?"

I sipped my water and rubbed my aching forehead while the angels loitered.

"Sophia, slow down. I can't understand a word you're saying."

My head whipped up at Martha's words. Setting down my glass, I drew closer, hoping to hear the conversation, but she moved into the living room and turned the television on, then navigated the channels until she found the local news. Slowly lowering herself onto the ottoman, she whispered, "Oh, my god."

It seemed there was some kind of explosion at a church in the city. The news anchor wasn't reporting much information yet because no one knew what had happened. All they were showing was an aerial view of the wreckage, a building completely burned to rubble.

Martha's sharp intake of breath brought my attention back to her. She dropped the phone and started to cry. Chamuel went over to offer Martha some comfort as the other angels stared. I took the opportunity to pick up the phone.

"Sophia, it's me...Jordan."

"Jordan!" she exclaimed. "What are you doing there?"

"It's a long story." I paused to look at the television screen. "What's going on?"

"Do you have the TV on?"

"Yeah."

"That church, the one that exploded in New York...it's the Sacrarium headquarters."

I sat down on the couch, struck by the gravity of the situation.

Sophia continued. "They're calling it an accident, a gas explosion. But it's not."

I didn't ask how she knew this. It was obviously inside information. Instead, I remained silent and turned to look at Michael. His face was so contorted by pain, anger, and sadness, it only confirmed my suspicions.

Satan had used the map in Michael's office to attack the Sacrarium and declare war.

"Was Sister Helen inside?" I asked, anxious to know.

There was silence on the other end, and I knew Sophia was holding back tears. Finally, the word I dreaded arrived through the receiver.

"Yes."

And just like that, the stakes were raised. I would fight in this war. No matter the cost.

Acknowledgments

There are so many I want to thank for helping to make my dream a reality. First, I must start with my family.

Mom, there are no words sufficient enough to express how grateful I am to have you in my corner. You are my rock, my best friend, and my all-time number one supporter. You believe in me when I don't even believe in myself. You push me when I start to doubt because you know I can do it. You jump in full-force, extending all your effort and energy. You were the first one I told about my book before I wrote a word and it was just an idea. Most people would be alarmed when their thirteen-year-old child describes Satan's fall, but you weren't. In fact, you encouraged me to be curious and to pursue my ideas, providing me with the proper tools to succeed. You were the first to actually read anything I wrote. When you told me how good my writing was, how it felt like you were reading someone else's book but had to remind yourself it was mine, I was determined to continue on because your excitement thrilled me. I mean it when I say it, I could never do this without you.

Dad, thank you for always being there, ready to help and support me in any way, no matter how crazy or absurd my ideas are. You were the second person to read anything I wrote, and I will never forget the look of enjoyment on your face after reading three chapters and wondering, "What's in the backpack?" Little did you know I intended for nothing to be in the backpack, but your question was the first and best critique I could ever receive since it helped to develop my story.

Anthony, thank you for being my brother and my stress reliever. Our countless excursions to movies, trips to conventions, and quests for collectibles is always the right amount of fun I need. The majority of my inspiration and research comes from the world of pop culture, and you're the one who I share that world with. I've always seen my book like a movie playing in my head, and when you felt that too, I knew I had accomplished what I set out to do. And you may not know this, but some of my best writing came from your advice and edits, so thank you for unknowingly pushing me to be a better writer.

Also, thank you to Uncle Frankie, Uncle Anthony, and Aunt Sherrill for being beta readers and book champions. You read, you fell in love with my words, and your enthusiasm revealed to me I had to start sharing this story with others. Thank you to grandma and grandpa for loving me and supporting me. I always want to make you proud, and I hope this book goes a long way in doing that.

A special shout-out to my cousin Nicole, who not only read early drafts but also committed herself to the cause. You have been there throughout the entire process, and I will forever appreciate the support you have shown me. In addition to Mom, you've seen me at my worst in great moments of self-doubt and fear, but you've also seen me at my best and cheered me on. I know we're family, and sticking around through thick and thin is in our DNA, but you went beyond that to help me succeed.

Pop, a big thanks goes to you as well. You started this journey with me years ago, giving my characters life and my ideas power through your drawings. Thank you for your patience by redrawing things until I found the right shade of blue. Thank you for your detail oriented mindset by perfecting every stroke of calligraphy. Although you never knew the full extent of my story, I am so happy you were a part of it, and continue to be a part of it through your drawings and memory. I wish you were around to read my book because I know you would love it. But even though you're not here in person, your spirit is with me each and every day, so I know you must have read it because you've been with me as I've written each word. Thank you for your love, support, and acceptance throughout my life. I march to the beat of my own drum, and you always appreciated that and encouraged me to do it. This book is a product of that encouragement as I continue to be uniquely me.

Thank you, Albert, for not only reading and critiquing, but also raising me. You've been there since the beginning, all the way back to when I had to go to reading camp with the nuns. Ever since, you've been an important part in helping me learn and grow intellectually as a person. Our philosophical talks are always intriguing, and I must say you do give the best book recommendations when it comes to research. I appreciate your additional help with proofreading the pronunciation guide and glossary. They definitely needed some work, and I'm glad these components can now benefit other readers.

Thank you, Franklin, for always being a great mentor and friend.

You were the one who set me on the path of graphic design, and I will always be grateful for that. You gave me the tools and resources that allowed me to learn how to design, create, and edit my own work. This book would literally not be a book without the knowledge and training you passed along. Also, thank you for your work on the book trailer. I appreciate the time and effort you put in. You made an awesome video that everyone can enjoy.

A special thanks to Bryony Leah (www.bryonyleah.com), editor extraordinaire. The universe was working in my favor the day I randomly discovered your editorial services because you are an excellent editor and an amazing person. You have been a believer and champion of my book from the first time you read it, and in the time since, you have become such a good friend. You are so dedicated to polishing and perfecting that I can rest easy knowing you have gone through my book not once, but multiple times. I appreciate you and your work so much, especially as you not only contributed your editing magic to my book, but also to countless query letters, book descriptions, and synopses. Thank you, thank you, thank you!

While we're on the topic of editing, I must say thank you to Nancy Allen, beta reader turned copyeditor, whose questions, comments, and critiques were the absolute best. You pushed me and made me think about story elements that never crossed my mind. I appreciate all the hard work you put in to reading and editing, and I am so grateful you were willing to do this. It took me months to get through your edits, but it was a truly wonderful experience that has since made me a better writer.

Thanks to Kimmie and M.E. for being beta readers. Your comments were so helpful as I continued to develop my story and they definitely contributed to the final product. Also, thanks to Starr, Erin, and Mike for being readers as well.

I want to extend a huge thanks to Jude Naples and Sue Paré. The both of you are always willing to assist me with design and formatting questions, and I cannot thank you enough for giving me the opportunity to work with you. I was able to create an early form of my book with the tools and resources you provided, and I will forever cherish that experience since it was the first time I held a physical copy of my book in my hands.

Thanks to Adrianne (www.adriannetamararachne.com) for being a fantastic artist. The symbol artwork and concept art you did for this trilogy was amazing, and it was only a small glimpse into the work you can do. Our collaboration was truly beneficial because it made me realize what I wanted my book to visually look like.

Another shout-out to three of my college professors, M.E., Eleanor, and Scott, who contributed to my learning and made me a better scholar. The material each of you taught in your classes influenced my thinking and imagination, and subsequently contributed to this book. All of you made me a better writer by pushing me. All of you made me a better thinker by allowing me to explore and discover new ideas. Essentially, all of you helped spark a curiosity in me that has made me a better person who can view the world from multiple angles. You all are great inspirations. Thank you for the hard work and countless hours of teaching.

If you're reading this, I want to thank you, the reader. You picked up my book, and that alone means the world to me. I hope you are able to enjoy this book as much as I do, and I hope you can find something inside these pages to connect with. A large part of why I published it is because I wanted to share this story with others, so I am excited you can now be a part of the journey too.

Wings up!

WANT MORE OF
THE EMPYREAN TRILOGY?

VISIT **WWW.SARAMSCHALLER.COM** FOR:

PRONUNCIATION GUIDE

GLOSSARY

STORY GUIDES

AUTHOR UPDATES

AND OTHER EXCLUSIVE CONTENT

7-7-20